MUM'S THE WORD

The Truth about Motherhood

Compiled and edited by

Sarah Webb

MUM'S THE WORD

First published 2007

by New Island

2 Brookside

Dundrum Road

Dublin 14

www.newisland.ie

Copyright © Editorial content: Sarah Webb 2007

Copyright © Individual contributors 2007

The authors have asserted their moral rights.

ISBN 978-1-905494-74-3

British Library Cataloguing Data. A CIP catalogue record for this
book is available from the British Library.

Book design by Inka Hagen

Printed by Colour Books Ltd., Dublin

10 9 8 7 6 5 4 3 2 1

This book is dedicated to my dear friend
Carolyn Thornton, her husband, Simon,
and their children, Olivia and Matthew.
With love and respect.

Contents

Acknowledgments

I'd like to start off by thanking the amazing Irish women writers who made this book possible, all thirty-four of you. In alphabetical order:

Mary Bond, Colette Caddle, Marita Conlon-McKenna, Tracy Culleton, Judi Curtin, Denise Deegan, Martina Devlin, Clare Dowling, Anne Dunlop, Anne Enright, Helen Falconer, Anne Marie Forrest, Tara Heavey, Suzanne Higgins, Kate Holmquist, Lucinda Jacob, Cathy Kelly, Cauvery Madhaven, Mary Malone, Jacinta McDevitt, Katy McGuinness, Sinead Moriarty, Saffa Musleh, Vanessa O'Loughlin, Sharon Owens, Siobhán Parkinson, Julie Parsons, Morag Prunty, Martina Reilly, Anne Marie Scanlon, Ho Wei Sim, Kate Thompson, Orla Tinsley and Alison Walsh.

This is the second charity collection I have compiled and edited (*Travelling Light* was the first) and it's you, the writers, who have made the whole experience so interesting, fulfilling and downright fun. Thank you for donating your time and your talent to this collection. I know how busy you all are and it means such a lot to me. (And I promise I won't ask again for at least another year!)

Special thanks must go to Martina Devlin for not telling me to shut up when I went on and on about the book, and to all the Irish Girls who supported this project from the very start. You know who you are. Thanks for all your support.

The wonderful team at New Island has been behind this project from its conception. Thanks to Deirdre for her eagle eyes, Edwin for his sound business mind and artistic sensibilities, Tom for making everyone in Ireland aware of *Mum's the Word*, Inka for the wonderful cover design and the rest of the dedicated team.

Conor Byrne, Director of Fundraising at the National Children's Hospital, Tallaght, has been fantastic from the very start. When we first talked about doing a book in aid of cystic fibrosis research in the hospital, he was full of enthusiasm and great ideas. And thanks also must go to Mothercare for coming on board and giving their financial backing to the project.

To the staff at Tallaght Hospital, who continue on a daily basis to make life that little bit better for sick children of all flavours (especially salty CF ones!).

To the team at TV3 for hosting the *Mum's the Word* Writing Competition and for their interest in the whole project. And thanks to everyone who entered the competition.

To the team at Today FM for all their support, especially Jenny Kelly and Mairead Farrell, who provided the wonderfully honest introductions, and Ray D'Arcy.

To Róisín Ingle for her early interest in the project and her unsung encouragement to young writers.

And finally, thanks to Ben, Sam, Amy-Rose and Jago, my sisters, Kate and Emma, and my dad for all their support. Most of the work on this book was done at night, so thanks for your patience, and I'll return all those phone calls at some stage, I promise. And most especially to my mum, who has been doing tireless voluntary work for the National Children's Hospital since I was born and still is, more than thirty years on, even though we all keep asking her to stop. A true inspiration.

Introduction

Sarah Webb

I didn't know much about cystic fibrosis until 2004, the year my great friend, Carolyn, had her third baby, Matthew. Her second child, Andrew, died when he was one week old, so Matthew was a very special baby. But from the start, he wasn't a well child.

When he was nine months old, Matthew spent two weeks in The National Children's Hospital, Tallaght and eventually they discovered what Carolyn had suspected from quite early on: Matthew had cystic fibrosis. She rang me from the hospital to tell me the news and I had no idea what to say. I just wanted to give her a hug. After putting down the phone, I immediately rang my mum. One of Mum's friends had lost an eight-year-old daughter to cystic fibrosis, and as tears flooded down my face, she explained the reality of the disease to me. I kept picturing little Matthew's perky face with his bubble curls; it was difficult to believe he was really so sick.

That evening, I started to trawl the internet for information on cystic fibrosis. I found that it's Ireland's most common life-threatening genetically inherited disease and that Ireland has the highest incidence of cystic fibrosis in the world. It's a disease that affects the glands and damages the lungs, digestive tract and reproductive system. People with it are prone to constant chest infections and malnutrition. I also found there is no specialised building in Ireland to treat cystic fibrosis patients; as adults, they are lumped in with all the respiratory patients in St Vincent's Hospital in Dublin. Consequently, Ireland has the lowest cystic fibrosis life expectancy in the developed world.

Then, quite by chance, I met Orla Tinsley. I was talking to the pupils in the Temple Street Hospital School on World Book Day a few years ago and Orla happened to be there. We got talking and she allowed me to read some of her work. It was astonishing – raw, intense, full of vivid imagery. It was about being a teenager with cystic fibrosis and I've never forgotten it. I was delighted when Orla agreed to write a piece for this collection, 'I Have a Mother, She Is Mine'. She's currently writing a memoir and is a talent to be reckoned with.

I wanted to do something small to raise funds for cystic fibrosis research and also to raise awareness of a disease that touches so many Irish families, either directly or indirectly. All over Ireland, women like Carolyn are looking after children with cystic fibrosis on a daily basis. Banging their backs, getting them to take enzymes with their food, giving them drugs and antibiotics, darting in and out of hospital, all the while trying to juggle family life.

So I decided to put together this collection with the support of my writer friends, the good people at New Island and Conor Byrne at The National Children's Hospital, Tallaght.

This book is dedicated to Carolyn because despite everything, she is one of the most upbeat and positive people I know, plus she's a great mother. That's what gave me the original idea for *Mum's the Word*: a book about real motherhood in all its glory.

I am honoured to have been the very first reader of the thirty-five pieces in this collection. I laughed, cried, sighed and with each and every one felt privileged to be sharing such personal, honest and uplifting true stories.

I do hope you enjoy *Mum's the Word* as much as I enjoyed editing it. Thank you so much for buying this book.

A Letter from Matron

Dear Friends,

On behalf of the National Children's Hospital, sincere thanks to you all for sharing your true life stories with so many readers.

I have no doubt all mothers will identify with this book, from first-time mums to those of us who have seen our children grow to adults and can now sit back and know that all the hard work was worthwhile. I often look back over the years and think of all the children cared for in the National Children's Hospital and how, like so many nurses and doctors, I too shared in the joys and sorrows of parents.

The National Children's Hospital was established in 1821 and is the second oldest children's hospital in Europe. For many years the hospital was situated in Harcourt Street and moved to Tallaght in 1998. Over 65,000 children come through our doors annually. Our emergency department is a busy place, where 32,000 children were cared for in 2006.

Children rarely come to hospital alone and our philosophy of care is family centred in partnership with parents or guardians. Hospital can be a frightening place for both parents and children and the environment can contribute greatly to the psychosocial effects of hospitalisation on both the child and parents.

Voluntary funding plays a huge role in our children's hospital. Government funding goes towards the day-to-day running of the hospital and new essential equipment.

There is little left over for the many comforts that the hospitalised child and parents require or the latest equipment on the market. Modern equipment makes tests and procedures quicker and easier to use, therefore making the experience less stressful for children.

A simple armchair and a blanket beside a sick child can greatly benefit the child and mother or father. Any parent who has sat watching their child in the lonely hours at night, waiting for morning but fearing the news it might bring, can vouch for that. However, armchairs and little comforts sometimes have to be balanced against the need for essential equipment in our budget. Funding is also important for our dedicated research teams; with your extra support, they can research paediatric illnesses such as cystic fibrosis.

When you buy this book, be assured not only of an excellent read, but that you are helping children from all over Ireland to better hospital care and a more positive experience of hospital for them and their parents.

Again, I would like to thank all you writers for your contribution to *Mum's the Word* and all you readers for your contribution to the National Children's Hospital.

Sincere thanks and kind regards,

Maura Connolly
Matron of the National Children's Hospital, Tallaght

A Few Words from Two New Mums

Jenny Kelly, Today FM

I have been a mum for all of seven months now, although between you and me, I don't feel I've earned the right to call myself that...yet.

Before my baby arrived I read every book going – books on being pregnant, books on giving birth, after birth, on rearing methods, possible routines to get her into once born, weaning, toilet training...you name it, I had read it. As far as the theory went, I had it covered from birth to age three. I'd worry about the rest at a later date.

Close friends with children tried to warn me – they told me to just go with the flow, to relax into it, enjoy my time bonding when he or she arrived, not to put so much pressure on myself. But to be honest, that didn't make any sense to me – that wasn't how I operated. If I didn't know how to do something in work, I normally went online and researched it, so I put the same foolproof method into having a baby. How could I go wrong?

And then Kate arrived.

This tiny person with magic eyes. It was as if my father's side of the family were all in her, staring out at me. I felt like I was her and she was me. I went blank. I knew nothing. And it scared the hell out of me.

I remember when she was only a day old and I was sitting on the edge of my hospital bed peering in at her as she lay all cosy, cocooned in her little Perspex crib. One of the midwives came into my room and asked me whether everything was OK. I quickly mumbled something to her; the truth was that I had been waiting to ask someone's permission to pick her up.

For the first time in years I felt totally out of my depth. Actually, that doesn't come close to describing how I felt. I felt terrified. Clueless. Scared. Upset. This was not how I imagined I would feel. And that was the problem – I had never really thought about what I would feel like after I had a baby. What being a mum meant. And suddenly I wasn't in control any longer. So I cried. And cried and cried. Between crying I got on with feeding her, bathing her, changing her and feeding her some more. And miraculously, they allowed us take her home from hospital. Alone. Without a nurse. Just the three of us. Dear God.

The first night home, I gave her diarrhoea after I ate some chilli. That nearly sent me over the edge. I honestly thought I should bring her back to the hospital for her own safety, because it was obvious I wasn't any good at this mothering lark. And then I remembered what everyone kept saying to me whenever I asked them how the hell I was going to be a proper mum: 'You'll just muddle through.' And here I am seven months in, muddling through, being a mum, having the time of my life with gorgeous Kate – the one person I know who can make me smile in the morning.

That's my story so far. So whether you're a mum or have had a mum, I think you'll enjoy the other mothers' stories in this book. One thing I do know – being a mum rocks!

Mairead Farrell, Today FM

The Easter Bunny normally brings Easter eggs to our house, but this year he was extra generous and brought us the best gift we could have wished for. The gift came in the form of a bouncing 8 lb 1 oz baby boy, Dara.

Towards the end of your pregnancy, everyone offers you advice. The sadists will have a gleam in their eyes when they tell you how much you'll struggle with the lack of sleep. The 'mother earths' will tell you what to pack, what to eat, what to say to the doctor and almost what to call your baby.

My advice to you is: listen to none of it. At 6:15 p.m. on Easter Monday, Doctor D'Arcy (no, that's not a mistake) plonked a baby on my tummy, asking, 'What is it?' I was hoping he'd know. My suspense was short lived when he announced we had a son. When we saw him, we just knew his name was Dara.

My first thought after twelve hours of labour was, 'Can I have some toast please?' I was absolutely starving! Eamon, my husband, was packed off to the shop to buy tons of chocolate and Lucozade. As soon as my belly was full, the love story began.

Forget your wedding day and all the hype that goes with it, this was the happiest day of my life with not even a close second. Sure, you're tired, sure, there's pain involved, but you'll soon forget that because ladies, you'll be head over heels in love.

The only advice I'll offer to expecting mothers is have some toast on stand-by; the rest comes naturally. We're all born to be mothers. I hope your experiences are as fantastic as mine.

Sinead Moriarty moved to London after university, where she worked as a journalist. Having always wanted to write a novel, she joined a creative writing group and began to write her first book, *The Baby Trail*, which was subsequently translated into twenty languages. She now lives in Dublin with her husband and two young sons. She is currently working on her fifth novel.

Take Two
Sinead Moriarty

The difference between your first and second pregnancies is akin to the difference between black and white. There is no comparison. They are two completely different experiences.

During your first pregnancy, you take long naps when you're tired. During your second pregnancy, you pass out face down, fully clothed, on the pillow at any given opportunity. Even five minutes is not to be sniffed at.

During your first pregnancy, when your back begins to ache, you languish for hours in scented bubble baths reading magazines while listening to calming whale music. During your second pregnancy, you're lucky if you get time for a five-second shower before your toddler upends all your make-up down the loo.

During your first pregnancy, your partner won't let you lift a teapot. During your second pregnancy, you're left to carry the shopping home with a toddler strapped to your back.

During your first pregnancy, your partner goes to all the check-ups with you, holds your hand and listens intently to the obstetrician. During your second pregnancy, he has a lot of meetings on.

During your first pregnancy, everyone makes a huge fuss – seats are given up, cushions are placed behind your back, foot-stools are provided for your swollen ankles. During your second pregnancy, you're lucky if you get the foot-stool to sit on.

During your first pregnancy, you eat healthy meals you never would have looked at before. Spinach becomes your best friend. When you get up in the morning, the first thing you do is make a healthy fresh fruit smoothie before heading off to work. At dinnertime you eat lots of green vegetables and avoid soft cheese and pâté like the plague. During your second pregnancy, you eat whatever is fast, accessible and gives you instant energy. Chocolate biscuits, cereal and leftover fish fingers become your staple diet. Cooking takes up precious time that could be spent sleeping.

During your fist pregnancy, you care how you look. You hunt for pretty, stylish clothes that flatter your new round shape. During your second pregnancy, you know you look like Shrek, so you wear big tents.

During your first pregnancy, you try not to eat for two and kid yourself that you'll get back into shape as soon as the baby's born. During your second pregnancy, you know you'll never fit into your skinny jeans again, so you eat for Ireland.

During your first pregnancy, you discuss baby names for hours. You read baby name books, always taking care to analyse the prospective nicknames that could be formed from any given name. A straightforward name like Richard suddenly becomes a potential minefield of Rich, Richy, Dickie, Dick, Dickster. Days turn into weeks which turn into months, until eventually you have a shortlist, which you agonise over before finally choosing the child's name. During your second pregnancy, you forget to name the child and when they are born you look at them panic stricken, hastily name them after your granddad – and regret it for the next thirty years.

During your first pregnancy, your mother listens sympathetically to your moaning. During your second pregnancy, she reminds you that the women in Africa give birth while working in the fields and not a word of complaint out of them.

During your first pregnancy, you wonder who the baby will look like, what colour hair they will have, what school they will go to, what type of personality they will have, what career path they will follow. You assume they will be a world leader or the curer of cancer. During your second pregnancy, you wonder how long it'll take before the baby sleeps through the night.

During your first pregnancy, your partner listens patiently to all your aches and pains. He is interested in the fact that your rib cage is expanding as the baby grows. He is immensely sympathetic, massages your back and brings you cups of tea in bed. During your second pregnancy, he's heard it all before, he's exhausted and his own back hurts from lifting the toddler. If you want a cup of tea, you can make it yourself.

During your first pregnancy, you watch your bump grow with fascination and awe. You follow each step, mesmerised by the development of the foetus. You feel blooming, beautiful, maternal, alive… During your second pregnancy, you feel like a big fat blob.

During your first pregnancy, the nausea is bearable because you can just curl up in bed all weekend, have early

3

nights during the week and if needs be pull a sickie in work. During your second pregnancy, you don't even have time to throw up.

During your first pregnancy, you think your life won't change that much, the baby will just slot in. During your second pregnancy, you store up on DVD box sets because you know you won't be stepping foot outside the door for six months.

During your first pregnancy, you describe all the stages to your partner, who listens, enthralled at the baby's progress. He asks you to wake him up when the baby kicks so he can feel it. He beams at you and says, 'That's the next David Beckham in there.' During your second pregnancy, he's as desperate for sleep as you are. Unless the house is on fire and your life is in danger, don't even think about waking him up.

During your first pregnancy, you go for pedicures and long lunches with girlfriends. During your second pregnancy, you chase after a hyper toddler, change dirty nappies, wipe snotty noses and sing 'The Wheels on the Bus Go Round and Round' four thousand times a day.

During your first pregnancy, you fret about child care. You want a nanny who is a former *Blue Peter* presenter with a degree in paediatric nursing, is a cordon bleu chef, loves going for long walks, knows every nursery rhyme ever written and thinks television is the root of all evil. During your second pregnancy, you'll hire anyone without a police record.

During your first pregnancy, you read all the baby books available and are determined to have your little one in a routine and sleeping through the night at six weeks. During your second pregnancy, you laugh hysterically when people mention routine.

During your first pregnancy, you pack pretty nightdresses with matching dressing gowns and satin slippers for hospital. During your second pregnancy, you pack XXX-large T-shirts and ear plugs.

During your first pregnancy, everyone asks you how you are. During your second pregnancy, no one cares.

During your first pregnancy, you think the horror stories you hear about forceps and stitches are exaggerated. During your second pregnancy, you know they aren't.

During your first pregnancy, you're excited all the time. During your second pregnancy, you're worried all the time.

During your first pregnancy, you invite everyone into hospital to see the baby. During your second pregnancy, you nail the door shut.

During your first pregnancy, you have the nursery ready weeks in advance. You spend hours painting and decorating the perfect room for your baby. Bunnies and teddies abound. During your second pregnancy, you turn the cot mattress over.

During your first pregnancy, you go to hospital laden down with beautiful baby clothes, booties, hats and mittens purchased in fancy baby shops called Petit Bateau and Mon Cheri. During your second pregnancy, you go to hospital with a 12-pack of babygros from Tesco.

During your first pregnancy, you can only try to imagine the miracle of having a baby. During your second pregnancy, you know what joy and happiness await you when you see that beautiful little scrunched up face for the first time.

Cathy Kelly is the author of nine novels, including *Past Secrets* and *Always and Forever*. She lives in Wicklow with her partner and their twin sons. In 2005, she became an ambassador for UNICEF Ireland.

Children Is a Language
Cathy Kelly

On my kitchen wall is a picture that sums up motherhood for me. It's a photo of a mother and a baby girl, perhaps a year old, with shining dark eyes full of mischief and fun. Her hair is delicately braided with fuzzy blue hairbands and her chubby little hands are raised joyfully because she doesn't need to cling onto her mum for support.

Mum will take care of her, right?

And that's what motherhood is about: taking care of your children no matter what and giving them the confidence to know that whatever happens, Mum will be there.

That absolute confidence means that the devil-may-care toddler can attempt the 'look, Mum, no hands!' leap from the kitchen table because she knows that Mum will catch her.

Being the open arms ready to catch your children from any and every fall is part of the mothering deal.

You would give up your own life for them. But what if that wasn't enough? What if you couldn't help them?

It's unimaginable, isn't it? And yet it happens every day on our planet to parents who are just like all of us, but are born into a different world.

But for the accident of birth, they could be any of us.

The little girl in the picture on my kitchen wall is from Mozambique. I took that photo over two years ago when I visited Africa with UNICEF, and now I wonder if she's still alive.

Every day I look at her, I regret that I never even found out her name. She was one of scores of beautiful children I met in a mother and baby clinic in the Xai Xai province in southern Mozambique. It was day three of my tour of this beautiful but poverty-stricken African country, and my head was reeling from spending time at a hospital where men, women and children are treated for AIDS. Parents with HIV-positive children gave the UNICEF team the thousand-mile stare of people in a living hell. There was no guarantee that they'd get life-saving anti-retroviral drugs (ARVs) for their children or themselves. Sitting in the hospital in the heat, I felt faint for the first time in my life at seeing the AIDS pandemic up close and personal.

Here, AIDS isn't a word on a newspaper page: it's part of daily life, with one in seven people infected with HIV. The disease has wiped out almost an entire generation, leaving hundreds of thousands of children orphaned and turning grandparents into parents.

And then we left the hospital and drove along dusty tracks to the mother and baby clinic, where, suddenly, I felt gloriously at home. Here, amongst the mothers and their babies, I belonged. My twin sons, Murray and Dylan, were twenty months old and the world of small children was my world. The clinic in Xai Xai shared so much with the one in Dublin's Rotunda Hospital, even though thousands of miles separated them.

There was the same crying of outraged babies, the same tiredness of weary mothers and the same drone of names being called with calm efficiency. Immunisations were being given, contraception was discussed and babies squealed with shock when the needle went in.

The difference was geographical, but the mother love was the same. Only the problems were vastly different.

Mozambique has one of the highest mortality rates in the world and the beautiful babies I saw had a 20 per cent chance of not living beyond the age of five. As in much of Africa, malaria is the top killer, followed by acute respiratory infections, malnutrition, diarrhoea and measles. None of these should kill a child in the twenty-first century.

When it was time to go, I took out my camera to take some photos of the babies. My boys had just made that quicksilver leap from babyhood to sturdy toddlerhood and some part of me still yearned for those baby days. Photos of these imperious little beings, smiling and squealing by turn, would be my baby fix. As I clicked the camera on, the mothers in the clinic all held up their babies up for a photo. Because your own baby is always the most beautiful, right?

Up till then, the mothers had been busy with their babies and hadn't paid too much attention to the newcomers. Now, we were all women together: smiling, gesturing, laughing at the infants' antics.

Children is a language. I had only a few words of local dialect, and I probably said those incorrectly, but it was immaterial. A woman who knows how to caress a baby's delicate head and murmur soothing words in one language can make herself understood to parents and children in any language. A smile is still a smile whether it's in English or in one of the twenty-two dialects spoken in Mozambique.

I took photo after photo and then took one of the little girl with blue hairbands. Pure joy of life shone out of her, and keeps shining up on my kitchen wall.

I can't pass it without thinking of the infant mortality rate in much of Africa and try not to wonder which of the mothers I met will be grieving for their child in a few years' time.

Smug motherhood is one of my pet hates – that annoying belief that only if the other person had a child, they'd understand what was previously incomprehensible. Yet the world of UNICEF is undoubtedly in sharper focus in my life because I am a mother of two sons.

When we visit the local GP for the nth time over a cough or a rash, I'll think of the people on our planet who live hundreds of miles from a doctor, who couldn't afford to buy any medicine the doctor might prescribe even if they saw him and who rely on local – and sometimes medically risky – remedies to protect their kids.

I can see our lives through the prism of theirs and it makes me both desperately grateful for what I have and fiercely sad for what they don't.

In Mozambique, I met mothers who face problems that I dare not imagine. HIV-positive mothers desperately trying to get their beloved HIV-positive kids on the life-saving ARV drugs that can mean the difference between life and death.

One morning, I watched an elegant woman sit gracefully on a chair in the day hospital with her fragile seven-year-old daughter in front of her. The little girl was beautifully dressed in a white *broderie anglaise* blouse and skirt, almost like a party dress. Yet there was no party in her life. She had been diagnosed with HIV six months previously. Her mother was HIV positive too. The little girl held onto her stomach nervously while her mother clutched her handbag tightly with slender fingers. Neither of them were on ARV treatment.

These expensive drugs are still not widely available. Who gets them is a complex decision based on factors like blood count and whether the patient will be able to take the drugs correctly for the rest of their lives.

During the trip, myself and the team met lots of smiling people who thanked UNICEF for their various projects (the day hospital is funded by UNICEF at a cost of $200,000 a year), and in pidgin Portuguese (Mozambique was once a Portuguese colony), we replied. With this sad-eyed woman and her small daughter, pretty in her white party outfit, there was nothing any of us could say. There was nothing *to* say.

In Mozambique, 270,000 children are orphans because of AIDS. They care for their dying parents and then they have to care for their brothers and sisters as well as trying to protect their tiny families and feed them.

Like handsome young Andreas, who was just thirteen when his mum and dad died. When we met him, Andreas was eighteen, the head of his household, mum and dad to his four siblings. When his parents died, the youngest were four-year-old twins. As a mother of twins, I can't imagine how a thirteen-year-old would cope with being a parent. But Andreas, standing tall and proud beside the cane house he built for his family, said, 'We get on all right. We all help.

Our neighbour helps us. Kuvumbana help us.'

Kuvumbana, which means 'unity' in the local language, is a UNICEF-funded voluntary group of people living with HIV/AIDS who support children orphaned due to the disease.

Orphans in the West have social services and extended families to take care of them. In Mozambique, the adult population is being eroded due to AIDS, so the extended families are often elderly grandparents. There's little legal framework in place, so kids don't even have a system to get lost in. They drop out of school and are vulnerable to abuse and child labour. Not only have they watched their parents die, but they've had to grow up instantly.

On one of our last days in Mozambique, the UNICEF team visited the Fidel Castro school where there was a huge welcoming party to greet us. It hit me again that day: kids are the same the world over. Creed, colour or geography are immaterial. School kids giggle, climb trees to show off, admire the UNICEF jeep, shake their heads and laugh. Pale, freckled people with blonde hair are thin on the ground here, so they think I'm funny looking. I admire the little girls' gorgeous braids and they touch my hair.

They proudly show us their UNICEF schoolbags with 'my future is my choice' printed on them. The kids treasure their bags in a way that makes me feel ashamed of Western materialism.

The parents' council wants to talk to us and say thanks. Not thanks-with-their-hand-out-for-more, but a grateful thanks of strong people who are standing there shoulder to shoulder with non-governmental agencies like UNICEF trying to put their country back together again.

Paper decorations and tablecloths with floral displays

are laid on in the school to welcome us. The local community, led by the velvet-voiced Celesto Antonio Lange, sings to us. We've got one word of their dialect: *kanemambo*. It means thank you. They laugh uproariously at our pronunciation, shake our hands and proudly admire their kids.

'Thank you,' says one speaker. 'There is a big difference between before your help and after. Your help has given us life in our hearts and for our families.' Translation can do weird things to language, but that's what they said.

For my sons' first birthday, I decided to write them a letter each telling them how much I loved them, how much magic they'd brought into my life. Because what if one day I never came back? How would they know how much their mum adored them?

Who'd teach them all the things that only a mother knows? Who else would tickle that soft spot under their chins, or pretend that 'the claw!' is coming, in the voice that only I can do?

No letter would tell them.

That's my greatest fear, next to something happening to them, that I won't come back one day and they'll grow up without me to protect them.

Yet while I am here, I have the luxury of taking care of them. Working with UNICEF has shown me people who are powerless to protect their children purely because of where they live. In our world, geography is destiny. Perhaps one day it won't be and mothers and fathers will be able to take care of their children irrespective of where they live.

Anne Enright has written short stories, novels and essays to great acclaim. Her collection of stories, *The Portable Virgin* in 1991, won the Rooney Prize that year and other short stories have been widely published, including by *The New Yorker* and *Granta*. Her novels are *The Wig My Father Wore*, which was shortlisted for *The Irish Times*/Aer Lingus Irish Literature Prize; *What Are You Like?*, which won the Royal Society of Authors Encore Prize; and *The Pleasure of Eliza Lynch*. She has also written about her experience of parenthood – *Making Babies: Stumbling into Motherhood*. Her new novel, *The Gathering*, is published by Jonathan Cape.

Birth
Anne Enright

Amniotic fluid smells like tea. When I say this to Martin, he says, 'I thought that was just tea.' Of course, a hospital should smell of tea: a hospital should smell of bleach. Unit C in Holles Street smells of tea and a little bit of ammonia; whether human or industrial is hard to tell. There is a lot of amniotic fluid in Unit C. At least three of the women have had their waters broken that afternoon, and as the evening approaches we sit draining into strips of un-bleached cotton and watching each other, jealously, for signs of pain.

There is a little something extra in there, sharp and herbal – green tea maybe, or gunpowder tea. Pregnancy smelled like grass. Sort of. It certainly smelled of something growing; a distinctive and lovely smell that belongs to that family of grass, and ironed cotton, and asparagus pee. But the smell of tea is beginning to get to me. There are pints of it. I'm like some Birco boiler with the tap left open. It flows slowly, but it will not stop. For hours I have been waiting for it to stop, and the mess of the bed is upsetting me. It upsets the housekeeper in me and it upsets the schoolgirl in me. The sanitary pads they hand you are school issue and all the nurses are turning into nuns.

The breaking of the waters was fine. The nurse did whatever magic makes sheets appear under you while other things are folded back, and the obstetrician did something deft with a crochet hook. There was the sense of pressure against a membrane, and then pop – a bit tougher but not much different than bursting a bubble on plastic bubble wrap. It felt quite satisfying, and the rush of hot liquid that followed made me laugh. I don't think a lot of women laugh at this stage in Unit C, but why not? We were on our way.

After which, there was nothing to do but wait. As the afternoon wears on, the pink curtains are pulled around the beds. The ward is full of breathing; the sharp intake of breath and the groaning exhalation, as though we were all asleep, or having sex in our sleep. One woman sobs behind her curtain. From the bed beside me the submarine sound of the Doppler looking for a foetal heartbeat and endlessly failing – a sonic rip as it is pulled away, then bleeping, breathing; the sigh and rush of an unseen woman's electronic blood.

Then there is tea. Actual tea. The men are sent out, for some reason, and the women sit around the long table in the middle of the ward. It's a school tea. There is a woman with high blood pressure, a couple of diabetics, one barely pregnant woman who has such bad nausea she has to be put on a drip. There are at least three other women on the brink, but they stay in bed and will not eat. I am all excited and want to talk. I am very keen to compare dressing gowns – it took me so long to find this one, and I am quite

16

pleased with it, but when I get up after the meal, the back of it is stained a watery red. I am beginning to hate Unit C.

After tea is the football. Portugal are playing France and, when a goal is scored, the men all come out from behind the curtains to watch the replay. Then they go back in again to their groaning, sighing women. I keep the curtain open and watch Martin while he watches the game. I am keeping track of my contractions, if they are contractions. At 9:35, Martin looks at me over the back of his chair. He gives me a thumbs up as if to say, 'Isn't this a blast? And there's football on the telly!' At 9:35 and twenty seconds I am, for the first time, in serious pain. I am in a rage with him for missing it, and call to him quietly over the sound of the game.

A woman in a dressing gown comes to talk to me. She is very big. I ask her if she is due tonight but she says she is not due until September, which is three months away. She is the woman from the next bed, the one with the Doppler machine. They couldn't find the foetal heartbeat because of the fat. She stands at the end of the bed and lists her symptoms, which are many. She has come up from Tipperary. She is going to have a caesarean at thirty-one weeks. I am trying to be sympathetic, but I think I hate her. She is weakness in the room.

When I have a contraction I lurch out of bed, endlessly convinced that I have to go to the toilet – endlessly, stupidly convinced, every five minutes, that there is a crap I have to take, new and surprising as the first crap Adam took on his second day in the world. This journey to the toilet is full of obstacles, the first one being Martin, whose patience is endless and whose feet are huge. When I get into the cubicle at the end of the ward, I sit uselessly on the toilet, try to mop up the mess and listen to the woman on the other side of the partition, who is louder than me and who doesn't seem to bother going back to her bed any more.

This has been happening, on and off, for a week. There is nothing inside me by way of food; there hasn't been for days. I am in what Americans call pre-labour, what the Irish are too macho to call anything at all. 'If you can talk through it, then it's not a contraction,' my obstetrician said when I came in a week ago, convinced that I was on my way. This week, she says she will induce me because my blood pressure is up, but it may be simple charity. Ten days ago I wanted a natural birth, now I want a general anaesthetic. Fuck aromatherapy, I would do anything to make this stop – up to and including putting my head in the road, with my belly up on the curb.

A woman answers her mobile. 'No, Ma, nothing yet. Stop calling! Nothing yet.' Pain overtakes the woman two beds down and the curtains are drawn. When they are pulled back, you can tell she is delighted. Oh this is it. This must be it. Oh oh I'm going to have a baby. Then more pain – agony, it looks like. 'Oh good girl! Good girl!' shouts the midwife as the man collects her things and she is helped out of the Ante-Room to Hell that is Unit C. I am jealous, but I wish her well. The room is full of miracles waiting to happen, whether months or hours away. Another bed is empty – the woman on the other side of the toilet partition, is she in labour too? 'She went out, anyway,' says Martin. 'Hanging onto the wall.'

It is a theatre of pain. It is a pain competition (and I am losing). Martin says that Beckett would have loved Unit C. We wonder whether this is the worst place we have ever been, but decide that the prize still goes to the bus station in Nasca, the time we went to Peru and didn't bring any jumpers. All the paper pants I brought have torn and I sit knickerless on the unbleached sheet, which I have rolled up into a huge wad under me. My bump has shrunk and gone slack. When I put my hand on it, there is the baby; very close now under the skin. I just know it is a girl. I feel her shoulder and an arm. For some reason I think of a skinned rabbit. I wonder are her eyes open, and if she is waiting, like me. I have loved this child in a drowsy sort of way, but now I feel a big want in me for her, for this particular baby – the one that I am touching through my skin. 'Oh, when will I see you?' I say.

This could be the phrase of the night, but instead it is a song that repeats in my head. 'What sends her home hanging onto the wall? Boozin'! Bloody well boo–oozin'.' I stop getting out of bed every five minutes and start breathing, the way they told us to in the ante-natal class. I count backwards from five when the pain hits, and then from five again. Was I in labour yet? Was this enough pain? 'If you can talk, then it's not labour.' So I try to keep talking, but by eleven o'clock the lights are switched off, I am lurching into sleep between my (non)contractions for three or five minutes at a time and Martin is nodding off in the chair.

My cervix has to do five things: it has to come forward, it has to shorten, it has to soften, it has to thin out, it has to open. A week earlier, the obstetrician recited this list and told me that it had already done three of them. In the reaches of the night I try to remember which ones I have left to do, but I can't recall the order they come in, and there is always, as I press my counting fingers into the sheet, one that I have forgotten. My cervix, my cervix. Is it soft but not short? Is it soft and thin but not yet forward? Is it short and hard but open anyway? I have no sense that this is not a list but a sequence. I have lost my grasp of cause and effect. My cervix, my cervix: it will open like the clouds open, to let the sun come shining through. It will open like the iris of an eye, like the iris when you open the back of a camera. I could see it thinning, the tiny veins stretching and breaking. I could see it opening like something out of *Alien*. I could see it open as simple as a door that you don't know you've opened until you are halfway across the room. I could see all this, but my cervix stayed shut.

At 2:30 a.m. I give in and Martin goes off to ask for some Pethedine. I know I will only be allowed two doses of this stuff, so it better last a long time. I want to save the second for the birth, but in my heart of hearts I know I'm on my way to an epidural now. I don't know why I wanted to do without one; I suppose it was that Irishwoman macho again. Mná na hÉireann. MNÁ na hÉireann. FIVE four three two…one. Fiiiive four three two one. Five. Four. Three. Two. One.

Once I give in and start to whimper, the (non)contractions are unbearable. The Pethedine does not come. At 3:00 a.m. there is a shrieking from down the corridor and I realise how close we are to the labour ward. The noise is ghastly, Victorian: it tears through the hospital dark. Someone is really giving it soprano. I think nothing of it. I do not wonder if the woman is mad or if the baby has died, but that is what I wonder as I write this now.

Footsteps approach but they are not for me, they are for the woman from Tipperary who has started crying, with a great expenditure of snot, in the bed next door. The nurse comforts her. 'I'm just frikened,' she says. 'She just frikened me.' I want to shout that it's all right for her, she's going to have a fucking Caesarean, but it is forty-five minutes since I realised that I could not do this any more, that the pain I had been riding was about to ride over me, and I needed something to get me back on top or I would be destroyed by it, I would go under – in some spiritual and very real sense, I would die.

The footsteps go away again. They do not return. I look at Martin, who is listening, as I am listening, and he disappears silently through the curtain. At 3:30 a.m., I get the Pethedine.

After this, I do not count through the (non)contractions or try to manage my breathing. I moan, with my mouth a little open. I low. I almost enjoy it. I sleep all the time now, between times. I have given in. I have untied my little boat and gone floating downstream.

At 5:00 a.m. a new woman comes along and tells Martin he must go home. There follows a complicated and slow conversation as I stand up to her (we are, after all, back in school). I say that I need him here, and she smiles, 'What for? What do you need him for?' (For saving me from women like you, Missis). In the end, she tells us that there are mattresses he can sleep on in a room down the hall. Oh. Why didn't she say so? Maybe she's mad. It's 5:00 a.m., I'm tripping on Pethedine at the raw end of a sleepless week, and this woman is a little old-fashioned, in a mad sort of way. Wow. We kiss. He goes. From now on, I stay under, not even opening my eyes when the pain comes.

I think I low through breakfast. They promise me a bed in the labour ward at half ten so I can stop lowing and start screaming, but that doesn't seem to be happening really. I am sitting up and smiling for the ward round, which is nice, but I am afraid that they will notice that the contractions are fading and I'll have to start all over again, somehow. Then the contractions come back again and by now my body is all out of Pethedine. I spend the minutes after half past ten amused by my rage, astonished by how bad I feel. Are these the worst hundred seconds I have ever been through? How about the next hundred seconds – let's give them a go.

At twelve o'clock, I nip into the cubicle for one last contraction and we are out of Unit C. The whole ward lifts as we leave, wishing us well – another one on her way. I realise I have been lowing all night, keeping these women from sleep.

The room on the labour ward is extremely posh, with its own bathroom and a high-tech bed. I like the look of the midwife, she's the kind of woman you'd want to go for a few pints with. She is tired. She asks if I have a birth plan and I say I want to do everything as natural as possible. She says, 'Well you've made a good start, anyway,' which I think is possibly sarcastic, given the crochet hook and the Pethedine and now an oxytocin drip. Martin goes back to pack up our stuff and I start to talk. She keeps a half-ironic silence. For months, I had the idea that if I could do a bit of research, get a bit of chat out of the midwife, then that would take my mind off things – what is the worst thing that anyone ever said? or the weirdest? – but she won't play ball. I run out of natter and have a little cry. She says, 'Are you all right?' I say, 'I just didn't think I would ever get this far, that's all.' And I feel her soften behind me.

I don't remember everything that followed, but I do remember the white, fresh light. I also remember the feelings in the room. I could sense a shift in mood, or intention, in the women who tended me with great clarity. It was like being in a painting. Every smile mattered; the way people were arranged in the space, the gestures they made.

I have stopped talking. The midwife is behind me, arranging things on a stand. Martin is gone, there is silence in the room. She is thinking about something. She isn't happy. It is very peaceful.

Or: She tries to put in the needle for the drip. Martin is on my right-hand side. I seem to co-operate but I won't turn my hand around. The stain from the missed vein starts to spread and she tries again. I am completely uninterested in the pain from the needle.

Or: A woman walks in, looks at me, glances between my legs. 'Well done!' she says and walks back out again. Perhaps she just walked into the wrong room.

Even at a low dose, the oxytocin works fast. It is bucking through my system, the contractions gathering speed: the donkey who is kicking me is getting really, really annoyed. The midwife goes to turn up the drip and I say, 'You're not touching that until I get my epidural.' A joke.

A woman puts her head round the door, then edges into the room. She says something to the midwife, but they are really talking about something else. She half turns to me with a smile. There is something wrong with one of the blood tests. She tells me this, then she tells the midwife that we can go ahead anyway. The midwife relaxes. I realise that, sometimes, they don't give you an epidural. Even if you want one. They just can't. Then everyone has a bad morning.

The midwife goes to the phone. Martin helps to turn

me on my side. The contractions now are almost continuous. Within minutes, a woman in surgical greens walks in. 'Hi!' she says. 'I'm your pain relief consultant.' She reaches over my bare backside to shake my hand. This is a woman who loves her job. Martin cups my heels and pushes my knees up towards my chest while she sticks the needle in my spine, speaking clearly and loudly and working at speed. I am bellowing by now, pretty much. FIVE, I roar (which seems to surprise them – five what?). FOUR. THREE. (Oh good woman! That's it!) TWO. One. FIVE. They hold me like an animal that is trying to kick free, but I am not – I am doing this, I am getting this done. When it is over, the anaesthetist breaks it to me that it might be another ten minutes before I feel the full effect. I do not have ten minutes to spare – I want to tell her this, but fortunately the pain has already begun to dull.

The room turns to me. The anaesthetist pats down her gown and smiles. She is used to the most abject gratitude, but I thank the midwife instead, for getting the timing spot on. The woman who talked about my blood tests has come back and the midwife tells me that she is finishing up now, Sally will see me through. This is a minor sort of betrayal, but I feel it quite keenly. Everyone leaves. Martin goes for a sandwich and Sally runs ice cubes up my belly to check the line of the epidural. There is no more pain.

Sally is lovely: sweetness itself. She is the kind of woman who is good all the way through. It is perhaps half past one and in the white light, with no pain, I am having the time of my life. Literally. Karen, the obstetrician, tells me my cervix has gone from practically zero to eight centimetres in no time flat. The heavens have opened, the sun has come through. Martin is called back from the canteen. He watches the machines as they register the pain that I cannot feel any more. He says the contractions are off the scale now. We chat a bit and have a laugh, and quite soon Sally says it is time to push. Already.

For twenty hours women have been telling me I am wonderful, but I did not believe them until now. I know how to do this, I have done it in my dreams. I ask to sit up a bit and the bed rises with a whirr. Martin is invited to 'take a leg' and he politely accepts, 'Oh, thank you.' Sally takes the other one and braces it – my shin against her ribs. Push! They both lean into me. I wait for the top of the contraction, catch it and ride the wave. I can feel the head, deliciously large under my pubic bone. I can feel it as it eases further down. I look at Martin, all the while – here is a present for you, Mister, this one is for you – but he is busy watching the business end. Karen is back and everyone willing me on like football hooligans, Go on! Go on! One more now, and Push! Good woman! Good girl! I can hear the knocking of the baby's heartbeat on the foetal monitor and the dreadful silence as I push. Then, long before I expect it, Sally says, 'I want you to pant through this one. Pant.' The child has come down, the child is there. Karen says, Yes, you can see the head. I send Martin down to check the colour of the hair. (A joke?) Another push. I ask may I touch, and there is the top of the head, slimy and hot and – what is most terrifying – soft. Bizarrely, I pick up Martin's finger to check that it is clean, then tell him he must feel how soft it is. So he does. After which – enough nonsense now – it is back to pushing. Sally reaches in with her flat-bladed scissors and Martin, watching, lets my leg go suddenly slack. We are mid-push. I kick out, and he braces against me again. Karen, delighted, commands me to 'look down now, and see your baby being born'. I tilt my head to the maximum and there is the back of the baby's head, easing out beyond my belly's horizon line. It is black and red, and wet. On the next push, machine perfect, it slowly turns. And here it comes – my child; my child's particular profile. A look of intense concentration, the nose tilted up, mouth and eyes tentatively shut. A blind man's face, vivid with sensation. On the next push, Sally catches the shoulders and lifts the baby out and up – in the middle of which movement the mouth opens, quite simply, for a first breath. It simply starts to breathe.

'It's a girl!' Sally says afterwards that we were very quiet when she came out. But I didn't want to say the first thing that came to mind, which was, 'Is it? Are you sure?' Newborns' genitals are swollen and red and a bit peculiar looking, and the cord was surprisingly grey, and twisted like a baroque pillar. Besides, I was shy. How to make the introduction? I think I eventually said, 'Oh, I knew you would be.' I think I also said, 'Oh, come here to me, darling.' She was handed to me, smeared as she was, with something a bit stickier than cream cheese. I laid her on my stomach and pulled at my T-shirt to clear a place for her on my breast. She opened her eyes for the first time, looking into my face, her irises cloudy. She blinked and found my eyes. It was a very suspicious, grumpy look and I was devastated.

Martin, doing the honours at a festive dinner, cut the cord. After I pushed out the placenta, Karen held it up for inspection, twirling it on her hand like a connoisseur: a bloody hair net, though heavier and more slippy.

The baby was long. Her face looked like mine. I had not prepared myself for this: this really astonished me. 'She looks like me,' and Martin said (an old joke), 'But she's got my legs.' At some stage, she was wrapped rigid in a blue blanket, which was a mercy, because I could hardly bear the smallness of her. At some stage, they slipped out, leaving us to say, 'Oh my God,' a lot. I put her to a nipple and she suckled. 'Oh my God,' said Martin. I looked at him as if to say, 'Well what did you expect?' I rang my mother, who said, 'Welcome to the happiest day of your life,' and started to cry. I thought this was a little over the top. In a photograph taken at this time, I look pragmatic and unsurprised, like I had just cleaned the oven and was about to tackle the fridge.

I am not stricken until they wheel us down to the ward. The child looks at the passing scene with alert pleasure. She is so clear and sharp. She is saturated with life, she is intensely alive. Her face is a little triangle and her eyes are shaped like leaves, and she looks out of them, liking the world.

Two hours later I am in the shower. When I clean between my legs I am surprised to find everything numb and mushy. I wonder why that is. Then I remember that a baby's head came out of there, actually came out. When I come to, I am sitting on a nurse. She is sitting on the toilet beside the shower. The shower is still going. I am very wet. She is saying, 'You're all right, you're all right, I've got you.' I think I am saying, 'I just had a baby. I just had a baby,' but I might be trying to say it, and not saying anything at all.

Cauvery Madhavan has three children who, despite their concerted efforts to the contrary, keep her sane. She is a columnist with the *Evening Herald* and has written two novels.

A Right Pair
Cauvery Madhavan

The learning curve for mothers is actually a series of hair-pin bends with frightening gradients and terrifying conse-quences should you lose control – of yourself, that is – so it is imperative at the start to get one thing right: you are the trainee and your children the demanding task masters who may or may not be sympathetic as you attempt those goody-two-shoes things that fall under the collective diffi-culty called mothering skills, like patience, calm and under-standing.

My own schooling in this regard has been varied, with unexpected lessons learned along the way. You learn the basics quickly enough, but advanced theory is not that easy to grasp. For instance, when is a kiss not just a kiss and a sigh not just a sigh? When do the fundamental things never ever apply? It is when the stars of your show, the artistes formerly known as angels, grow into veritable thespians and are able to communicate all that they feel in as mute a fashion as possible. Your children will quickly teach you how deafeningly loud sign language can be.

Often you will find that each of your children has their own special bodily signals. Your teenage daughter might be able to control the upward roll of her eyes to the extent that when they are about to annoy you for the nth time by heading towards the ceiling, she can, before you say a word, have them back where they belong, all round-eyed and innocent, presumably giving you her attention.

Your teenager has effectively said what she wanted and is now ready to counter any reprimand about her ocular activity with a well-timed, ever so soft sigh. Any comment on this nearly imperceptible exhalation, and quick as a flash her eyes are at it again. Don't interrupt, you say. I didn't say a word, she insists. You point out the thing with the eyes. Now she lets out a deep breath. At this juncture, if you are foolish, you might let your serious lecture on her disproportionate contribution to the phone bills dissolve into a farce about eyeballs and breathing patterns. But if you have been a good student, you know that in fact this is the time to walk away from confrontation, into your bathroom (en-suite ideally), where you can calm down by briefly indulging in some therapeutic eye-rolling yourself.

Coping with your children's takes on disappointment needs parental nerves of steel. Boys seem to specialise in this manoeuvre. Take, for example, the complete and utter dejection that your ten-year-old son's shoulders can convey. That desperately acute droop, followed by a hanging head and compounded by the listless kicking of an imaginary football, is wordlessly telling you he can't believe you are the sort of penny-pinching mother that would deny him the pleasure of replacing the two emperor marbles that he lost in a match in school with giant new marbles from the corner shop. Any urging on your part that he should use his innate skills to win them back the next day is met with hot tears of the instant variety. Your arm around his sagging shoulder is roughly shrugged off. He has said what he wants to say. Don't touch me. If you can't buy me my marbles, you don't deserve me.

And when is a kiss not a kiss? When it is being very reluctantly granted at the school gate by a wooden-faced five-year-old, who is punishing you for having confiscated her four Barbie dolls and their one-legged Ken from her school bag. No angry words here, no sulks and definitely no tears – just a very subtle eye for an eye.

Occasionally your children can do a collective on you, like when you enthusiastically model the outfit that you plan to wear for the school's fundraising race night for them. Believe me, the complete silence and total paralysis of body language on their part can only mean only one thing.

Once in a while, when motoring along on that aforementioned learning curve, your children might insist on a short halt at a lay-by full of memories to make sure you remember what it was like to be a child. This happened to me the time my first-born fell in love – with an unsuitable stiletto heel from the wrong side of the shop.

'How do you know I will end up hurt?' she demanded. 'You've never worn one in your life.' That's when I snorted, to no effect. She continued to flit excitedly from shelf to shelf, longing for and admiring every orthopaedic nightmare in the shop. I padded after her in my sensible walking shoes, bristling like a hedgehog with PMT, trying to do a quick tot-up of all the pairs of ankle-twisters and toe-maulers that I had ever worn over the years.

'Fourteen,' I said to her through clenched teeth. 'Seventeen if you include wedges and clogs.'

'Mum, what are you on about? Look, can I try this?' she said, holding out a dangerous four-inch steel-capped horror of a shoe. She saw the look on my face. 'Okay,' she sighed. 'I know. Too tarty.'

Instantly, I had a new worry. What was her definition of a tart? 'There is an age for everything,' I muttered.

'Yeah, and I'm old enough now for heels, proper high heels. Dad said so too.'

'Here is a nice pair,' I said, picking out a compromise.

'That's the sort of shoe you'd wear!' she replied in dismay.

'And what's wrong with that?'

Her eyes rolled. 'Please, Mum, you and Dad agreed.'

'Well, don't cast any aspersions on my ability to wear stilettos then. I've worn plenty in my time, young lady.'

'What?'

'Oh, never mind,' I said, deciding, in all my cunning, to go along with it. 'Okay, try it on,' I said, pointing to the shoe in her hand. She won't be able to walk ten steps in it, I thought. The excruciatingly acute angle, the flimsy support, the impossible pinpoint of the heel, the pain – I knew she'd come to her senses immediately. I watched and waited. She strutted in front of the mirror, confident and delighted.

'They must hurt,' I prompted. 'Horribly uncomfortable, aren't they?'

'Mum, I'm a teenager now,' she replied. 'It's no problem to me.'

Three hours and many shoe shops later, she has what she wants – her first pair of heels – and I have relived memories of getting my first pair. We head for some coffee and cake and I moan as we dump the bags and sit down at last. 'My feet are killing me.'

'You need to wear sensible shoes,' she says. Then she grins. 'Thanks, Mum, you're the best.'

Some lessons that you get from your children are mere updates to get you up to speed on the newest trends, like, for example, the latest in good manners. I fear my children have good manners coming out of their ears – in one ear and out the other. Perhaps the mother in me, expecting perfection, wants them to nod enthusiastically as I give them the standard lecture on how to answer the phone, or how to control the rolling eyes and shrugging shoulders or how to stop a while, say hello and make a minute or two of conversation with the neighbour's mother-in-law who has called in for a cup of tea. I want them to be well mannered and polite all the time, every time and they are happy to oblige – except when their notion of what constitutes good manners deviates in the most worrying fashion from my own views.

There is nothing more annoying than being called old-fashioned by your children. Let your friends have a slice first, I hiss as they all dive in for the pizza, but I am laughed off by all, friends included, and told to chill, relax, lighten up. The eldest begs me with an anguished look – Please, Mum, mind your manners and don't make a scene. Defeated, I leave them to fight over the stray pepperoni slices, which they do with much whooping and loud laughter.

Good manners are no longer as straightforward as teaching your children where to keep their knife and fork, for situations are more complex now – are they allowed to lick their fingers when eating barbequed spare ribs? The cutlery debate sums it all up: my children live in a different world than I did as child. I rolled my eyes to get a laugh;

they roll theirs when they want to be cheeky. I think nine o'clock in the evening is the latest my teenagers should call their friends' homes on the phone, but I have to, as they would say, like, get real. So I have learned to let some things go, but a few basics I just cannot compromise on and saying please and thank you are two of them.

Politeness never goes out of style and good manners can be judged with a timeless yardstick: thoughtfulness and consideration for others is what it is all about. What I am working at is to get them to be well mannered with their siblings, but the feedback from all three is that brothers and sisters are sub-human and therefore don't count.

Sometimes your children can teach you lessons on how not to try your hand at being democratic socialists. My household was sailing along happily, everybody pitching in on my motherly command, when I foolishly decided that our three children needed to learn the value of hard work and the associated pleasure of money well earned. What better way than to pay them for small jobs around the house? Within a month, jobs around the house were suddenly either coveted or despised and in the time that I spent deciding who would do what and, more crucially, who would get paid how much, I could have done most of the little jobs myself.

At first, it was all eagerness and enthusiasm on both sides, until that very spirit of honest enterprise that I wanted to inculcate in them turned on me in a most disconcerting fashion. The son whizzed around the lawn quite happily at the start of spring, but by early summer he was muttering about the front and back lawn being two separate jobs. The daughter agreed to vacuum the car, but then she began doing it with alarming frequency in order to feed her mobile phone dependency. There was a time when I grumbled about the dirt in the car – suddenly I had to insist that it was clean enough. Meanwhile, the youngest, then aged seven, told all and sundry of her battle against age discrimination – the job opportunities were non-existent, she complained.

My plans for honest enterprise had been overshadowed by cut-throat business tactics. The older two fought over the more lucrative jobs. The cushy numbers were coveted – suddenly, everyone wanted to iron for four hours non-stop in front of the television. I struggled to think of appropriate jobs for the youngest, but refused to submit to requests from her that she be paid to tidy her own room. Complications arose when they sometimes subcontracted parts of a job to a brother or sister without permission – should I pay the main contractor below the agreed price for a job poorly done and let her sort it out with the errant brother or sister? Or would the ensuing argument between the three drive me so demented that I may as well have paid the full price and bought my peace in advance? Should I have grinned and put up with it when they dropped my chores to do nixers for the neighbours for twice the money?

It was supposed to be a learning experience for my children – hard work does pay and all that sort of stuff. But I ended up learning the lesson instead – admittedly copping on a bit too late – that my kids were making easy money for jobs they should be doing anyway.

But of all things, the most important instruction that I have received from my children is that when all else fails, try a little bit of bad behaviour. I plead guilty to indulging in this technique occasionally.

Say I am stuck in traffic in the little cage that is my car and my children are going for each other like baited bears. Do I chide them cheerfully, counting to ten between attempts, thus missing my only chance in the day to listen to the radio? Oh, no! I do to them what they are doing unto me – turn up the volume, match them decibel for decibel and then sit back, relax and enjoy. I get pin-drop silence, every time.

I confess to having perfected the following methods as well: when it comes to throwing a tantrum in the shops, I have embarrassed them well before they embarrass me. I harangue them with questions of great importance when they are on the phone to friends, getting them to commit on difficult issues when they are thus distracted. When they are fighting over the last chocolate doughnut or prawn cracker, I have often calmly begun to eat the item myself, silencing them and removing the object of the argument in one fell bite. When my daughter complains about a punch received from her brother, I have advised her to gouge his eyes out. This is based on the principle that they never do as they are told.

Here is another of my procedures that you could try, but it requires advance planning. First, it is necessary to have secreted away a good book, a flask of tea and slice or two of chocolate cake in your bedroom. Then wait for a day when you have slaved over a family-sits-down-together meal. At the first hint of trouble over the veggies or who kicked who under the table, be on guard. When cutlery has morphed into weapons-grade steel and the gravy is finding its own level on the tablecloth, put your head in your hands and wail inconsolably. Then march off to your bedroom, saying you don't want your dinner, slamming the door as you go. Plump up the pillows, fish out the goodies and savour the moment. The effectiveness of this ploy wears off if used more than twice a year.

The last time I did this, I was awarded a bonus. After an unprecedented two-hour lull in hostilities amongst the siblings, my five-year-old knocked at the door. She walked in with a confident smile and a bowl of chocolate cereal in hand. 'Would you like today to be Mother's Day?' she asked sweetly. Who said bad behaviour doesn't pay?

Vanessa O'Loughlin is the busy mother of Sophie (7) and Sam (2 ½). The founder of Inkwell Writers' Workshops (www.inkwellwriters.ie), she has been writing for the past seven years.

Every Second Counts: Kyra's Story

Vanessa O'Loughlin

I'm lucky. I was lucky the day Robyn was born, a healthy 7 lb 6 oz, and, I'm convinced, already smiling. I was lucky the day I put the kettle on when she was sixteen months old, but didn't wait for it to boil. I was lucky that I heard a sound, like the TV remote hitting the floor maybe, or a toy falling, and went to investigate. Lucky that I didn't wait a second and finish what I was doing before going to see what was up. Because that day, seconds counted. Every single second.

It was a Thursday, about five o'clock. August. A beautiful sunny day, all the windows open, the birdsong loud even inside the kitchen, dust particles fairy dancing through beams of sunshine. Our accountant had popped over for a chat with my husband, who was on his way home from work early to meet him. He was sitting in his shirt sleeves at the kitchen table and I was just putting the kettle on as Robyn ran into the living room to play. She had only just learned to walk and was still tottering, delighted with her newfound freedom, and had greeted him with a pirouette in her new summer dress and a cheeky *hi-ya*.

Even today I still don't know what made me rush to her. She's my firstborn, so I was as protective as any first-time mum, but little ones make lots of noise when they're playing, and the odd crash certainly wasn't unusual. But that day, something was different. There was a silence after the crash that wasn't normal.

Before I reached her, I knew something was dreadfully wrong. She was lying on her back beside the fireplace, her long dark hair tumbled across the floor, a blue duck egg of a bruise already appearing on her forehead. Shaking all over, she looked like she was having a fit, hands clenching and unclenching like a pulse. And she wasn't breathing. I tried to stick my finger into her mouth, thinking she was holding her breath, an old trick. No go. Before my eyes, she began to turn blue, her soft brown eyes open, glazed, unseeing.

I screamed. Scooping her up into my arms I ran screaming back through the kitchen, instinctively heading for my dad, who was in the stable yard washing his car. Whenever I think about that day, I thank God that I wasn't alone. My husband, Henry, had just arrived, met me in the yard and immediately took Robyn into his arms, laying her on one of the garden tables, trying to clear her airway. Years before, he'd done a first aid course, practised on a doll not much bigger than our baby. And as my dad called an ambulance, Henry started CPR.

I ran for my own phone, trying to call my brother (a junior doctor) and my uncle (a GP). I couldn't even focus on the numbers, let alone make the calls. I'm normally the cool one in a crisis, but not that day. Our accountant tried to calm me, made me stand still, control my breathing. But it wasn't any good. And as a breeze picked up clouds of dust in the yard, the dogs running around yapping wildly, reacting to our stress, Henry continued to work on Robyn.

But I'm lucky. Lucky Henry was there. Lucky he knew CPR. Lucky he got her breathing again. Lucky my dad was on hand to dial 999. Lucky an ambulance was able to prioritise our call, already halfway to our house on another call.

We live right on the N11. The paramedics were at Robyn's side in about three minutes. Bags open, equipment spilling over the cobbles, two professionals bending over her. A rapid assessment of what had happened. No time for pleasantries, no time for hypothesis. Oxygen mask on.

She was still shaking violently.

I remember them lifting her tiny body like a rag doll onto the stretcher, scrambling in behind her. Then the doors slamming, the sound of tyres on gravel, the smell of disinfectant. I gripped her hand tighter. Sirens on. Four minutes to Loughlinstown Hospital. She needed to be stabilised before she could be taken anywhere else.

Robyn was violently sick in the ambulance, inhaling the vomit under the mask. But that was the least of our problems. The nightmare was only beginning. I felt so totally useless, talking to her, cradling her cold hand in mine, my eyes fixed on her face, on her blank lifeless eyes, willing her to fight, willing her to come back from wherever she had been taken. Could she even hear me?

With no paediatric speciality at Loughlinstown, it took the emergency team who waited for us what felt like an age to find a vein. We watched as they cut off her new dress, trying her feet, arms, groin and even shaving off her beautiful hair to try her scalp, but with so little oxygen in her system, the veins were closing. And she was only sixteen months old. A baby with tiny baby veins. She moaned at every attempt, feeling the pain, lost and confused somewhere we couldn't reach her. Eventually an anaesthetist was called from theatre and managed to get a line in. We both breathed a shaky sigh. An hour and a half later, she was heavily sedated, stable enough to move to a paediatric hospital.

But there were no intensive care beds available in Crumlin or Tallaght, so they couldn't take her. Standing in the heat of the corridor, burying my head in my husband's chest, gripping his arms, I stamped my foot in frustration, screaming into his shirt. What could we do? I didn't care if she was on a trolley for a week once she was somewhere where they could treat her. How could this happen? How could they have no beds? She was a baby, for God's sake, she'd fit under someone's desk.

Then the call came that Temple Street had a bed.

With the anaesthetist from Loughlinstown and the emergency transfer team on board, there was only room for one of us in the ambulance. Henry went with her. I felt like a failure, but I couldn't do it. I felt like he was holding it together, would be more use to her than I would be. So I missed the drama that was to unfold on the way.

Hooked up to a confusing array of equipment, Henry held Robyn's hand, the reassuring pip of the heart monitor giving him something to focus on as the medical team chatted about mundane things, the weather, the soccer, anything to keep him calm. The summer evening traffic was relatively light ahead of them, clearing as they headed for Blackrock. It was one of those sticky evenings when everyone wanted to get home to mow the lawn, have a few friends in for a barbeque, wind down into the weekend.

Then the pip stopped.

Flat line, they call it on *ER*. Because that's what it is. A flat line on the screen, a long, high-pitched flat beep. No output. No beat.

To this day, every time Henry passes the spot in Blackrock where the ambulance pulled over, he goes cold. Each member of the medical team registered the change and reacted simultaneously. Heart massage. Adrenaline. More oxygen. A top-class trauma team thinking as one, working as one. Doing everything they could. Doing more than they could.

But it was no good.

Flat line.

Henry watched as they exchanged glances, reading their expressions. Willing them to be wrong. This was it. After everything, she'd gone. How could it happen like this, how could her little life end on the Rock Road? The anaesthetist turned to him, the sweat running into his eyes. 'I'm so sorry, we're trying...'

Pip pip pip. As quickly as her heart had stopped, it restarted. A microsecond of complete astonishment, and then they moved. Fast. Lights, sirens and a call ahead to clear the toll bridge, straight through to Temple Street.

I was waiting on the pavement with my dad outside the hospital, but she was rushed past me so fast I didn't see her. Henry climbed out of the back of the ambulance shaking, white.

I never smoked in front of my parents, but up in the Relative's Room, my dad asked if he could get me anything. I asked for twenty Marlborough Lights and chain smoked them over the next two hours, pacing the floor, waiting for news. My dad rang everyone he knew who might be able to help. My brother and uncle arrived. No one was smiling.

Then my uncle called Dad outside. He'd been updated by the team looking after Robyn. Dad's face was ashen as he closed the door gently and gestured for Henry and myself to sit down with him.

'You've both been such wonderful parents…' He didn't get any further. Henry rushed from the room, his amazing calm finally cracking.

Dad had been told to prepare us for the worst.

Ten minutes later, a doctor came to see us. I don't know exactly what she said or how she said it; all I remember is hearing, 'Your daughter is very, very sick.' 'Swelling or bleeding on the brain' and 'it is very likely that she will be severely brain damaged or brain dead', 'the next forty-eight hours are critical.'

They didn't think she'd survive the night.

I couldn't think about losing her. Perhaps it was a coping mechanism, but her leaving us, dying, just wasn't on the agenda. Through the cigarette smoke in that hot, stuffy little room, I looked at my dad. Images of spoon-feeding Robyn at eighteen crowded into my head. Of life with a severely brain damaged child, of growing old with a baby locked in an adult's body.

Then they said they needed to get her to Beaumont to do a CT scan. It was the only place where they could assess the extent of the damage to her brain. We couldn't go with her because of the equipment and the personnel that were needed to transport her. And they thought that she might not survive the trip.

The doctor spoke so softly, so gently that I almost couldn't hear her. She was in the Intensive Care Unit, it would be a shock, but the equipment was essential and she was still heavily sedated and couldn't feel anything. I finally tuned in – this could be our last chance to see her. She might not survive the trip to Beaumont. Henry and I followed the doctor's white coat through the long, white, bright corridors to say our goodbyes.

Wrapped in tinfoil, tubes and wires everywhere, she looked nothing like our baby. Her face was blue, swollen dramatically, a collar supporting her neck, two tubes protruding from her mouth. I felt like she wasn't mine, like I'd lost her already, like my life had changed completely and utterly in a few short hours. We'd never get her back the way she was – there was no way of getting out of this without some level of loss.

So Beaumont next. Another ambulance, another transfer. This time on her own, with a dedicated team, but without her mummy or daddy. We arrived ahead of the ambulance, drank more coffee in cardboard cups in the Relative's Room, smoked more cigarettes, waiting again to find out how sick our baby was. I was cold, exhausted, almost comatose myself with shock, wore a path on carpet tiles with pacing. But the news was better. At eleven o'clock we were told that there did not appear to have been any bleeding on the brain. But she wasn't out of the woods – she'd had a forty-minute seizure that had deprived her brain of oxygen. There was no way of telling how it would affect her.

1:30 a.m. and we were back in Temple Street, assigned a room beside ICU, huddling together in the small bed. Henry closed his eyes and instantly fell into the deepest sleep of his life. Pure exhaustion. I slept fitfully, sweating in the airless room, listening to fights on the street outside, my imagination in overdrive, waiting for the phone to ring, waiting for a nurse to arrive and tell me she'd gone.

At 6:20 I woke up and went to check on Robyn. Pulling on the scrubs, tucking my long hair into the cap, I prepared myself for the worst. As I walked around the corner of the ICU a nurse met me, a serene smile on her face. I looked over her shoulder and saw Robyn, still pale and sickly but sitting up in bed. Waking up moments before, she had started to pull the tube from her mouth, demanding her bop bop and the Teletubbies. I looked in disbelief at the nurse and she smiled.

I cried like I've never cried before. I held Henry so tight he thought he was going to need a respirator. Robyn is eight now, in second class and has just done a test at school that puts her intellectually in the top 2 per cent of children in Ireland.

I'm lucky that Henry came home early that day. I'm lucky he'd done a first aid course. I'm lucky the traffic was light. I'm lucky that they had an intensive care bed in Temple Street. I'm lucky Robyn is a fighter. I'm lucky.

Kyra would like to thank everyone who helped saved Robyn's life, from the workmen on the N11 who cleared the traffic to allow the ambulance through to the paramedics and doctors who treated her. She is particularly grateful to the team at Temple Street Hospital.

Orla Tinsley is a student studying English and Greek and Roman Civilisation in UCD. After developing a worrying addiction to *Murder She Wrote* at the age of eight, her parents bought her a typewriter. The ink set and that was it as far as any serious lawyer-type job was concerned. She has written several pieces for *The Irish Times* and other publications about the treatment of cystic fibrosis patients in Ireland and also some about teen issues. She loves writing short stories, poetry and general musings.

I Have a Mother, She Is Mine
Orla Tinsley

I used to think I was adopted. In my early teens, while strolling along Grafton Street, I looked around for possible birth mothers. My mother and I have never had a sparkling relationship. When I tried the Marsha Brady thing, she was playing Morticia Adams; when she was Jackie Kennedy, I was the Girl, Interrupted who accompanied her. We rarely found an equilibrium to keep us both afloat. When I was sinking, I reached for any hand but hers and I came to the conclusion, as only a wise fifteen-year-old can, that not everyone gets on with their mothers.

At fifteen and sixteen, a lot of girls I knew were sleeping around, getting high, drunk and passing out nightly. I didn't have the slightest desire to humiliate myself in such a manner, as I respected myself and my parents. My mom didn't seem to realise that it could have been so much worse. We clashed regularly, plates fell, hair pulled, doors slammed and throats panged from our yelling. It baffled me. Your mother is the one person you're meant to have the strongest connection with, but for a while there, on a daily basis we wanted to kill each other.

One thing that tweaked incessantly at my brain was her

inability to understand me. It seems like typical teenage stuff, but there's a minor twist. I have cystic fibrosis, the charity the funds from this book will support. It's a long-term chronic illness and sometimes, when life goes too fast, it can get you down. I had a penchant for spending time in my room when I was younger. Losing myself in Emily Dickinson or even my own writing was cathartic for me. I wasn't dwelling, I was dealing.

She called it 'anal gazing'. After countless clashes and an extensive period of 'anal gazing', which to me was an attempt at starting a first novel and not a practice in morbid mulling, she took me to a psychologist 'for a chat'. The woman said that she had never witnessed two people so desperate to claw at each other in all her twenty years in that profession. In her office, the tension crept out like a detonated grenade, seeping higher with every moment. We left the place in silence. Somewhere between there and our house, I ended up on a mucky road in the middle of nowhere watching the sun bounce off the car bonnet as she drove off. It was mostly my fault. There was a lone sheep in the field across from where I stood and I watched it. I imagined living in its field, eating grass all day. After ten minutes, just as the tears were being snorted up my nose, she came back. The door swung open in silence. I glanced at the sheep and sat in like a folding down box, exact and rigid. I knew I was learning a lesson; I just wasn't quite sure what it was yet. We drove home and didn't speak for the next two days.

Having an illness as a child was never really an issue. While you question impulsively with stark curiosity, answers are more readily accepted than in later years. As a teenager it becomes more difficult – anyone who says it doesn't is just plain lying. Excess baggage had already accumulated and the desire to rebel was so fresh. My revolt came one Sunday dinner when I announced that the carnivorous life was not for me. I decided I wanted to be a vegetarian. Seeing those cows standing vacant and unassuming in the fields around our house set it off. Watching them chew on their grass as possible members of their family lay massacred on our sizzling hot plates made me want to hurl. My life-altering decision was met with attempted straight faces that cracked into sniggering disbelief. I was told to 'cop on' as the goodness I needed daily was more important than any cow. My mom, being a nurse, knew these things. I hated her for it. It seems so stupid now, but, like most teenagers, I was convinced I knew everything, that I had everyone figured out. Years later, I understood. My mother was not telling me what I couldn't do, but merely showing me how much I could do, if I only had the courage to comprehend some limitations that I just couldn't fight.

In hospital, I see a lot of mothers in vulnerable positions, some nearing the end of their lives and others neurotically convinced that the end is nigh when it is quite clear they will live to see next week's episodes of *Shortland Street*. I watch their children, now mostly fully grown adults, bring in their favourite things. Regular appearances are made by archaic hot water bottles, fresh-smelling editions of *Woman's Way* and the best grapes they can find. Some want more specific things, like that toasted sandwich from Roly's or the pink Foxford woollen blanket they saw in Avoca. They want it and usually get it. In a desperate attempt to make a loved one feel better, any need is pandered to, even the ridiculous. The clue to the severity of the ailment is usually whether they would rather have you driving half an hour to get *that* sandwich, or allow a lesser sandwich to suffice while that half an hour is spent mulling over the mundane with you. The more demanding are usually easy to spot. They're lying up, clutching their hip, when in fact it's their toe that's broken. With a flash of a bedpan, their mobility miraculously increases. I've often empathised with the children and think perhaps I would be one of those standing in line in Avoca for that blanket, but that lady is not my mother. However willing I would be to fight off the Avoca-ites, she would never ask such a thing of me. She knows how much work it is on the other side, as a nurse and as a mother.

In May 2006, the theatre group I'm part of set about exploring xenophobia and racism through physical theatre and minimal vocals. It was a project that spanned many months and we ended up doing two exchanges. Firstly, 'The Italians', as they were collectively called – and yes, the friendly labelling was ironic given the topic at hand – came to our native Newbridge. We worked from ten to six for a solid week devising and meeting with people and hearing how they came to Ireland. Two families we met stood out in particular. One was a Zimbabwean mother of one. She was twenty-three, her child was five. She spoke about the squalid conditions she lived in, a local hotel that had been converted. The situation was illuminated in my mind because I remember the uproar that had gripped our little town when the news broke that our new high-class hotel was to be used to house 'refugees'. Hearing the circumstances in which they lived would surely silence any of the people opposing them now. She and her little girl shared a room with twenty other people, some of whom slept on the floor. They took turns. There were cockroach-like insects everywhere and oftentimes her little girl would wake in the night screaming as they crawled along her body. But the woman had to stay there. The second story was of a mother, daughter and son from Romania. There they were considered well off, but political turmoil changed that. They were lucky in the sense that unlike the Zimbabwean mother, they did not travel in a sealed container; they could afford a plane. But that didn't save the father, who was taken just as they boarded the plane. The mother's yellow eyes possessed a green hue that seemed so foreign but shot straight at me, and a wave of shame came over me, like it was my fault. They had discussed what to do if this sort of thing happened – they must keep going. They did. Those eyes seemed to glaze over as she told us, He is presumed dead. And although the Zimbabwean woman had not looked me in the eye once, all of a sudden the lives of these two women consumed me. Someone from the group asked, 'How do they keep going?' The Zimbabwean lady, her ethnic beauty putting our pasty faces to shame, looked up at this point and shook as she stuttered in apparent disbelief, the only emotion we had seen from her other than fear. 'I have a child. She is mine.' She flattened us.

A few months later, we began extensive exercising on the stage in the glorious grounds of Theatre de Lemonia in Florence. I knew I wasn't 100 per cent. I was trying to sweat it out in our clogged-up hostel by night and keep my energy up in the 40-degree heat by day. So much of our hostel reminded me of St Vincent's Hospital, where I attend at home. It was cheap, at just €7 per night, and the rooms were small and cramped, with no air conditioning.

The windows on the corridors could only open a miniscule fraction, just enough to allow an oozing of dead heat to surge through the air. The rooms stank of body, of that perfumed odour of overworked people who were constantly on the go. It's funny how similar that smell is to inactive, unwell people surrounded by bedpans, nose-burning disinfectant and sweat. At night, bodies seemed sprawled so close together that the heated breath of another tickled the hairs on your arm. At least they were still alive. During this time my mother and I texted a lot. I kept it to a minimum and said I was fine, but I did mention the bathrooms. Having been so used to the heated musk of someone else's dirt, freshly shed, punching as I walked into the shower room in hospital, the shower rooms there, with their unopened windows, didn't faze me. The poisonous atmosphere was eerily familiar to me, but of course voicing that to my friends would have been a little strange and so I refrained. The cliché is true – if you haven't been there, you couldn't possibly know. At least there were no dirty nappies rolled up beside the toilets.

I moved to a hotel near the end of two weeks. My two amazing friends walked half an hour in the 40-degree heat to find one for me and then, after trekking back to get a slightly disorientated version of me, endured a further hour of my ridiculous I-know-what-I-want trait. We left the hotel they had chosen, amid disparaging grunts from the receptionist, and went to find a bigger room in a more suitable establishment. With my arm around each of them and a feeling as though a Looney Toons anvil had been dropped on my chest, we strolled through peculiarly large flocks of pigeons and witnessed a bizarre argument between a jewellery-laden Italian woman and an ice-cream seller. They were flinging money and ice cream on the floor, trying to outdo each other. Everything was surreal. Instead of a Mary and Joseph journey, it was more of a Christ-and-his-crucifix-like walk, except there were two Christs, and I was the crucifix they were dragging affectionately along.

Eventually we found a hotel to my liking. This means it had to have (a) room service and (b) more than one round tower-type slit for a window. The check in woman must have seen how pasty and limp I was, despite my bug eye sunglasses. There was no room in the hotel, but she gave me an apartment for a ridiculously low price. Judging by her vampish red lips, Rita Hayworth hair and the worrying number of young women hanging about, it occurred to me that this might be some type of Italian Moulin Rouge. At this stage I felt as though I was breathing through a McDonald's straw, so it was evident to anyone watching that I'd be pretty useless in any can-can routine. I hoped I looked mysterious and Brigitte Bardot-like, though I suspect now that it was more washed-up rock chick coming down from some substance or another with a wan alabaster face, glassy eyes and cracking lips. Attractive.

Once safe inside, the boys had to leave for the theatre. I was dehydrated and that super duper room service wasn't answering, so I decided to venture out for some water. It cost me €5 and I had no change left after paying for the room. All I kept thinking as the Italian shopkeeper was whooshing me out was why in blazes didn't I just fill out that credit card form. I needed food but I had just slipped on his floor, in the middle of his pizzeria. He didn't like it. Red faced and slurring verbs, I felt my way back to the hotel.

A maid saw me stumble in from the shop and despite not having a word of English understood that my shaking hands meant that I was having a severely low blood sugar fit. I passed her, smiled and nodded, feeling a little stoned. She grabbed at me in some frantic Italian that made me turn and try to decipher her hand gestures, but I couldn't stand any longer. I sunk down on the cool marble step and took a long suck through my ever narrowing lungs, which were now like those measly straws you get with cartons of Ribena.

I looked at her. My eyebrows raised and mouth twisted in a weary half smile. Why did I get myself into these situations? What did she want? My hands convulsed as though conducting their own bizarre orchestra, straight and jerking like a wizard shooting sparks of magic. She spoke again. *Juizzz, jusss.* Juice? Did she say juice? Yes! Juice! *Si! Si!* Please! She left and didn't come back. I went up to my room and searched for jellies, with all the ability of a frantic tortoise.

The phone rang twice and it was a male voice spouting Italian. I spoke to him in muddled French. It had no effect. A knock came and I wondered if it was some Mafia guy sent up by Hayworth in search of a mot. My head felt heavy and woozy. The door opened and I held my loaded bottle of still water, ready to swing just in case. Into the frame stood the small Italian maid. She was dressed in a blue dress with a white frilly apron. There was something so elegant about her. In her hand was a tray with a carton of orange juice and the most scrumptious chocolate wafer biscuits. She spoke no English – she just handed me the tray. This woman had just saved me from going into a coma. I wanted to hug her but knew that was a little extreme and the last thing I needed was a screaming maid on my hands. If anyone came, I would appear drunk and nonsensical because of my low blood sugar. I put down the tray quickly and clasped her hand as she left. She spun around, alarmed, her eyes emanating fury peppered with embarrassment. Her cheeks reddened. I looked at her and smiled. I held her hand for a minute. I said, '*Gracias*.' She seemed to understand. I lasted one night and then they sent for the ambulance.

Passing the spectacular architecture in an ambulance felt sinful. I felt as though I was being cheated. I could see the inside of an ambulance in any country, but I couldn't see beautiful architecture like this, nor could I indulge in the equally interesting markets that we were going to the next day on our afternoon off. When I reached the A&E I was confident and cognisant. I was used to hospitals; this was a universal disease, nothing could be as bad as Vincent's. I was wrong. After twenty minutes of tests, a burly lady reminiscent of the Italian mama character of Dolmio pasta ads came in. This nurse shattered my sense of control by performing a basic procedure wrong on me and causing quite a bit of emotional and physical damage. While it only takes an hour to get a bed in Italy, you can't discount the value of nursing care from competent nursing staff.

My knight in shining armour, Michaela, the director of the Italian theatre group, assumed the role of protector. He communicated with my mom by phone, conversed with me and then translated to the nurses. My mom instructed and guided them, calmly and with a collected coolness that set me in awe of her. I had never really seen her in action before.

After the Italian mama incident, I was upset. She had tried to tranquilise me. Luckily, I had heard the words *tranquille, tranqille* being uttered and was suspicious of the two nurses, one who sat on the side of my bed facing me, one arm over me, blocking my body, the other quite tightly clasped upon my arm. At first I thought she was being motherly – after all, the second nurse was holding her sweaty palm against my brow. This physical comfort, while comforting in the beginning, began to have an eerie feel to it.

My suspicions were confirmed as Mama waddled in, brown eyes dead and white gloves covering those stumpy fingers. The whispers of '*tranquille*' began like some demented harpies. There she was, à la Norman Bates, leaning over me, arm raised, green-needled syringe in hand. (Green translates as the biggest possible needle.) *Tranquille*, she seemed to hiss. I pleaded, I pushed. They had me, I couldn't budge, so I played the insanity card. All I knew was that with oxygen stats as detrimentally low as mine at that moment, that 10 ml syringe would have comatosed or killed me. So I growled at them, which turned into a type of *rarr*. Hardly a beastly one, more the Cowardly Lion's feeble attempt to scare Toto before Dorothy slaps him on the nose and says, Shame on you, why don't you pick on someone your own size. And why didn't she? She fingered my arm for a vein as I calculated. She lunged towards me, and with one fell swoop I got it. I grabbed the needle and syringe without injury and shook it in sheer desperation at her, saying, 'No, no, no, no!' My voice created Italian nuances in a ridiculous attempt to communicate that I wasn't going to hurt her. She grabbed the syringe and suddenly she knew how to speak English. Her wise words were, 'Why you go on holidays if you know you have this illness?' I looked at her and was so fraught with panic that I gave in and sobbed. She sighed, fed up with me, and left the room.

Her followers stayed, rubbing my brow and stroking my hand. It must just be what they do, I thought. Michaela returned and his eyes popped from slit peas to flattened pods when he saw what a cumulus I was. What happened? I heaved it out amid fractured breaths and sniffing convulsions. Right then, I wanted my mom. Michaela left the room. For the next twenty minutes, unintelligible Italian bounced from the walls of the corridor outside, and at one point the nurses with me went red and the one whose hand had now been replaced by a cloth on my brow sniggered uncontrollably. Mama re-entered with Michaela. She stood beside the bed with spite and bitterness in her eyes. 'I am nice,' she muttered. I shoot her a bewildered look which bounced off Michaela and his eyes seem to propel her. He looked straight at her and she turned to me. 'I am sorry.' She released a breathy sound that permeated the end of 'sorry', then fled in disbelief and hopefully some sense of shame. Michaela got me some crackers.

Two days later I was stable in a specialised hospital and watched Italy win the World Cup in my own little room. The yelping cheers of Italian throughout the ward were beautiful. Nurses whooped, forgetting themselves, and paraded around with the Italian flag blazing on their backs and in their eyes. The noise kept me awake all night. I imagined the motorcyclists jetting by screaming *Italia*, like when they won the semi-final and we jumped and punched the air with them. It was the most beautiful sound, much like the excitement I felt when I knew my mom was coming. My mother wanted to fly over the minute I got ill, but as a matter of pride I kept putting her off. Eventually she decided to come anyway, which, typically, was the right decision.

The next morning my mother came to Florence, one of the most beautiful cities in the world. She passed the jewellery, Il Duomo and the gelatos to get to me. The night before she came was like Christmas Eve to me, I was that excited. She met Michaela at the airport, an Italian man she had never met before, and after seeing me briefly rushed, on my demand, to see the performance I was meant to be part of.

The next two days were spent squabbling with hideous insurance men. The stereotypical role of mother is to give birth and then mind them until they are brassy and big enough to tend for themselves. When they become old enough to do this is debatable. I know some thirty-year-olds who still can't take responsibility for themselves and some thirteen-year-olds who are so organised that I just can't be around them. Mothers are there as clandestine conveyers of wisdom to help you along the way. It seems the older you get, the more you need their advice and ability to pull you in when you are ever so gleefully skiing off track, oblivious to the snowball about to topple you.

Sometimes letting that snowball flatten you is no harm; it makes you appreciate the shovellers much more. That term may not sound eloquent, but I say it with the most esteemed respect. Those people who would break their backs trying to get you out of that avalanche, and seem to manage to, just before your toes fall off. My problem with my mom was not that she didn't understand me – it was that she understood too much of me. Being a nurse, she knew more than me, mostly about the medical side of me. She knew the dangers, the possibilities, the probable outcome before I did. She knew not just because she was a nurse, but because she was my mother and she'd been watching from a most difficult position, from day one, with two juxtaposing viewpoints.

I've heard fellow colleagues talk of her as 'the best nurse they've ever worked with' and I constantly run into people who praise her – former patients, friends or relatives of them or even doctors who recognise the second name, even though the hospitals are miles apart.

We used to practise attempted murder on a daily basis, but now we're only up for it every few months. The good behaviour increases daily on both sides. Maybe I'm calming down or growing up, but when banging doors and mascara smears stain the surroundings, I remember the most vital thing – I have a mother, she is mine. That keeps me afloat.

Siobhán Parkinson is a children's novelist, writer-in-residence at the Marino Institute of Education and co-editor of *Bookbird*, a journal of international children's literature. *Something Invisible* (Puffin) was shortlisted for the Bisto Book of the Year award and for the Irish Children's Book Award. *Blue Like Friday* (Puffin) has recently been published. Siobhán lives in Dublin with her husband and grown-up son.

From Public Property to Public Enemy: Mothering Through

Siobhán Parkinson

When you first become a mother, you become public property. At first, it's admiration all the way, and myrtle mixed in your path like mad. But then you start to notice that the myrtle has faded and in its place have come drifts of advice – not the occasional gem of good sense scattered carelessly at your feet where you might pick it up for yourself and feel you had discovered something. No, advice comes in truckloads – noisy, opinionated truckloads, in the main.

In fact, advice wouldn't be all that bad. The trouble is, it's instructions that people feel they have to issue to the new mother. They tell you to read this book, they tell you that that book is rubbish, they tell you to pick the baby up when it cries, on no account to pick the baby up except at predetermined times, to breastfeed till the 'baby' is four, to wean the baby early, to give solids instead of a bottle if the baby is hungry, not to put anything in the bottle except milk (or breast milk, in the case of the breastfeeding police), to put the baby in a cot from day one, on no account to let the baby into your own bed, on no account to let the baby sleep alone in a cot, to play soothing music to the baby, to play maths CDs to the baby, to read to your baby, to get your baby's sticky paws off that good library book, to lay the baby on its back/front/side, to wrap the baby tightly, to clothe the baby loosely, to make sure its little head is covered, on no account to put shoes/slippers/socks on its freezing little feet, to speak only medieval Latin to the baby, to put its name down for a Gaelscoil at conception – oops, no, too late, your child will have to be educated by the parish, oh *dear*, how will you ever show your face at the gym?

And so on and on and on until you feel you want to have a spot of postpartum depression just so you can crawl into a nice safe hospital bed and put the covers over your head so you can't hear and people will stop giving you bloody advice.

The advice/instructions keep coming right through the teething, toilet training, toddling and tantrums stages, and then it starts to slacken off a bit. I don't know, maybe people get tired of telling you stuff that you are plainly going to ignore, or maybe they are not so expert in three-year-olds. Maybe they managed to smother/mislay/overheat/forget their own littl'uns by that stage. Apart from the pro- and anti-child care terrorists, most people ease off a bit once your child hits playschool. By the time you have a hoary old Senior Infant on your hands, you are either, by some sort of silent consensus, adjudged a Fit Person to bring up your own child, or a sort of role-flip occurs and people start telling you how to defend yourself against the monster you have reared.

But actually, you hadn't noticed you'd reared a monster. You had got kind of fond of the little tyke. Now that all that night feeding, toilet training and tantrums are over, you thought the child had turned out rather well, pretty smart actually, cute almost, winsome to a degree. How wrong can you be?

A mother is a nice, warm, loving, milky, huggy sort of a creature, though one who has probably temporarily lost a grip on herself and on whom we are practically compelled to pour out advice and baby clothes and gurgling sounds. Everyone loves mothers (poor dears). It is obligatory. You have to love your own mother, you see, so by extension, you have to love the concept of 'mother'. It's a cultural requirement. As we all know, it goes with apple pie in the utterly-beyond-criticism category. But luckily for the media, the neighbours, people-who-hate-you, society-at-large and your mother-in-law, there is another category which is a sort of inside-out version of 'mother', and that is 'parent'.

I don't quite know how or when the transition occurs, but once you become a parent instead of a mother, you are suddenly fair game. 'I blame the parents' replaces advice-orhoea. It probably starts when your child goes to school and you overhear teachers muttering viciously to each other about 'parents'. You notice they are not using that high-pitched squeaky voice people have been using with you for the past four or five years. On the contrary, there is an alarmingly venomous quality to the snarl with which the word 'parent' is uttered/spat out.

You look around you and you notice there is not a slice of apple pie anywhere in your vicinity. Oops, category change. You are now surrounded by things like 'non-marital families' and 'social fragmentation' as a cause not so much of your child's unhappiness/dyslexia/bad behaviour/asthma, but of all the problems associated with 'youth', from underage drinking to vomit on the street to vandalism, drug trafficking, lung cancer and car accidents. You could play 'spot the odd one out' there, and you might say, But 'youth' can't be blamed for lung cancer. And you would be right. Only problem is, 'youth' in general can't actually be blamed for any of the rest of the list either, but people like to talk in shorthand, so you will find it is all the fault of youth, and what is the fault of youth is ultimately the fault of parents. Parents had parents too, of course, so that is actually not all that logical. If we take that line of thinking to its conclusion, we could all just sit back and blame Adam and Eve for everything and there'd be no moral responsibility for anything any more.

Then comes a moment to make your blood freeze. You are chopping onions for an innocent family stew, perhaps. Or maybe you are ironing your darling's rugby shirt (there are mothers who do these things, I've read about them in books) or whatever trivial motherly task it might be. The radio happens to be on, and over the airwaves comes a voice of sickening gravitas, freighted with menace: 'Do you know where your sixteen-year-old is at this moment?' it asks in the kind of tone the vice-principal used to use when requesting information about your knowledge of the state of your stockings when you were thirteen. Your heart sinks. Fear's icy fingers grip your psyche. Where is he? Why don't I know?

Well, of course you don't know, because he is sixteen and he is (thank God) able to walk, and he has a really important thing to be doing. It's called growing up. It's called learning to be independent. It's called taking responsibility for yourself. It's called standing on your own two feet. It's called hanging out with your friends. It's called not bloody ringing up your mammy every five minutes. And this is just when you thought you'd got it right, you'd learned to loosen the apron strings, to let him go paddling off into the shallows of adult life. You thought you were doing so well!

You ask yourself, What has happened? Where did I go wrong? How come I was a heroine/mother/wonder only a few years ago, and now I am a hate-figure/parent/social problem?

Well, look. There is only one piece of advice you should take when your baby is small, and that is to enjoy this time, not because your baby is going to grow up and away from you, but because you are going to be shuffled off into the deadly parent category pretty soon, and you may as well bask in the glory while you can.

If the glory has started to fade, here's another piece of advice that's worth taking: tell the lot of them to go to hell. Because do you know what is better than a new baby? It's a new adult, that's what. This is one secret the old wives/breastfeeding police/day care terrorists never reveal: your baby is going to grow into a wonderful, witty, beautiful, intelligent, carefree, delightful young man or woman. Yes, he or she will do one or more of the following: they will be rude, will wear awful clothes, will stay out too late, will drink too much, will have appalling table manners, will drive too fast, will have unsuitable relationships, will listen to unbearable music, VERY LOUDLY; he or she, let's face it, may even do something awful. There could be trouble, there could – God forbid – be tragedy. But that is life – it is not some sort of judgment on parents, it is not because you were/were not married to your child's father; it is not because you had a Caesarean/IVF/natural birth in a tank of tepid water with dolphins/adopted a baby from Russia/Ethiopia/South America; it is not because you did/didn't lay your baby on their back/front/side, or didn't read enough stories to her, or did or didn't forbid him to play with toy guns, or let him or her watch too much/too little TV.

By and large and in the main, though, we are lucky and they do survive and they do turn out OK. And the great thing about a child turning out OK is that OK in a young human being is like nothing else imaginable: OK in human terms is FABULOUS. Your run-of-the-mill young man, your ordinary young woman, your fairly well-balanced and averagely talented twenty-one-year-old is no less fantastic and wonderful than your new baby was. In fact, he or she is far more of an achievement.

Of course, he or she is their own achievement, but hey, you're their mother. You had a hand in that. And just look at that: isn't he/she great? As for you – you have survived them all: the youth police, the *Liveline* experts, the professional amateur psychologists, the woman from Clontarf, the ASBO merchants, the educationally correct lot, the 'I blame the parents' brigade. Aren't you bloody marvellous!

Julie Parsons has been a mother for thirty-one years and a grandmother for three. She has also given birth to five novels: *Mary, Mary*, *The Courtship Gift*, *Eager to Please*, *The Guilty Heart* and *The Hourglass*. Her sixth, *I Saw You*, will be joining its siblings in spring 2008.

'And, I Love You.'
Julie Parsons

She wriggled out of me like a large, wet fish. Twelve hours of labour. Not bad for a first baby. It was a beautiful Sunday, the last day of August 1975. I had woken at about two in the morning. Pain. A familiar sensation. Part of my monthly cycle since I was fourteen. Low down in the back and the groin. Wow, I thought as I struggled from sleep. This is it.

The hours passed slowly. The pain got worse. The nurses in the Rotunda offered, in those pre-epidural days, Pethadine. I resisted. Then gave in. Nasty stuff, that drug. Made me feel as if I was drunk, disorientated, unable to focus or concentrate. And even worse, it had absolutely no effect on the pain. Like a hot iron, I thought in a lucid moment. As if someone was moving it towards my back, slowly, slowly, then quickly. Holding it there for five, ten, fifteen seconds, then slowly moving it away. A few minutes of respite. A few minutes to gather my breath, gather my strength. Then the pain would begin again. The hot iron would move towards my back. I could almost smell the singeing flesh. Through the tall windows that gave onto the tennis courts behind the hospital came the sound of a ball. *Thwock, thwock, thwock*. It bounced from tightly strung racquet to racquet. I couldn't see who was playing, but I could hear their voices. Happy, carefree, accompanied by great shouts of laughter.

While inside my body, in the protective dark, my baby was beginning to move from the great muscle that was my womb, down into the birth canal.

'Push. Go on, push,' the midwives urged.

I had been taken over by a force that was outside me. All the books I had read comforted that as soon as the pushing started, the pain would stop. I would be safely into the second stage of labour. The worst would be over. But somehow it wasn't happening like that. The pain had not gone away. I struggled to sit up. I wanted to see what was happening. And then, with a surge of something muscular, something beyond my control, I could see. What was this creature that was separating itself from my body? For a moment I couldn't imagine what it could be. An elf, an imp, a dark spirit? What was it?

'Look,' the midwife turned. She was holding something loosely wrapped in a pink hospital towel. I saw two feet, two legs, and incongruously large, the sign of a girl.

'Here.' She put her in my arms. I looked down at her small face, crumpled like the petals of an Oriental poppy as it bursts from its protective sheath. My baby's head was covered with a fuzz of pinky gold. Her small eyes were milky blue. She waved her little hands and the darker pink of her tiny mouth twisted towards my mothering smell.

'See if she'll suck,' my own mother said when she came to see us a couple of hours later. I supported my baby's floppy neck and awkwardly pushed her towards my breast. My nipple was flat and dark, like a field mushroom. She opened her mouth and fastened her little lips around it. Mother and baby joined again. The temporary rupture of birth forgotten as her skin met my skin.

No way to speak sensibly of the intensity of that bond. I felt as if I too had been born in the hours after her birth. Born into a world of feeling, of closeness, of pure and unadulterated worship of this tiny, perfect creature whose every movement filled me with joy.

Why had I not known that motherhood would be like this? Why had I ever scoffed and mocked at the women I saw bending over prams, with expressions on their faces that set them apart from women like me? Now I too was at one with them. I knew that the world did not begin and end with me. That I had been, literally, transformed. But I also knew now with a frightening clarity how vulnerable I would be forever more. As I held my baby, gazing down into her sleeping face, I could feel the fear seeping through me. What would I do if anything ever happened to her? How would I bear the grief of losing her? Would I ever be able to let her move away from me? To allow her to move beyond the protective encircling of my arms? And I remember with stunning clarity the first time it happened. She must have been about four months old. We were sitting at the table. I was drinking a cup of tea. She was as always snuggled close, her warmth and mine as one. She was waving her arms and making those familiar little sounds of pleasure. But suddenly something was different. She was moving. Away, out into the world. Towards the table, towards the teaspoon shining in the morning sun. Towards the rest of her life. I felt the gap between us. The cold air between her warm little back and my warm tummy.

'Ah,' I thought, 'this is the beginning.'

And now she too is a mother. And I am a grandmother. My love for my granddaughter is of the same quality as my love for my daughter. Surprising, unconditional, without the words to express its nature. And somehow the future has changed again. It lies ahead, a bright shining path stretching beyond my gaze. A whole new world of opportunity and excitement.

A message on the phone. I hear a deep breath, a piping voice.

'Hi, it's Em'ly.' Pause, deep breath, 'Will you come and visit me? Will you watch a DVD with me?' Longer pause, deep breath. 'Will you play with my Sylvanian fam'lies.' Another pause, another deep breath. 'And,' pause, 'I love you.'

Katy McGuinness took to writing after earlier careers as a lawyer in New York and a film producer in London and Dublin proved incompatible with family life. Katy writes for *The Sunday Tribune* and *The Gloss* and is taking an MA in Creative Writing at Queens University Belfast. She lives in Dun Laoghaire with her husband, architect Felim Dunne, and four children, Esme, Talulla, Milo and Ellie.

Ellie
Katy McGuinness

'Her eyes are slightly slanted.' And with those words, everything changed.

Seven years ago, when our daughter Ellie was born, the obstetrician was able to tell us, almost immediately, that she had Down Syndrome. The paediatrician confirmed this an hour later. The telltale signs – to the professionals, not us – were her facial configuration, floppy muscle tone and the distinctive line on her palm.

Over the next few days, as Ellie was subjected to a barrage of tests, we started to glean, piecemeal, some information as to what this meant. From the medics, most of what we got was perfunctory: 'She'll do everything all your other kids do, just slower – everything will take her just a bit longer to learn', 'as syndromes go, it's not a bad one', 'prefer a Downs to x other disability any day' and so on.

The most reassuring conversation I had was with a busy midwife who took the time to come and have a cup of tea with me on Day 2 and tell me about her fabulous sister with Down Syndrome who was the centre of their family, great company, earning a living and a fabulous cook to boot.

I was and remain full of admiration for those of our friends who were brave enough to make it across the threshold of the maternity ward when I'm sure they would rather have stuck pins in their eyes. And for those who celebrated her arrival at a time when all I wanted to do was put a pillow over her beautiful little face. Of course, I couldn't tell anyone that that's what I wanted to do, or that was what I was planning, not even my husband. But I spent many hours looking at a sleeping Ellie and thinking that however much we loved her – and we did, from the very first moment – she would be better off dead. And for the first few mornings after her birth, my first thoughts were ones of hope that she had died in the night.

The majority of our friends did all the thoughtful, generous things that you do for anyone with a new baby – minded the other children, cooked meals, bought beautiful gifts. The room was a bower of flowers. Some people of whom I would have expected more were cowardly and insensitive, barely unable to contain their relief that this had happened to us and not them. They are no longer friends.

Gradually I abandoned thoughts of infanticide. Good, kind people – friends and family – came and sat and talked about nothing much. Pretending to listen, I was busy planning where Ellie was going to live when she was twenty-five before I had even managed to take her home from the hospital. I worried about who would take her clothes shopping at fourteen and make sure that she didn't look frumpy. I worried about whether she would have friends and whether people would be cruel to her. I made a vow that she wouldn't be allowed to wear sandals and white ankle socks beyond the age of six. (As it turned out, she was out of them by four.)

I remember very clearly anyone who told me a positive story about Down Syndrome, even if they were made up. I stored them up in the bank of good news. Often I would listen to these stories about fabulous children with DS and then ask, 'So what is she doing now?' There would an embarrassed silence and it would turn out that the child had died, from a heart condition, or leukaemia, or pneumonia. Now that I had made up my mind that Ellie was staying and was going to be the best-dressed, brightest child of all time, this wasn't what I wanted to hear.

We had been advised to tell our other children that Ellie had Down Syndrome from the outset. We did, explaining as it had been explained to us, that she would do everything that they did but that it would all take her a little longer to learn. Over the next few months, our children were constantly spotting other people with Down Syndrome and helpfully pointing them out to us. They did seem to be everywhere we went.

Once we got Ellie home, we came into contact with our local early intervention support services. For the first time in our lives, we had a social worker that came to visit us regularly. Sometimes we found her visits helpful, when the information she brought with her was practical. When she tried to get us to talk about our feelings, we clammed up. We kept our crying to ourselves. I kept my tears for solitary walks down the pier. I grew to cherish the darkest, wettest, windiest mornings when there would be the slimmest chance of meeting anyone I knew and I could rage against the elements and the unfairness of it all. My husband cried in the car, on his way to and from work. We tried not to weep in front of each other.

We began attending our local early intervention programme when Ellie was about six weeks old and started to meet other parents of children with Down Syndrome. We latched on to one mother whose child was a year older than Ellie as our role model. We ordered a lot of books from Amazon and spent many hours surfing the net for more and more information. At times we have felt overloaded with knowledge. We know too much about too many things. Sometimes, we try hard to forget.

By virtue of being Ellie's parents, we have met many other families with a child with Down Syndrome. We are in the club. In the early days, it was all war stories. There was a gallows humour to be derived from revelling in the terrible things that people had said to us about our children. I knew I had made it into the inner circle when I was invited on a Down Syndrome mummies night out – 'Pizza and a glass of wine', I was told, 'and then later, when we've had too many, we all cry.'

Of course there were going to be tears, because however many people tell us how privileged we are, how our children are angels, a gift from God, and special, and very affectionate – some of which is true, some of the time – we also know that we are facing into a lifetime of battling on behalf of our children, for their rights, their needs, their security, their education, and everything else that you can think of. Battles for which we didn't sign up.

During the months that followed Ellie's birth, I must have heard all the best lines:

From a paediatrician (not mine): 'Hey, double whammy – DS and a heart condition.'

From a friend: 'Are you sure? She doesn't look it to me.'

From another, not an expert: 'She's very mild.'

From a mother-in-law (again, not mine): 'It's not on our side of the family.'

When Ellie was about six months old, I thought my head would burst with the amount of information about Down Syndrome that it contained. I started to ease off a bit and focus on the immediate. More importantly, I started to concentrate on Ellie and the fabulous child she was becoming. I have always found the early months with a new baby the most difficult, and the most boring. Selfishly, my rewards come and my interest is piqued when I start to get reaction and feedback. We started taking her to weekly speech therapy sessions and working on her homework. The physiotherapist visited regularly and gave Ellie exercises. She started making progress in respect of all her developmental milestones. I began to realise that everything I'd been told about her doing everything that our other children did, just slower, was true.

Ellie started to walk at eighteen months. Her first word, 'No!', came soon after. She started attending a specialised speech therapy pre-school three mornings a week just before her second birthday. At three she joined the same Montessori school that all her siblings attended. At three and a half she started swimming on her own in a pool with armbands. At four she won a rosette in the under-five lead rein class at the local gymkhana.

At five she started in junior infants at our local Educate Together mainstream primary school. The school has a great track record in inclusiveness and seems to have an ability to make a virtue out of difference. Ellie has a special needs assistant and gets an hour of one-on-one resource teaching per day. Her vocabulary runs into the thousands of words and she can read a couple of hundred. We are still working on counting to ten without leaving anything (usually five) out.

Ellie has become an enthusiastic Special Olympics athlete, participating in gymnastics, basketball and horse-riding clubs. Her brother and sisters are encouraging all this in the hope that there will be a role for them as travelling supporters or chaperones in the future.

As I write this piece, I can see Ellie running outside with her sisters and brother, playing some horseracing game, in fits of giggles every time she falls over. Floppy baby indeed. This morning she spent at least an hour bossing her dolls and berating them for not concentrating on their numbers. Later she'll be looking for stories and her favourite *Simpsons* episode before changing her clothes, applying her make-up and telling us that she's off to Wesley or Bondi with her boyfriend, Tom.

I know people with Down Syndrome who are great footballers, athletes, musicians and artists. Many pass state exams and some go on to third-level education. In a salsa club in Havana I saw a young man up front with the band making some pretty fancy moves. The range of skills and talents is no less diverse than in any other cross-section of society. People with Down Syndrome are individuals with very distinct personalities – just like any other group. Which is why I hate it when people say to me, 'Very affectionate, aren't they?' Cliché and generalisation are lazy and insulting.

Ellie has, touch wood, been lucky health-wise. Half of children with Down Syndrome have some form of heart condition. Ellie is not one of them. Aside from a tendency to chest infections that has landed us in hospital on several occasions – memorably, one year, from Christmas Eve until New Year's Eve – she is a robust child. Despite her good health, we still find ourselves attending more than our fair share of medical appointments and her dentist has warned us that she is looking at a long and expensive orthodontic career.

The range of capabilities of people with Down Syndrome is vast. From the start, we decided to push Ellie hard and putting effort into developing her speech and communication skills has been hugely rewarding, though scarily expensive. Seven years on, I can honestly say that the addition of Ellie to our family has been a positive one. I think that it has made us all take a hard look at our priorities and adjust them accordingly. It has certainly changed the way we vote – canvassers get a rough ride at our front door. I hope it has made us better and more tolerant people. Without doubt there are trials and battles ahead, but we are entering into them determined to do the very best for Ellie and to maximise the potential of her every opportunity. If this makes us vociferous and militant, then so be it. Bring it on.

A version of this piece previously appeared in Image Magazine.

Helen Falconer lives in north Mayo. She is married to Derek and has four children, Jack, Molly, Imogen and Seán. Her novels *Primrose Hill* and *Sky High* are published by Faber.

For My Little Girl
Helen Falconer

If it could be just you and me
Together
Somewhere, anywhere…alone on an island in a glassy sea,

Fruits falling like jewels,
Sand pale as snow,
Thin skewers of tropic light piercing the quiet blue of
shark-less pools;

Just you and me in that hot little land,
My only job
To watch you wallow in safe water, run, heap up soft white
castles in the sand,

Your only job to grow…
I would be pure happy.
I would discard all other places: idle worlds you'd have no
call to know.

I Was a Girl
Helen Falconer

I was a girl of smiles and promise,
I was so pretty and clever and full of fire,
Ideas sang in my head; I was a genius
And my soul a choir.

But then I had my son, my darling one,
And he my son has robbed me of my light.
Oh how I do adore him for this wrong,
Because he burns so bright.

All that was mine by right I give to him:
My life, my blood, my song, my child's heart.
All that I had that gloried now grows dim –
I burned but now am dirt.

Dear child, I love to see you shine and dance,
A poor dark thing before your blaze I lie;
I mourn my empty fire (such brilliance!)
And fear how cold I'd be if yours should die.

Having lived most of her adult life in the cities of Dublin and Melbourne, *Anne Marie Forrest* has recently returned to her native County Cork with her husband, Robert, and two young daughters, Lucy and Sylvie. She is the bestselling author of the novels *Who Will Love Polly Odlum?*, *Dancing Days*, *Something Sensational* and *The Love Detective*. Anne Marie writes a weekly column for Cork's *Evening Echo*. Her website is www.annemarieforrest.info.

For Sale:
Baby Shoes. Never Used.

Anne Marie Forrest

Once, when challenged to write a story in just six words, Hemingway came up with the title above. Years and years ago, back in my teens, when I first came across it, I remember marvelling at its brilliance; at how he ingenuously managed to capture so much drama together with the full gauntlet of human emotion in just six tiny little words.

But reading them now, I have a problem with the 'for sale' part of his story. It simply doesn't ring true. You see, I could never imagine selling my baby's unused shoes – a tiny little pair of baby blue basketball boots given to him by his aunt on his birth. In fact, I still have them, seven years on, as I do his toys, his little baby clothes, his photos, the cards received on his birth and on his death, his birth certificate and even his death certificate. The day his death certificate arrived in the post, some months after his death, was one of the worst. When it plopped through the letter box, I opened it, not realising at first what it was, only to be faced with the official version of my child's life – Occupation: None, Martial status: Single. It was like reading a life unlived. But of course, that's just one version. There are other versions of his life. The one I particularly like is the lengthy one my husband penned for our son's funeral, part of which reads, 'Darragh loved nothing more than to be held; to curl up in bed with Anne Marie talking dreams and stories, or to stroll round the Mercy Hospital in my arms watching the Melbourne cityscape unfold.'

There was never a baby more wanted than our baby and our relationship started long before he was born. I'd spent so much of the preceding months buying him little baby things, talking to and about him (from the first scan, we knew he was to be a boy and we'd named him Darragh) and imagining his future.

But Darragh lived just five days after being born. Weighing in at nearly 11 pounds, he was healthy and happy those first two days, and during that time we had the normal but amazing experience of being first-time parents. I spent hours just staring at him, absolutely bowled over by him and by how much I loved him. The first time I breastfed him was one of the most satisfying experiences of my life and, to this day, remains one of my favourite memories. But everything changed on the third day when – out of the blue – Darragh began fitting and was whisked off to ICU. When I saw him there, great big fellow that he was, I wasn't too worried for him – God no! – despite all the tubes he looked so healthy compared to the tiny little babies in the incubators on either side (in truth, I was worried for them). On the fourth day, we learned he wasn't going to live due to the severe hypoglycaemia he'd suffered. On the fifth day, we brought him to the park (our only family day out with him) accompanied by two nurses, the consultant and a care worker and there, on a glorious afternoon as people enjoyed ordinary, everyday pleasures, we witnessed our child drifting away from us forever. Every parent's worst nightmare had come true for us. Our baby was dead.

How does a parent make sense of such an event? I don't know. All I know is that I never have and never will, not if I live to be a hundred. I stopped trying a long ago. There is no sense in it. But do I wish he was never born? Absolutely not. Those five days were the best and worst of my whole life. As for the months that followed, they were truly horrendous: going home to an empty house (a friend having thoughtfully removed the cot, the changing table, etc.); that first never-ending night – having to cope with the pain of engorged breasts knowing that the child I should be feeding no longer needed the milk; the agony of passing a baby in a pram in those early months – I'd sooner have crossed the street than chance setting eyes on another baby's face (and I did – all the time); and hearing news of other births. I wouldn't wish those months on my worst enemy, but still I couldn't not wish to have had those five days with our son.

When something so pointless happens, perhaps it's only human to try and find some good in the experience. So seven years on, did I learn any lessons? Did it change me? Did it change me for the better? Has any good come out of it?

I like to think so.

It's doubtful our daughter Lucy would be here today. She was born exactly a year after her brother died. Experts caution parents that they should allow themselves time to grieve the death of a child before trying for another baby, but sometimes a woman instinctively knows what's best for her and having another baby was the best thing for me. Having Lucy was my salvation. It didn't stop me grieving, but it did distract me from it somewhat.

When people, as they're wont to tell parents of small children, tell me, 'Enjoy them while they're young,' I feel like replying that I don't need to be told, that I do enjoy every moment of them. And I do. Not for a second do I take Lucy or her younger sister, Sylvie, for granted and I like to think that I'm a better parent to my two girls than I would otherwise have been.

Some of our closest friendships today stem from around that time. While some people were conspicuously silent, others, some mere acquaintances, became die-hard friends for life through their kindness. Going through what we did gave me a better appreciation of how good friends are worth their weight in gold.

Knowing I got through something most people never will have to go through means I'm confident that I'm up to coping with what life throws at me, and that's a good feeling.

I like to think I'm more sensitive too. True, I have little interest in partaking in conversations so favoured by other mothers – how their birthing plans were never followed; how long their labour was; how they had to have a section against their wishes. I know these are normal conversations, but I don't want to be part of them, even though I can top almost every story: a twenty-hour labour, followed by an emergency Caesarean, followed by the death of our child, followed by tests to assess the risks of the same thing happening to any future children, followed by two subsequent Caesareans (and, happily, two healthy babies). And that's the important thing, isn't it? As long as a woman leaves a hospital with her baby, does any of that other stuff really matter? Sometimes, reading the birth columns, I notice entries from parents announcing the birth of their first child and I wonder at their optimism – their easy assumption that more will follow. But then, I guess parents need to be optimists. Otherwise how would they dare do what they do? I guess what I mean when I say I'm more sensitive is that I'm more aware of the enormous trials people experience in life in general, and in attempting to be parents, and in being parents: women with fertility problems who have gone through IVF time and time again and still haven't conceived; the unsung heroes and heroines bringing up children with mental and physical handicaps; single parents raising families alone; women and men who've never found that person with whom to have the children they so desperately want.

Before, I was vaguely apologetic for my lack of faith, but now I'm not. If I can give others the courtesy of accepting that they do believe in God, then I expect they should accept that I find it impossible to believe in a god in a world where awful things randomly happen to good people every day; a god who could – for example – allow a baby to be born into this world, a baby so wanted, and so loved, only to have him die five days later.

Before Darragh died, I used to wonder at my good luck. I enjoyed my life, I loved my husband, I had nothing to complain about. Up to that point, my husband and I had both breezed through life, somewhat unreflectively – neither of us had ever experienced any hardship, not to mind tragedy. Our son's death could have had the opposite effect on our relationship, but we were lucky and, in the months that followed, we were at our closest. Of course, we squabble like most couples do (and we probably squabble more than most), but I know what my husband is made of and I know the value of our relationship. Now I appreciate everything I have more acutely, even when, or perhaps more so because, I know it all can change in an instant.

Years ago, I remember someone asking me what attracted me to my husband and, after some thought, I replied that it was his sense of humour. This rather solemn person nodded her head and said, 'Yes, I thought as much,' in a manner that suggested she didn't think very much of my answer. But now I truly understand the value of a sense of humour. I rate it up there with kindness and strength. The root word of 'humour' is '*umar*' in Latin, which means to be fluid and flexible like water, and that is what humour is about. It's staying flexible so you don't get broken by the difficulties you confront. You can't control the external events in your life, but you can control how you look at them. Give me someone with a sense of humour any day over a gloom merchant!

So, yes, to answer my own question, I guess I did learn some lessons through Darragh's death, but I'd give anything not to have learned them.

To those who know someone who has lost a baby, the important thing, I think, is not to avoid them and not to avoid talking about the baby. It's not as if you're going to suddenly remind them or make them sadder by mentioning what's already on their mind.

I truly hope nobody reading this has, or ever will, go through what we went through, but if there is, then the only advice I have is that old cliché, 'time is a great healer', as witnessed by the fact that I can write all this without shedding a single tear, something I would once never have believed possible. I don't seek 'closure' and from time to time I still rail at the unfairness of Darragh's death (unfair to him most of all), but now I can remember him fondly, happily – as we all do. Recently, Lucy announced that there were six in our family and, baffled by her maths, I asked her who she meant, so she called out her list: Mum, Dad, Darragh, herself, Sylvie and Milo (a stray dog the girls have turned into a pet). Somewhat reluctantly, I guess I could include Milo, but of course she's right about Darragh – he is still very much part of our family.

To end, I'm going to do the unthinkable and amend a genius's words:

Most Prized Possession: Baby Shoes. Never Used.

Marita Conlon-McKenna is a hugely successful Irish children's writer and her debut adult novel, *The Magdalen*, was a number-one bestseller in Ireland. Her latest book is *The Hat Shop on the Corner*. She lives in Blackrock with her husband and four children and is the chairperson of Irish PEN.

The Real Mummy

Marita Conlon-McKenna

The girl next door knew everything. She knew how to play hopscotch without standing on the chalk lines or falling over. She knew how to play elastics without getting tangled up in the complicated manoeuvres that 'cat's cradle' required and she knew how to disappear up to the forbidden freedom back fields without our mothers spotting us.

My sister and I had our strengths, but she could not only run faster than us, but could run rings around us at times. She was a fountain of knowledge about things that we hadn't a clue about: Elvis Presley, motorbikes and how to pout your lips correctly to put on lipstick and how to kiss a boy.

She was blessed with an older sister and brother and was obviously privy to discussions which we could never know about, given that there were just the two of us, aged seven and eight, with little more than a year between us.

The line between best friends and best enemies was thin, as I discovered one day when I got nervous about an expedition she was planning up the back fields with a group of us kids. We had gone to play in her house, something we rarely did. Everyone had to bring something – a blanket, food, a drink – she convinced us, as we'd be gone to the fields for hours. It would be a great adventure and no one would miss us. As far as our parents were concerned, my sister and I were strictly forbidden from playing anywhere near the vast acres of open fields. Getting my courage up, I told her this and she began to call me names.

At eight years old, I felt nervous, out of my depth about making jam sandwiches and a Tupperware of orange squash and running off to the secret place for a picnic where the tall willows and catkins grew, where I was not allowed to play.

'I'm going home to my mummy,' I called.

'She's not your mummy,' she answered loudly in a know-it-all voice.

'Don't be so stupid,' I laughed. 'My mummy is my mummy!'

'She's not your mummy!' she repeated, her face taunting me. 'Not your real mummy.'

'She is! She is! She is!' I yelled back.

'You didn't come out of her tummy.'

'She's my mummy!' I insisted, torn between wanting to kill her and feeling scared with a strange sense of foreboding deep in my stomach. I had no idea what she was talking about or telling me and I turned tail and ran out her kitchen door and down the high side passage towards her blue garden gate, wanting to get away.

'And your daddy's not your daddy!' was her parting shot.

'You are a dirty rotten liar,' I shouted back. 'A dirty rotten liar!'

I stood at my garden gate, hating her, wanting to race inside and scream at my mother about what a brat she was and the awful thing she had said to me, wanting my mother to take me in her arms and tell me my friend was a liar and that she was a bold girl and had made the whole thing up.

I stood at our gate looking up the path towards our house, at the rosebushes my father had planted and the big lilac tree my mother loved so much, wondering why she had said it, wondering could it possibly be true. I couldn't let my mother, who was busy in the kitchen cooking, see the doubt in my eyes.

I ran upstairs and hid in my bedroom, trying to make sense of it. Maybe the girl next door was right! People were always saying I looked different from everyone else in the family. Could it be true? Whenever I went out with my parents and sister for a walk or shopping or a family outing, people would regularly stop us and ask, 'And where did you get her from?'

It always seemed to come up in conversation; people remarked how my sister looked so like my dad but I bore utterly no resemblance to anyone in the family, with my blonde hair and tanned skin. My mother and father both had black hair and my sister had a mop of curly dark hair too, while my hair was straight and long and almost white blonde. Even my mother's eyebrows were black, drawn in with a black pencil, and my dad's eyebrows were black and hairy too, while mine were so fair, along with my eyelashes, that you would hardly see them. My mother had reassured me that she had been fair when she was small too but after a bout of scarlet fever her hair had fallen out and grown back black.

I hunched on the floor, trying to work the puzzle of the girl next door's words and the hair colour out. My mother found me an hour later when the tea was ready and asked, 'What's the matter?' Not wanting to hurt her with the awful words, I finally told her what the girl next door had said.

'She said that you are not my mummy.'

I waited for my mother to protest vehemently. I saw pain in her eyes as she told me about how many years she had waited for a baby. She explained how the nuns had told her about a special baby in the orphanage that needed a mother and how herself and my dad had gone to see for themselves and walked along all the baby cots in a row, and found me with my blonde hair and blue eyes. They had wrapped me up in a blanket and had taken me home to this house with the roses in the garden and the purple lilac tree. A year later, they heard about another baby that needed a mummy and daddy and they had gone and fetched my sister.

'I am your mummy,' she said fiercely, and at that moment I knew it was true and I need never ever doubt it again, no matter what anyone said or did.

The next summer, when I was nine, one day she went up to Peggy's, the local hairdresser in the small seaside town where we had a house. Once a week, like all the mothers we knew, she went for her usual shampoo and set. It was a woman's place, herself and the other mothers sitting in under noisy beehive hairdryers with their curlers in their hair, chatting about husbands and children and reading magazines while we kids rushed in and out, borrowing money for ice cream and comics as we breathed in the scent of shampoo and hairsprays and kept out of the way of the hairdresser's floor brush as she swept up curls and hair.

'I'll be a bit longer than usual today,' she told us as my sister and I played on the path. 'So be good.'

We ate orange ice-pops and played I Spy and pored over the toys in the toy shop window and watched the men buying tobacco and cigarettes in Paddy's. Bored, we waited and waited in our summer T-shirts and shorts. Eventually, as the shop began to empty, we stepped inside. Peggy, with her pink lipstick and shiny pink plastic earrings, was almost finished. Our mother was sitting in the chair as she sprayed her hair with a fine mist of hairspray, my mother's face reflected in the mirror with her new blonde hairdo, her fair, un-pencilled eyebrows and blue eyes holding my gaze in the glass. We both held our breaths. She looked so different.

'What do you think?' she asked, nervous.

'You're beautiful,' my sister and I said in unison, running into her arms.

She looked beautiful, the most beautiful mummy in the big wide world.

Over the years, time and time again friends of hers and then later mine would remark how alike we were and how clear it was to see we were mother and daughter. It made us laugh, thinking of Peggy's Hairdressers and that long ago summer day.

But as I grew up I, too, learned that real motherhood is about more than hair colour and words; far more. Sometimes *real mummies* do not give birth in a hospital but are handed a small stranger, a baby in a blanket, and find it in their heart to make that baby their own. Real mummies like mine.

My real mummy held me when I fell off a bike and smashed my kneecaps and had to get stones and gravel picked from my skin before I got stitches.

My real mummy listened to my spelling and tables and homework night after night all through school and encouraged me to study and read and cheered when my first book got published and told me she'd always known that I could do it.

My real mummy told me stories of banshees and spirits, of fairies and mermaids, that made my spirits soar and my imagination take flight.

My real mummy showed me how to bake a cake, make a beef stew and sew a button on my shirt and knit a rather wonky scarf.

My real mummy showed me how to plant a bulb, sow seeds and applaud when snowdrops and crocuses burst through the grass and the lilac tree was covered in purple flowers.

My real mummy showed me how to walk and talk to a dog, be kind to animals and say a prayer for the gift of their friendship when they went to that great paradise in the sky.

My real mummy visited the hospital day after day, afternoon and evening, during the long hot summer I was eighteen and was too sick to care about anything.

My real mummy showed me how to laugh and dance and sing when things are good, but more importantly, when they are bad.

My real mummy asked me *did I love him* when I told her about the boy I kissed who made my heart spin, and smiled when he put a diamond ring on my finger and asked me to marry him.

My real mummy hugged me close when I told her that I too was going to become a mother.

My real mummy held each of my four children in turn as if they were the most precious gift in the world.

My real mummy showed me how to pray, to ask for what I need and give thanks for what I have.

My real mummy cheered as my children learned to crawl and walk and talk and sing.

My real mummy taught me in time about getting old and frail and facing the end of days.

My real mummy helped me to learn a hundred thousand things that mothers and daughters will always need to know.

My real mummy taught me about dying and how in some strange way, being a mother never ends.

Judi Curtin was born in London and raised in Cork. She studied at UCC before training as a primary school teacher. She is the bestselling author of *Sorry Walter*, *From Claire to Here* and *Almost Perfect* as well as the popular Alice books for children. She and Roisin Meaney are working together on a novel for children which will be published late in 2007. Judi lives in Limerick with her husband and three children.

Moving Swiftly Along

Judi Curtin

Fifteen years ago, a wise friend gave me some advice. 'Being a mother is hard,' she said. 'And if you don't think you could make a madeira cake while breastfeeding a baby, then you have no business getting involved.'

This was an interesting comment in many ways.

How well did that woman know me anyway?

Didn't she know that I'd never in my life managed to make a madeira cake, even without the encumbrance of a suckling infant in my arms?

And besides, since I was already a few months pregnant, my friend had perhaps left it a small bit late for the offering of this precious gem of wisdom.

Six months later, my baby boy arrived, and life changed forever. The doting father and I learned the joys of broken nights, early mornings and endless, endless nappies. Still, as far as I can remember, it was great fun – so much so that within four years, two beautiful baby girls had joined our happy household. We muddled along somehow. We learned how to fasten those complicated baby sleepsuits without resorting to language unsuitable for a baby's ears.

We made cookies, we accidentally spatter-painted the walls and we all threw tantrums at various stages.

Things were great, and after a while it became impossible to imagine a life that didn't involve the petty hassles and unspeakable joy of being around small children.

In due course, baby number one found his feet and set off for playschool, followed a year later by his younger sister. These were momentous events for all concerned, and each new milestone was marked with suitable ceremony. However, for me, these first blows were softened by the fact that there was still one small child at home, waiting for me, needing me.

Life rolled on, and before long, the dreaded day came close, the day my youngest child, my little baby girl, was to start playschool.

Much, much too soon, the big morning arrived. My baby had been up since dawn, prancing around in her best clothes, demanding to know why I was still in my night attire.

Despite my best delaying tactics, the time to leave was quickly upon us. I walked as slowly as I could while being dragged along the footpath by my eager scholar. When we got to the school, she raced inside, keen to see what was going on.

Was it selfish of me to half wish that I could have been mother to one of the tearful children clinging to parents' legs and begging to go home? Would it have hurt less if baby had at least pretended that she was going to miss me?

A small boy sat in a corner, sobbing as if his heart was going to break. I knew exactly how he felt.

I advanced towards my daughter for a final hug and kiss and was rewarded with a very brief, 'Bye, Mum,' before she returned to an elaborate construction of bricks.

I strolled into town. Where were all the friends who'd once invited me to adult-only coffee mornings? Why hadn't I planned my morning properly? I had a lonely cup of coffee in an almost empty café. I bought a cream cake but couldn't enjoy it when it dawned on me that I had no greedy toddler to share it with. I told myself that I was being foolish, but still I allowed myself one small, self-indulgent tear.

I wandered around the shops without interest before going home – to my silent, empty home. I did all the things that had been denied to me since my first baby was born seven years earlier. I had a twenty-minute shower, uninterrupted by children beating on the door wanting stuff. I left my toilet bag on my bed, knowing it would still be there, untouched, when I returned. I watched TV without first having to wrestle the remote control from a pair of small sticky hands. None of this helped, and it was a very, very long three hours.

Embarrassingly, I was the first parent at the school at pick-up time. Passers-by gave me strange looks as I paced outside the gate, trying not to look suspicious. After a while, I could resist no longer and I peeped through the classroom window and watched my baby. She was using thick red crayon to write on a huge sheet of paper. Her blonde curls slipped over her face as she concentrated fiercely. I hoped she'd look up, but she didn't. She had far better things to do than to check to see if her sad mother was lurking outside.

Finally, she skipped out. She hugged and kissed me and waved a page of scribbles in my face. When we got home, she snuggled on my knee and fell asleep, one warm baby hand resting on my cheek.

That was seven years ago. Time has passed and many things have changed.

Baby's first page of scribbles is yellowing in the attic. Now she can write whole pages of real writing – even in Irish.

I have learned how to make madeira cake. Though I never did try it with that suckling infant in my arms.

Recently I noticed a strange silence and realised that the *Teletubbies* theme tune is no longer rattling around my brain.

Baby will soon be a teenager, like her older brother and sister. Those intense loving moments will increasingly be punctuated by times when she will see me as the architect of all that is wrong in her life. It will be less, 'Mum, can you help me with this?' and more 'Mum, get out of my life.'

Nowadays she will still snuggle next to me on the sofa, and I dread the day when our only physical contact will be if our fingers accidentally touch as I hand over yet more money to buy flimsy scraps of fabric masquerading as skirts.

Soon the child who could once listen to me singing 'Lavender's Blue' for half the day will cringe if I dare to even hum along to a song on the radio.

It doesn't matter what I do – I know that soon my very existence will become a source of embarrassment to her.

This year she smiled shyly as she gave her dad and me the Valentine's card that she'd made at school. How long before such treasures are handed to pale surly youths who could never, ever love her as much as we do?

This morning, I watched her as she skipped happily off to school, her no longer quite-so-blonde hair flying in the wind behind her. And when she was gone, and the house was quiet again, I found that I was wishing myself back to that first day of playschool, back to that day that I had dreaded for so long. Why had I been so sad, when in truth I didn't know quite how lucky I was?

What part of my soul would I sell for one afternoon rolling out grey pastry in the company of that grubby, beaming child?

My wise friend was right, all those years ago. Being a mother is hard. But it's not about the mechanics of wrestling with an infant while simultaneously trying to be a domestic goddess. For me, the hard part is adjusting to what will happen when the babies grow up and leave. I've noticed that becoming a parent has a funny way of making time accelerate, and just when you're getting the hang of it, everything changes. One minute you're up to your eyes in baby rice and mashed bananas, and the next minute your house is full of grumpy teenagers.

And still, I know that in ten years' time, I will surely wish myself back to today. I will look around my clean, organised home and wish that it was once again full of rampaging teenagers. In the end, I fear that the silence will be too much for me.

But these thoughts really are too melancholy for a beautiful day like this, so I've come to a decision. I'm going to ignore all those e-mails lurking in my inbox. I'm going to shut down my computer, close the door on the messy kitchen and step around the overflowing ironing basket. I am going to surprise my daughter at the school gate.

Homework can wait as we go for hot chocolate in our favourite café. We will treat ourselves with whipped cream and extra marshmallows, and she will giggle and sigh and tell me about her day, and I will sit back and savour every single, precious moment.

Colette Caddle is the author of seven bestsellers: *Too Little, Too Late*, *Shaken & Stirred*, *A Cut Above*, *Forever FM*, *Red Letter Day*, *Changing Places* and *The Betrayal of Grace Mulcahy*. Her books are sold throughout the English-speaking world and have also been translated into five languages. Her new book, *It's All About Him*, has just been published and revolves around a single mother who is slightly obsessive about her child's health. Colette lives in County Dublin with her husband and two sons.

A Labour of Love
Colette Caddle

When I had my first baby, I was so ready to become a mother. I had been married for twelve years and I'd had all the wonderful holidays, late nights and long lazy mornings in bed. I was ready to give up our frivolous, carefree life and was looking forward to become a parent. Thanks to my new career as a writer, I would be able to stay home with baby – something I always knew that I'd want to do.

I had a textbook pregnancy – suddenly I understood why everyone used the word 'blooming'. I bloomed like no one had ever bloomed before. If there had been an Olympic category in blooming, I would have brought home the gold! My morning sickness consisted of one day when I felt a little off colour; I got no varicose veins, no stretch marks; I didn't even put on that much weight. You hate me now, don't you?

My favourite pastime during this golden era was reading baby books and magazines. I spent a fortune on the things and avidly consumed every word. I was well prepared for the birth and the baby and I knew exactly what I wanted.

I would try to give birth naturally, but if I needed medication, I wouldn't hesitate. All that mattered was that we ended up with a healthy, happy baby. I had decided to give breastfeeding a go too, but again, I wouldn't fret if it didn't work out.

But, you see, secretly I knew it would. I had read the books and I knew what to do.

I would make sure the baby latched on properly and never ever suffer from soreness or cracked nipples. I would follow the very sensible advice to sleep when my baby was sleeping and be full of energy when he awoke. I would burp him when he needed burping and he would never suffer from colic. I would exercise within days of giving birth and I would be back in my old clothes in no time at all.

Ha!

Any mother reading this is already falling about the place laughing, because they know the truth. Having a child may be a natural process, but it's also an unpredictable one and, at the end of the day, you just have to go with the flow. Once the baby comes along, your days of control are over. There's a new boss in the house, albeit a cuddly, sweet-smelling one.

But hang on a second! I'm getting ahead of myself. I'm completely glossing over the birth itself – would that I could have done that in reality!

Let's say that if the pregnancy was textbook, then the birth was a horror story. All those programmes I'd watched – and I'm not talking fiction – where women screamed for a couple of hours and then smiled beatifically down at their beloved newborn – what a load of codswallop! That's not how it worked at all! By the time my son was finally delivered – after eighteen hours – I was in total shock. Despite all my reading and my wonderful antenatal classes, I was not prepared.

I had looked forward to the classes hugely. It felt like a step closer to holding my baby in my arms and that thrilled me. The course was run by a team of midwives and a physiotherapist and, at the time, I found them useful, informative and entertaining. The aim, it seemed, was to boost our confidence and focus on the positive. But were they any help to me when I was in the delivery ward? I don't think so.

One indication that I wasn't totally prepared for the big event was when it came time for me to push, i.e. the final stage of labour. Now maybe it's just me. And maybe I am particularly stupid, but I *assumed* the idea was to push the baby *out* of my body, in the general direction of the midwife, that is. Not so, I was told irritably by that lady – I use the term loosely – I was to push down into my bottom. But of course! It was obvious! Just not to me. This seemingly obvious little nugget of information hadn't been mentioned in class. Or maybe I'd just nodded off that night.

And what about all that bunk about pelvic floor exercises? I can almost hear the collective groan. Isn't every mother sick to the teeth of hearing about pelvic floors? Well, I was. They went on and on about them and my mind usually started to wander when the subject arose and, sorry, but yet again, I blame Teacher. You see, I completely misunderstood the purpose of pelvic floor exercises. I thought they were to assist in the birth itself and that if I did these exercises it would help me to push in whatever direction we finally all agreed on. And so once baby made his appearance, and pain, euphoria and unbelievable tiredness took over, I never gave my pelvic floor another thought. What a mistake. After several weeks of discomfort and pain, my GP finally explained THE FACTS.

And so I'm going to make sure that none of you make the same mistake I did. Here is the truth:

YOUR BODY WILL NEVER BE THE SAME AGAIN UNLESS YOU DO YOUR PELVIC FLOOR EXERCISES.

There. Simple. Problem solved. I can see it now. Frenzied, manic clenching and unclenching being performed the length and breadth of the country.

So baby makes his entrance into the world – oh, hang on a minute, I'm doing it again, glossing over. I wonder what a psychologist would make of that? Okay, this is it, enough prevarication, time for the gory details.

My ordeal began when I was greeted in the hospital by the midwife from hell. She took great satisfaction in telling me that I hadn't started to dilate and I should go home. I refused. We had been told in antenatal classes that when your contractions are less than three minutes apart and last more than a minute, go to the hospital. They had and I had and now this woman wanted me to go home. It was not going to happen. After some discussion, she reluctantly agreed that I could stay, shunting me into a ward with the words, 'I'm going off duty now and I bet you'll still be here when I come back tomorrow.'

The contractions continued to increase in intensity and frequency and every so often the nurses – much nicer and more sympathetic ones – came to check on me, but it was to be a full six more hours before I started to dilate.

At this stage I was exhausted and demoralised – the initial euphoria of going into labour had long worn off. The nurse said they'd take me to the labour ward and suggested an epidural. I readily agreed.

An angel of a midwife took over my care and held my hand through that long night and my cup runneth over when the epidural worked like a dream. It was all going to be plain sailing from here on – wasn't it? Sorry, no.

My angel went off duty at eight, at which stage several women decided to go into labour at the same time and the ward was like a train station. Also, the baby's heart rate was erratic, so he was hooked up to a monitor and my husband and I eyed each other nervously as we listened to this terrifying machine. It didn't help matters that the only person available to stay with us through these difficult hours was an equally nervous student. Every time the monitor bleeped or I asked a question, she ran for help and I grew more and more convinced that something was seriously wrong.

Just when I thought it couldn't get any worse, it did.

The midwife in charge turned out to be the same dragon who'd greeted me the night before.

'Told you you'd still be here!' she said with an evil grin when she finally came in to see me. She scornfully dismissed all my concerns as hysteric nonsense and left again, leaving me in the hands of the terrified student.

Finally, at about 11:30 – twelve hours after I'd first started to dilate – I was ready to give birth. The urge to push was incredible, like nothing I'd ever experienced before. The student went running for Godzilla. It says everything about the state I was in that I was actually happy to see her. She examined me, agreed I was ready to push but told me I'd have to wait.

I goggled at her. Wait?

There was another woman in labour, she told me, and I'd have to wait until she finished. My husband and I looked at each other, gobsmacked. They hadn't told us *this* in antenatal class.

It seemed like hours, but it was probably only fifteen minutes later when she and the obstetrician came in and announced it was my turn and I was finally allowed to push. But still, things weren't going to go according to plan.

As I've already told you, I had the pushing thing all wrong and my little boy, who was obviously very comfortable in his cosy little pad, wouldn't budge. I cried with pain and frustration.

'Why do you think it's called labour?' the midwife said nastily.

Finally, the obstetrician suggested using the ventouse (suction cups for those of you who luckily don't know any better) and wearily, I agreed. That didn't work – does it ever? – and he said that he would have to use forceps. Again, I was past caring. The baby's heartbeat was all over the place and I was seriously beginning to doubt he would survive.

Minutes later, he was in my arms, seriously battered and bruised but, thankfully, alive.

To my dying day I will regret what I did next. In my defence, I was obviously in shock, but even so, what was I thinking? As I cuddled my son, tears of relief streaming down my face, I profusely thanked the monster who'd treated me so badly. Not only that, I apologised for being a difficult patient! Yes, *I* apologised to *her!*

I was wheeled up to the ward, my baby nestled close beside me, and despite my exhaustion, I couldn't take my eyes off him and it seemed he couldn't take his eyes off me either. It amazed me that despite the ordeal we'd just been through, he seemed both quiet and serene and eager to feed.

I was in a ward of four and we were all attempting to do the earth mother thing and breastfeed. I was the only one who succeeded without too much trouble – well, I suppose I was due a lucky break by then – and the general feeling of pressure and concentration in the ward equalled any exam hall.

Unfortunately, my talents stopped there. When it came to actually looking after a baby, I hadn't a clue. This was an area that got very little time in antenatal class, but we were assured that we would get some instruction after the birth. Unfortunately, the ward was completely understaffed and the nurses had a tough enough time getting through their basic duties without taking the time to teach us how to be mums.

As a result, my poor baby had to suffer my learning on the job and I will never forget the first time I had to change his nappy – he probably won't either.

I didn't get a demo of how to bathe him or clean the umbilical cord until the evening before I went home, and then I was too busy trying to keep a grip on the slippery sucker to take too much on board.

So I went home feeling nervous and ill prepared for the job ahead of me. How could anyone with an ounce of sense put me in charge of this precious little bundle? You wouldn't let someone out in a car on their own without lessons, would you? It's a funny old world.

I got through it in the end and, although it took me four years, I went on to do it all again. Thankfully, both my sons seem to be reasonably hale and hearty despite my clumsy ministrations and hopeless inadequacy and I have no regrets. Well, not many, and any rumours that I own a doll dressed as a nurse with several pins sticking in it are, of course, not true.

So have I any last words of advice for those of you thinking of taking the plunge into motherhood?

Don't do it.

No, just kidding. Go for it, but remember that every woman's experience is different. As for antenatal classes, by all means sign up. They won't really prepare you for what lies ahead, but you'll definitely have a laugh and, you never know, you might even learn something.

And years later you'll have your beautiful children and any painful memories will long since have faded just the way mine have. Now where did I leave that doll?

Ho Wei Sim is a Malaysian-Chinese woman who moved to Ireland ten years ago. Wei Sim wrote for a popular drama series by the Television Corporation of Singapore, and her award-winning short film was produced and shown on television and at the Galway Film Festival. She writes short stories and has contributed various articles to the *Irish Independent*. In her past life she was a corporate lawyer.

Four Women, Two Journeys, Three Countries

Ho Wei Sim

Ciara's foot is in my mouth. I feel her toes shoved against my lips and startle awake, wondering what the hell is going on, where the hell I am. Arms, legs, faces, bodies everywhere. I open my eyes and see the sole of Ciara's foot in my face. I try to turn around, and on the other side of me, Liadh stirs and swings her arm over, slamming it across my nose.

Oh right, we are in the couchette of a train – we are going home, home to see my granny. My little girls are with me. The curtain on the narrow window flaps crazily. I peer out and see my old world flashing by in the darkness – silhouettes of palm trees, then cars and buses waiting at train crossings, men on Vespas, the fluorescent lights of workshops, then shophouses, squatter huts huddled close to the railway line. The wind roars in my ears as I watch the silent pantomime, a thin slice of the rich life that makes up my bones and flesh, my blood. I am home and I feel the sweetness of the familiar in my stomach. I smile and I don't know I am smiling.

Ciara is sleeping the other way around, her face near my feet. Sometime during the night, I can imagine her deciding to sleep the other way around, instinctively finding space for herself. I reach for her and pull her towards me, lay her beside me. She is lost in sleep. I move my face into her hair and breathe in her smell. Liadh snuggles close, puts her arm around me. I turn and mould my body around hers and kiss her smooth cheek. I whisper in their ears. My little darlings. I let the warmth of their bodies envelop me.

I sit up gingerly, trying not to knock my head against the bunk above, and look at my two girls, my two miracles. The complete surrender of sleep. I don't do this – look at them and divide – their eyes, mouth, noses, cheeks, which part of them is me, which is Donal; which part of them is Chinese, and which is Irish. They are just my little girls. Liadh – the wide sweep of her cheeks and bones over her nose and then her fine eyes. Ciara, soft curly hair all tousled over her face, her long black lashes closed tight over her pink cheeks.

And then suddenly, we are here. The train pulls into the station, we get out, and soon we find ourselves standing at the front door of a Chinese shophouse – the inky blackness of the sky around us, the light of the corridor against the metal grating of the entrance. I am banging on the door, banging on the door of my heritage, my past. And then the door opens and she stands there, my granny – a little woman, little face, little eyes, little hands. She smiles. I smile.

We tumble in, buggy, suitcases, little people. I put Liadh and Ciara to bed. It is only 5:30 in the morning, too early to start the day. But our jetlag lends a surreal quality – in between two worlds – between wakefulness and sleep.

Between my new life in Ireland and the textures, smells of my old world; and for the children, a strange new world. The heat and the humidity, the smooth, cold cement floor, the voice on the Chinese radio station, the call to prayer from a mosque far away. My granny changes into a nice dress to mark the special day, a going-out dress though she is not going anywhere. She slips in her dentures in our honour. She makes my favourite Malaysian coffee and we sit down at the kitchen table. We sip our coffee silently, suddenly shy. Too early to start. Too late not to begin.

On this new day, we sit together at the kitchen table, preparing our day's meal, slipping back into our old routine. She peels the cloves of garlic, hands them to me. I chop them up; I have better eyes and steadier hands. She picks the leaves of the vegetables, I get up and wash them at the sink. And it's like it was always like this, two of us, sitting together, sometimes quiet, sometimes talking. And I remember a few years ago, when I was expecting Liadh, that special time expecting my first baby when everything is a hazard or a necessity. I sat here with my granny, conscious of the new life in me, tuning in to the sounds and movements of my baby, while listening to my granny's stories. These are her gifts to me, stories of lives in another time, of people I would never meet, of the home she came from so long ago. Tell me, Granny, tell me about your life in China, what it was like before you came to Malaysia, I used to say. In this unhurried way, we came also to talk about the name for my new baby. We talked and debated, and finally, in a quavery hand, she wrote on a thin piece of pink paper torn from the calendar on the wall. If it is a girl, she said, this is her name – 'Sook Yee', she wrote.

As I remember what it was like, the girls rush in. My granny smiles and nods in approval as they clamber up to sit on the stools around the table. These two little girls are now new additions to an old routine.

'Can I help, Mama?' Liadh asks.

'I want to help too,' Ciara pipes up.

'Here, Liadh, you can peel these carrots, and Ciara, why don't you wash these vegetables for me.'

'Don't you speak to them in Cantonese any more?' my granny says sharply. My granny doesn't speak English at all.

I feel abashed. I had been so good. Speaking to Liadh only in Cantonese from when she was born, scouring the shops for Cantonese books, CDs, cartoons, DVDs with Cantonese language options. Even playing Cantonese songs to Liadh, and to Ciara, as they fell asleep when they were a few months old in the hope that they would somehow absorb the language, their Chinese-ness, that somehow it would make that part of themselves come alive. And it had gone well for a time. Liadh could understand everything I said to her, although she would only answer in English, and had impressed everyone in the previous visits back to Malaysia. But as time went on, I found my own Cantonese failing me. 'How do I say "dinosaur" in Cantonese?' I found myself struggling. The truth is, being born to an emigrant Chinese family in Malaysia, we spoke mainly English and Malay at school, and English and Cantonese at home. Having little formal Cantonese instruction, English was the language I expressed myself best in. I even dreamed in English.

'I try to do that,' I say, but in my heart I feel I haven't tried hard enough. My granny says nothing. We work away, she is silent. Then the girls slip off to have a closer look at the people passing out the back door of the shophouse. Granny calls after them. 'Sook Yee,' she says. 'Sze Yee, come here,' she says in Chinese, holding out a piece of sweet potato for them to eat. But to my horror, they don't even react. They don't even realise they are being called. 'Liadh, Ciara, Tai Poh is calling you.' Tai Poh is the word for great-granny in Chinese. But the girls just stop and look blankly at me. My granny turns to me and says, 'Don't they know their own names?'

I am upset. I am upset for my granny, angry with myself and worried for my children – that they will have to pay the price for this one day. Not knowing, not recognising, their own Chinese selves. I feel I have betrayed my granny, and the Chinese-ness of all of us. And worst of all, it is all my fault. Yes, I feel the weight of that responsibility – that I am the only one who can help them know themselves. Living as a foreigner in Ireland, all the pain and the joy of that journey, I have come to realise how important it was for me to know what it means to be Chinese, to be Malaysian. To know where I end and where I begin. It has only been through knowing myself that I have been able to learn to live in Ireland, to be able to be separate and yet be at one with Irish people and this country.

My granny is a querulous, grumpy woman. She once said to my brother, 'Why aren't you married yet? Is it because you're ugly, or are you just gay?' She is the granny from hell. She has a tongue that will burn the wax off candlesticks. But I love her. I love her insults, I love her directness, I love her hard side, I love her intelligence. I know she has no time for fools and has no time for soft things, but I see the soft side of her that others don't often see, I see her love of children, and of plants, and her home.

This morning, at the kitchen table, we make our meal – roast duck, roast chicken, steamed chicken, roast pork. For my granny, no Chinese celebration meal is right unless it is a banquet of meat, meat, meat. Liadh says, 'Can we have spaghetti Bolognese for dinner, Mum?' I shush her hurriedly. It's a good thing my granny can't understand English. Then my granny announces, 'We are going to make dumplings. We must make dumplings for my two little white girls to eat.' These special dumplings are for good luck, to be served only on very special occasions.

I am struck by how much she has opened herself to Liadh and Ciara. How proud she is of them. She introduces them to everyone she meets. She calls them my two little white girls. To see her affection for them, when all her life she has been a narrow-minded, racist woman. I can see her reaching out towards them, and I am grateful.

There is a wall of photographs in my granny's house – the plaster on the wall chipped to reveal different colours through the decades – light blue, cream, pink. 'Liadh and Ciara, come and see, look at this.' I point out the people in the pictures, grand-uncles, aunts, cousins, people I don't even know.

Liadh points up at an old photograph, taken in black and white but coloured in as they used to do during those times. 'Who is this woman, Mum?'

It's a picture of my granny and my grandfather taken days after she arrived in Malaysia, fresh off the boat from her village in Taishan in China. She was twenty-one. She wore a white *cheongsam*, her hair in an elegant chignon, her lips generous and sensuous. She looks watchful, tense. My grandfather is handsome. He is square-shouldered and holds himself with confidence.

'Is that really Tai Poh, Mum?' 'Yes, it is.' I glance over to her. Now her hair is in tight curls like many women her age, in an 'old lady perm' she started to wear when she was only fifty. Where is that young woman in the picture, I wonder?

According to family folklore, that young woman was match-made to my grandfather and travelled thousands of miles across the ocean from China to Malaysia to marry a man she had never met. They were among the many Chinese people who left China for Malaya and other countries in South-East Asia or Hong Kong, escaping poverty to seek a better life. It was the year 1938. I pictured her coming off a flimsy boat, scanning the crowd anxiously, her hand holding all of her life's possessions in a cloth bundle, her heart holding all of her hopes and dreams.

It's ironic that two generations later, I left this part of the world to move to Ireland for exactly the opposite reasons. Malaysia and Singapore were affluent countries, not least by the efforts of generations of emigrant Chinese and Indians – we were at the height of the Asian Tiger economies. Life was good. Chrome and glass buildings, Starbucks cafés everywhere, shiny stores where you could shop to your heart's content. But I wondered, was this all there was to life? The materialism, that kind of driven and manufactured existence was the predominant flavour of Singapore life, and it bothered me. I dreamed of living in the country, with fields of green, grass and cows around me, closer to nature, closer to God, where family, friendship, love might have a bigger place in the order of things. I wanted a more meaningful existence.

'Take me to the Chinese grocery store near the market,' my granny says. 'I want to buy the ingredients for the dumplings.' And so we set off, the four of us walking through the streets of the town – the heat, dust, Toyotas whizzing by, past the tailor with the dummy in a Western suit that would be baking hot in this weather, past the Indian Muslim restaurant selling *roti canai, mee siam*, past the Indian lady in the corner selling tobacco leaves and betel nut – who flashes a disconcerting blood-red smile at Liadh and Ciara.

My granny's steps are slow and faltering, she leans on her umbrella, a disguised walking stick. She stops now and then, needing to sit down on a step, then again on another step just twenty paces way. That young woman in the picture is still here, braving life, a little more haltingly perhaps. I hold my grandmother's hand, I press it firmly. I take Ciara's hand, and ask Liadh to hold hers. And then the four of us, together, we cross the perilous traffic to the safety of the other side. I feel fiercely protective of my granny, of the young woman she was, crossing the ocean alone towards the hopes of a better life. If nothing else, I want my girls to know these are the hopes and dreams that carried them across time, across the oceans and continents to Ireland.

We arrive at the Chinese grocery store. On the floor, there are bags of barley, lotus seeds, rice flour, onions, dried squid. On the floor-to-ceiling shelves, there are bottles and cans full of condiments, soy sauce, rice vinegar, tins of luncheon meat, abalone, Milo. The old Chinese grocer calls out to my granny. He comes out to serve her himself, waving away his son like a little boy, save that the man is already in his fifties. This old grocer knows my granny from decades ago, probably having made that journey across the ocean as she did. She tells him what she wants and he gets them together quickly, tying each package together with a thin rubber band, swinging the package round and round the rubber band, and then letting the rubber band go with a decisive snap. He tots up the total in his head. Everything is done with a lithe efficiency.

Back home, my granny makes the rice dumplings. She adds water and kneads the dough with her hands, adding a little red colouring. The girls pitch in, making little pink balls of flour. I grind peanuts for the filling. My granny's fingers are no longer fleshy, and the skin is mottled. I have my mother's hands, my fingers are long and I am proud of them. One day they too will age, and I hope I will be as lucky to be making dumplings for my great-grandchildren.

'So, what was it like for to you come all the way from China, when you didn't even know the man you were going to marry?' I ask. To my surprise, she snorts in reply. 'Oh, that! That's nonsense. I was already married to your grandfather before I came here.' I am stunned. 'But that was what we were always told.' 'People will believe what they want to believe,' she laughs. 'Your grandfather's third brother came first and then worked to get enough money for his fourth brother to come. In the same way, the fourth brother got your grandfather here. Then when your grandfather was able to save enough money, he sent for me.' I am amazed. And it turns out she came here on a shining liner ship, not a flimsy boat.

'I wasn't afraid. When you are young, you are not afraid, you think you can conquer everything. I wandered about on the deck of the ship, looking at everything, everyone. And I can still remember this pork dish they served on board – it tasted wonderful.' She paused, remembering. 'When I came here, everything was so strange. I saw this man, skin dark as night – I had never seen anyone like that before, he was naked except for a piece of white cloth around his waist – and he walked down the street as if it was nothing at all. And then I realised, it was nothing at all, this was normal, for their people – the Indians. And in the marketplace, I went out with five cents that your grandfather gave me to buy some rice and vegetables for our meal, there were all these different people, I was sure I wouldn't be able to make myself understood. Malays, Indians, even the Chinese were different – from different provinces – Hakka, Teochew, Hokkiens, speaking all different Chinese languages. You know that man at the grocery store? Well, he ran a little stall back then. I wanted to buy some rice from him. I asked him, in Taishan language, and he answered in Hakka. I couldn't understand him, and he couldn't understand me. All I could do was give him my five cents and trust that he would give me the right change back.' She paused, thoughtful. 'Everything was strange.'

'We Chinese are a gambling people – we staked our life on this, thought we would have a better life here. We arrived here hoping for an easier life, but we struggled, it was very hard. And then just three years after I arrived, war came. The Japanese – oh, I will never forget it. We ran to the hills, your eldest uncle was just two, and I carried your second uncle in my arms, he was a baby, just two months old. I cropped my hair and wore men's clothes. We lived in the jungle for six months, on nothing but tapioca and tapioca leaves. Your second uncle screamed non-stop the whole time we were there. He was hungry and I had nothing to give him.' She paused. 'It was a terrible time.' I remembered the stories of torture, beheadings, executions when the Japanese occupied Malaya. She was silent for a long time.

'What I really wanted was for us to have been able to build our own house on some land, and I would plant some vegetables in the back and have some chickens. Just a place of our own. We never did.' She paused. 'But I'm not sad. I have more than I ever thought I would, and maybe what I don't, I was never fated to have.'

I cry for my granny, I cry for myself, the things we give up for our dreams, and the dreams that don't come true. And I am grateful for all that has been possible for me; what she wanted I have wanted too, and we have been fortunate to have been able to build our own house on our own land in the country, vegetable patch and all.

She puts the dumplings into a pot of boiling water. They bob up and down in the hot water. 'They are ready,' she says at last. She fishes them out carefully. I call the children. They run up, excited. 'Come and eat your dumplings.' My granny smiles her toothless smile. The dumplings are for good luck; they are full of her good wishes.

The girls look at them uncertainly. Liadh takes a tentative bite. Ciara throws one into her mouth, and a split second later, she spits it out.

My granny's smile disappears. Her face drops. 'Ciara!' I am horrified. My granny says nothing. Quietly, she gathers the bowls of dumplings, puts them in the sink and walks away.

'That wasn't very nice, Ciara.' 'But Mum, the balls were slimy!' she protests. She has a point, I thought, I always hated those dumplings myself. 'Well, Tai Poh made them especially for the two of you, and she was really hoping you'd enjoy them.' I give them a good talking-to. 'OK, girls, I know the food here is different, but I think you're really missing out if you don't try it.' 'It's too spicy,' says Liadh. 'Some of it is spicy,' I say. 'Spicy is good. OK, just try a little bit of everything, OK? And no spitting!' 'OK,' they nod. Still, I know for my granny, it is not just about the dumplings or the food.

The girls have been such good sports – falling into the rhythm of this life easily and without complaint. When the sweltering heat of the afternoon overtakes their enthusiasm for drawing or jigsaws, they fall asleep, only to awake later in a groggy stupor, unrested. Still they carry on, happy in their own way, going everywhere with me. As I roam the streets of the little town recharging my Malaysian-ness, they are my faithful companions, past the coffin shop, past the shop selling wooden clogs set out in rows on the floor, past the old cobbler, with his rubber soles and tools on the five-foot way of the corridor, past the monsoon drain where schoolboys poke at tadpoles in a thin stream of algae-filled water.

This is a completely different world from Ireland. I fit into my life in Ireland, yet I carry this other world within me, and few people in Ireland have any sense of this – not the colleagues in the law firm where I used to work, not the other mums on my school run, not the ticket-seller at the Leixlip train station with whom I have a brief conversation every week, not even my closest Irish friends, even though they are some of the loveliest people I have met. When I am here, when I speak Malay to the noodle vendor, or Cantonese or Mandarin to the hawkers at the marketplace, I slip into another part of me, like a beloved comfortable shoe unworn for too long. I meet old feelings, associations and memories from my past, like meeting an old friend in myself.

What can I say about what it was like when I first arrived in Ireland? Hailstones in May, like little bouncing Styrofoam balls on a street. Surreal. And after the safety and transparency of Singapore, I felt keenly the kind of grittiness in the streets and the people, a feeling of danger and unpredictability with everything. People walking in the street with their arms crossed over their chests. Rain that went on and on. I missed the thunderstorms in Malaysia when the rage of the storm hurled at us in a short sharp burst, the day returning to blue skies and hot baking asphalt all too soon. Here, the clouds pressed down on me. I missed the openness of my old world, an openness in so many ways, like its deep blue skies, tall, spacious. I missed the energy of my people, my country, how we looked outwards towards the world. I felt I came from a world where difference is the order of the day, to a world that tended towards homogeneity and sameness, where colours are muted and many thoughts and feelings are kept sheltered in people's hearts.

I miss my old world, but I love my new world too– when I drive along the country roads and the sun is so low in the sky it blinds me. Then my car swings around the corner and I am taken by surprise by the colours of the sky, a sunset that takes my breath away. I can see the sun setting every single evening from the patio of my home, over green fields, cows and horses in the next field. Driving on a winter morning, with a misty fog in the air, silhouettes of the bare beech and birch trees. Walking down Dun Laoghaire pier on a bright morning, wind through my hair, nodding to other people out walking. Grafton Street at Christmastime. The human-ness of the Irish people – when what is talked about seems much less important than the person you are talking to. I love the warm and reflective space in the minds and souls of Irish people. I love the easy banter accompanying every exchange, but I found the flipside of that – the reserve and privacy of people – a shock to discover, and painful to get used to. During some of my loneliest times in Ireland, it was ironic, in light of what my grandparents went through, that I found solace and companionship with my Japanese softball team-mates, when in history we might have seemed irretrievably divided, like the Jews and Germans, yet I connected with them most easily and more intimately; perhaps we are made of similar material. Forgiveness and prejudice, I wonder, in what places they belong.

'Look!' says Liadh. She points to a stall selling pancakes and the two of them run over, fascinated by the way the man pours his batter over the rows of pancake moulds, then scattering crushed peanuts and creamed corn over it, butter and banana slices at the end. 'Cool!' says Ciara. I am struck in that moment – I realise something about the way Ciara has been during this trip, seeing this new world, tells me it is as if she is merely a visitor here, that it would have been the same kind of wonder had she visited South America or India. Perhaps she is still young, but I didn't feel it was this way with Liadh. I wondered whether it was because Liadh was better with speaking Cantonese. Language is so close to identity and Liadh was always so much closer to her Chinese-ness in that sense. Or was this simply self-flagellation on my part, my guilt for not trying harder with the Cantonese with Ciara?

'This girl doesn't know me,' my granny had said that morning of Ciara. It's as if my granny is just another new person she has met. Ciara doesn't know my granny's place in her own heart, just as she hasn't let in her Malaysian-ness or Chinese-ness, not yet. And it doesn't surprise me; for a long time, I felt Ciara knew me as the person who cared for and provided for her, and it was not until much later that the penny dropped and she fell in love with me. Whereas Liadh loves easily, and in the same way seemed to attach to her motherland automatically. They are different. So perhaps it will take Ciara longer to learn to love her Chinese-ness, her Malaysian-ness. I think she will, in her own time.

I remember going to visit my motherland – to see my ancestral village in Canton where my grandparents were born. As the boat snaked up the Pearl Delta, I stood looking out at the windswept plains. I watched a woman on a bicycle, cycling up a narrow path with a big basket balanced behind her. I saw paddy fields, and rushes being beaten by the wind beside the orange-coloured water of the river. I wondered at the sights, I took in the different rhythm of that life, and still, I felt merely a visitor. It was only when I saw the prominent noses and generous earlobes of the men, the same as those of my father and my grandfather, that I realised, no, my roots go deeper. I am tied to this country whether I recognise it or not. And though in some ways I am different from the increasing number of mainland Chinese in Ireland today, we were made of the same material not so many generations ago. One day, their children in Ireland, overseas Chinese like me, might take a trip to China just as I had done.

'Mum, can we have pancakes, please!' the girls beg. They devour them. It is lovely to see them enjoying something I loved when I was a little girl. I wonder how things will turn out for them. In Ireland, people say they look so Chinese, while in Malaysia, people say they look so Irish. It is their difference that is picked up in either place; they will never blend in. A few years ago, I remember meeting a young woman, a GP, whose father was Malaysian and whose mother was Irish. Her father was also a GP; he had come to Ireland for his studies and had stayed on. I looked forward to meeting her, waiting to see how she turned out, waiting to see the Malaysian in her. She was lovely, but the subtleties in the way she related to me were so Irish. I was so disappointed because something in me wanted to see her Malaysian side, if only to give me hope for what was possible for my own girls. It was the week before Chinese New Year. She said, 'Oh, I just wish Dad would just give me the *lai-see* and get it over with'. The *lai-see* is a lucky red packet Chinese parents give to their children at Chinese New Year, the strongest symbol of the auspicious day. What she said seemed to capture the agony of a parent trying to pass on everything, all of our Chinese-ness, on that one day, and the ignorance and impatience of the child not knowing, not valuing, what it is that her parent fails to pass on and what she fails to receive.

Over the next few days, the girls discover more and more favourite foods. *Hokkien prawn mee* for Ciara. Noodle soup for Liadh. I am thrilled they share my passion for these noodles, for, as ever, it is not only about food. 'Mum,' says Liadh. 'We're Irish, and we're Chinese, so we're half Irish and half Chinese, right?' 'No, girls,' I say. 'You are all Irish, and you are all Chinese.' 'Huh?' she says. 'Let's say your Irish side is white and your Chinese side is red. Does that make you pink? You are not pink, because being pink will make you nothing, neither one nor the other,' I explain. 'You mean we're made of red stripes and white stripes?' 'That's it! I say. 'Oh…' Liadh says. There is a long pause. 'In that case, I think my red stripes are bigger than my white stripes.' I beam, delighted.

This is my inheritance from my grandmother – being an overseas Chinese growing up in Malaysia, the country that I love. Just as I took a trip to China to visit my motherland, one day my girls will make that journey to Malaysia, if only an emotional one. What they make of their inheritance is up to them. I can only pass on what I have; I can only do my best. What they are able or willing to receive is up to them. My hope is that they will not simply be visitors to their Malaysian past.

My granny sits in her favourite chair, staring into space, alone with her thoughts, as she is wont to do in the afternoon. I am making a longan and wintermelon drink. The smell of this dessert – woody, fruity – fills the kitchen. I taste it. It's good. I ladle it into a bowl and give it to Ciara to bring to my granny. Slowly, she walks over, carrying the bowl carefully with both hands. 'Tai Poh,' she says, 'for you.' My granny turns to her and smiles. She pats her on the head. 'Good girl,' she says. 'You are both good girls.'

My granny has the dessert and I can see her enjoying it with relish. I am glad. She comes over, joins the girls and me at the kitchen table. As we all chat, she cuts up little pieces of wintermelon sugar. She gives pieces of this to Liadh and Ciara to eat, hands it to them with her fingers. I remember her feeding me like this when I was a child. I remember their sweet and juicy softness between my teeth.

Today we are leaving. Our bags are packed. When we are ready to leave for the railway station, my granny presents Liadh and Ciara with a gold bracelet each. She puts the bracelets on them tenderly, and secures them with a piece of red string for good luck. I am glad they have something of her. Then I remember – the bracelets are not her only gifts to them. She chose their names. 'Yee' means 'family ties and relationships'. This gift will always be with them.

My granny turns to me and says, 'You know, I never thought I would have a great-granddaughter with curly hair.' She fingers Ciara's curly hair playfully. Chinese hair is usually dead straight. I laugh. I know what she means. I once realised that we are the inheritors of changes made by our predecessors. If my grandparents had not moved from China, my life would be completely different. Had I not moved to Ireland, my children too would have a completely different existence. And today, I realised one more thing – that our predecessors too may inherit from the changes we make. Through my children, my grandmother has gained a part of Ireland, something she would never have dreamed could happen.

We say goodbye to my granny. There are tears in her eyes, but she turns away to hide them. I give her a hug. Chinese families rarely hug; this is something I have in my own way inherited during my years in Ireland. I don't know if I will ever see her again. One day my granny will no longer be here, and this house will be boarded up, together with my roots and my past. But then, some precious things will always remain undiminished in our hearts.

I dedicate this story to my grandmother, Chon Chin Foon.

Anne Marie Scanlon is an Irish writer and journalist who lived in New York for over a decade. She has contributed to most of the Irish publications in the USA and currently works with *Irish Examiner USA*, where she writes features about fashion, cosmetics and lifestyle. She is the author of *It's Not Me…It's You (A Girl's Guide to Dating in Ireland)*. In January 2007, Anne Marie gave birth to Jack, the world's most beautiful baby™ (the dating guide works!). Anne Marie is currently working on a book about pregnancy and birth.

Morning, Noon and Night Sickness

Anne Marie Scanlon

The blood drained from the doctor's face as he looked at the results of the blood test.

'We're going to have to admit you,' he said. 'Your potassium levels are extremely low. Critically low, in fact.'

'Admit her?' my mother was echoing.

'Yes, immediately,' the doctor said, addressing her.

'Oh, could I not bring her back in the morning?' Mum asked. She wasn't really thinking. It was rush hour, it was raining and she has a quite remarkable sense of direction – the wrong direction. It was my job to navigate our way home, and in her panic she focused on how she was to get home in heavy traffic, in bad weather and having no clue which way to go. No doubt it was also easier to focus on her travel arrangements than on what the doctor was saying about her only child.

'Oh yes,' the doctor replied, 'you could bring her back in the morning, but equally, she could be dead by then.'

Poor Mum. I'd arrived from the United States, my home of the past ten years, at Heathrow in a wheelchair the day before. I was two dress sizes smaller than when she'd last seen me three and a half months earlier and I'd aged about ten years. Despite my repeated warnings about my appearance, I could see she was clearly shocked by the state I was in.

Now at this juncture I feel compelled to admit that I am a first-class drama queen. I enjoy a good drama, especially one in which I have a starring role. Show me a spotlight and I'll leap in ready for action, lights and camera. On this occasion, where I was suddenly starring in my own private episode of *ER*, I was utterly failing to react appropriately. I wasn't really reacting at all. Here was a doctor telling me I could at any second collapse from a coronary and I didn't appear to be bothered in the slightest.

'Do you understand?' the doctor persisted. 'It's not just that you could die, you could—'

'End up in a permanent vegetative state,' I interrupted, 'like Terri Schiavo. Yes, doctor, I know.'

The doctor hadn't the first idea what I was talking about, so I explained that Terri Schiavo was the American woman who had been at the centre of a controversy the previous year. Ms Schiavo was a bulimic who had been in a permanent vegetative state for fifteen years following a heart attack (during which her brain was deprived of oxygen) brought on by her bulimia. When her husband decided to cut off her life support, her parents protested and eventually even the Vatican became embroiled in the debate.

What I didn't bother telling the doctor – what I hadn't the energy to relate – was that the prospect of having a coronary didn't scare me. It would have been a blessed relief to lapse into unconsciousness. Words cannot describe just how awful I felt, and I had been feeling that way for far too long. For three and a half months I had been battling crippling nausea and constant vomiting. The prospect of relief, any relief, even if it meant collapsing from a heart attack, was a welcome one. I was worn down and worn out. I couldn't remember what it was like to feel well. I was malnourished, dehydrated and quite literally unable to function, either mentally or physically. The only relief I got was when I was asleep, and in the week or so prior to this visit to the hospital, I had been waking a couple of times a night to throw up. I was at a point where I couldn't take any more, and the doctor had the results to prove it.

You might wonder what was causing such extreme symptoms and why medical science was unable to alleviate them. The cause was no mystery. I was pregnant and had a condition called hyperemesis. In layman's terms, hyperemesis is basically morning sickness on speed. The doctors in the US defined it as a condition where you vomit more than three times a day on a daily basis. Good one. If I managed to count the amount of times I vomited on any given day, then that was a good day, a very good day indeed. What doctors can't tell you is what causes hyperemesis in the first place. I'd had it right from the start – the nausea began seconds after conception, long before it ever even occurred to me to take a pregnancy test.

The doctors in the US were, in a word, useless. Every two weeks I went to see the doctor. Every two weeks I reported that my symptoms had become more severe and every two weeks I was told 'it will pass'. It didn't. I became more debilitated with each passing day and soon was unable to be out of bed for more than ten minutes at a time. I didn't have the energy to shower or wash my hair. I couldn't work and my Baby Daddy was working abroad, hence as much use as a chocolate teapot. I have never felt as lonely or as alone in all my life. Finally, when I'd lost 8 lb in one week, I was admitted to hospital. I was put on a saline drip to rehydrate me and that was basically that. It was like putting a plaster on an axe wound. I'd already been getting backstreet rehydratration from my friend, a nurse, who would come around to my apartment and attach the drip to a standing lamp. The whole situation was bizarre, like a scene from one of those independent films that get lauded by critics but leave audiences wanting to slash their wrists with rusty razor blades. My friend the nurse was the first to admit that the saline drips she administered were fairly useless in the overall scheme of things, but as she said herself, 'they're better than nothing'.

When I was discharged after my first stay at the local hospital, I managed to make it as far as the front door of my building before I vomited in the gutter. After two subsequent visits to the hospital, where I encountered convicted felons from Rikers Island (shackled to their respective beds) and rodents (I don't know what scared me more, the bad guys or the mice), I was no better. I was worse. Much worse. By this stage I was getting daily phone calls from my mother in England, who was at her wits' end with worry, and from my friend Deborah in Ireland, who had become pregnant at approximately the same time that I had and was becoming increasingly concerned not just by my symptoms, but by my incoherence on the telephone (dehydration leads to mental confusion). Both were urging me to get on the first plane available, as were most of my friends in New York. I knew they were right, but I kept waiting until I felt a little bit better before booking the flight. I was too ill to wash myself – just getting to the airport seemed like an insurmountable task, never mind flying 3,000 miles.

After my third trip to the local hospital, my latent survival instinct kicked in. I was in a state of almost total collapse and I wasn't getting any help at all. Two days later, I was on a flight home to Mum. The morning after I arrived in England I woke up thinking I had wet the bed. I hadn't. I was bleeding heavily. As I made my way to the hospital with my mother, I was simultaneously terrified that I was going to lose the baby yet at the same time thinking, Finally the nausea and vomiting will stop. Finally I'll get some relief. To this day I feel guilty about thinking those thoughts, yet I can still understand why I did.

The doctors did not know what had caused the bleeding (which continued for a week). They checked the foetal heartbeat, which was reassuringly strong, and began the process that led to the discovery of my critically low potassium levels. That first night in hospital, things went from bad to worse. I could no longer hold down water and during the night I couldn't sleep and vomited violently approximately every twenty minutes. The doctors tried various medications to try to quell the vomiting, but I just threw them all back up. The only solace I had was that the woman in the bed opposite me was deaf and therefore wasn't disturbed by the hideous noises I was making while evacuating my insides. Finally, as a last resort, I was given IV steroids combined with oral medication, IM injections and suppositories. The next day I ate an entire cream cracker and didn't regurgitate it. The day after that I was able to have a cup of tea. I love tea and had sorely missed it in the previous months. The unbridled joy of being able to have a cup of tea was something I will never forget.

Like most women, I've struggled with my weight from time to time. I've had 'food issues', gone on diets, tried to cut out certain things, fallen off more food wagons than I could name. Until I got hyperemesis I'd never appreciated just how important food is. Not just the nutritional aspects, obviously – I knew that a sufficient intake of calories is essential for survival. I was well aware that you need certain vitamins and minerals to keep up some semblance of health. I knew these things but didn't practise them all that well – for years I've striven to eat a 'healthy diet' and for years I've failed miserably.

The thing I really noticed about the absence of food was how important meals are to daily routine and structure. I've never understood people who don't eat breakfast. I am more than fond of my bed and usually the only thing that gets me out of it is hunger – breakfast is the one meal of the day that I'm usually pretty good about. Normally I'd have tea (large quantities) and porridge with fruit and sometimes even yoghurt. When I became ill I woke up and…nothing. I woke up and had nothing to do. I just lay there in bed waiting until it was time to go back to sleep again. There was no structure to my day, no purpose. I was fit for nothing and that's exactly what I did – nothing. I couldn't mark the passage of time in any normal way. I was too ill to work, too ill to eat, too ill to do anything but lie there in what was close enough to being a vegetative state.

After months of being deprived, being able to drink a cup of tea was fantastic. Being able to drink a cup of tea and not regurgitate it five minutes later was, at that point, practically miraculous. After a week in the English hospital

I was released with a sackful of medication which included oral steroids to be taken on a decreasing scale over ten days. I now fully understand the appeal of steroid abuse. I felt wonderful. I had plenty of energy and, even more surprising, an appetite. Of course, I wasn't actually able to do very much or eat very much, but it didn't stop me trying. When I came off the steroids, reality hit me like a brick. The nausea returned, but thankfully it was intermittent and rarely as severe as it had been before. Thankfully, I was usually able to manage it with the medication I had been prescribed. Sometimes it proved beyond management and would be so severe that I would have no choice but to go to bed and lie still and wait for it to pass. Sometimes the vomiting reoccurred (and yes, on one or two occasions more than three times in the one day), but again, it was occasional rather than constant.

Having been an American size 2 with a flat stomach at 3 ½ months pregnant, I quickly gained weight (initially due to the steroids) and was soon looking like a woman who was either pregnant or enjoyed pies a lot. When I had first arrived in England, I looked gaunt and lined and was convinced that no matter what happened, my looks (such as they were) were gone forever. Happily, as I began eating again, my face began to fill out, the lines disappeared and I began to look like myself again.

As I write, my child is five days overdue. My face unfortunately continued to fill out, along with the rest of me, and it's hard to believe that I was so skinny and wretched only a few short months ago. The nausea and vomiting have continued on and off throughout the entire pregnancy and a few days ago I was violently ill for about forty-eight hours. One of my friends remarked that I'd had the worst pregnancy ever. I haven't. As far as hyperemesis goes, I was pretty lucky in that I responded to medication. There are women who don't. There are women who are unable to eat for their entire pregnancies and have to spend the whole time in hospital on drips to keep them alive. There are women who cannot endure the symptoms and opt to terminate the pregnancy. I know there are people who will be horrified at that and think it utterly selfish. Please don't judge. Until you've been that ill for that long, it's impossible to know how you would react yourself. Instead of judgment, the women who end their pregnancies deserve sympathy. What a decision to have to make. I'm only glad I was spared it myself.

I was damn lucky that the medication worked. I was even luckier that I could come to a country where I would get proper medication. Had I stayed in New York, I think my story would have had a different ending and not a very happy one. I am still in England, a move that was not made by choice but necessity. When I came out of hospital and began to recover, I was far too scared to return to the US. What if something else happened? (As indeed it did – my pregnancy has been like one long extended episode of *Holby City*.) I was afraid to return to my own home because I knew I would not get the same level of medical care there as I would here. I regularly hear people talking about how wonderful and advanced the health care system is in the United States. Maybe it is, if you have the money to pay for it. If you don't, you are in the unenviable position of living in a First World country receiving Third World health care.

Since I arrived in Britain I've noticed that the NHS (National Health Service) has been constantly criticised in the media. Now I'm aware that this isn't entirely baseless, but I have to say that the treatment I have received to date has been fantastic. The difference between the doctors here and those in the US is astonishing. Apart from everything else, the doctors, nurses and midwives in England give the impression that they actually *care* about me and my baby. I am not just another number to be processed; both my baba and I are real people.

I have yet to undergo labour and might change my tune afterwards. Having said that, although I dread the prospect of the delivery suite, I am confident in the ability of the doctors and nurses who will attend me. I very much doubt that I'd submit myself as happily to their colleagues Stateside.

When I first became pregnant, everyone told me that my life was about to change dramatically, that nothing would ever be the same again. I took that for granted. Mind you, I also took for granted that I'd have the best part of a year to get my head around the dramatic changes ahead. It didn't for a second occur to me that everything would change instantly – but it did. I'm still trying to come to grips with those changes – moving countries, moving home with Mum and battling with constant sickness – and any day now it will all change again. I'm terrified. I'm anxious, excited, worried, hopeful, apprehensive, curious and scared. I'm impatient for his arrival, yet worried that I won't be up to the job. I'm not ready and yet I am. Throughout it all, people have said to me 'it will all be worth it in the end', and I have no doubt they were telling me the truth.

Martina Devlin has written four novels in addition to a memoir, *The Hollow Heart*, about her attempts to become a mother via fertility treatment and her journey in coming to terms with childlessness. Her fifth novel, *Ship of Dreams*, has just been published and follows the fortunes of six survivors of the *Titanic* sinking. She is also a columnist with the *Irish Independent* and the *Sunday World Magazine*. Her website is www.martinadevlin.com.

Baby Hunger
Martina Devlin

I call them my baby hunger years as though in naming them I can control them – lancing their sting. I can't, of course, because the pain of infertility never recedes more than a few paces, although it does become more manageable in time. Not so manageable, however, that it can ever be eradicated, a bittersweet reality which childless people have to learn to live with.

I spent two years having fertility treatment in an attempt to give birth – looking back, I marvel how I ever survived them. My three failed attempts at in-vitro fertilisation (IVF) made a wasteland of my life for a time as my marriage, the home we shared and my dreams of becoming a mother all slipped through my fingers.

In the raw desolation of the aftermath, when I realised it had all been in vain – our hopes had been stored in a sieve – I saw no point in a life barren of motherhood. My days seemed purposeless. What did I care about sunrise or sunset, Christmas or summer, if I couldn't hold a baby of my own in my arms?

And beyond the grief was something darker again – a sense of unease. A suspicion of worthlessness. Natural selection had intervened to deselect me, so there must be something wrong with my genes. I felt flawed, an outsider, a sub-standard woman, and for a period I wanted to crawl into a cave and be left alone to die.

But I survived. I survived because grief alone doesn't kill people, even if you imagine it must be impossible to live with such pain. As time went by, I learned to enjoy life again – it continues to amaze me that this should be so. But I'll never forget – never make sense of – that savage time when a torrent of emotions possessed me: betrayal, incomprehension, rage and, above all, heartache, the wrenching bereavement of childlessness. Don't believe people who say you can't miss what you've never had. My heart knew to feel cheated.

Yet my story started on a positive note. I was just married and my husband and I were keen to start a family. Putting the cart before the horse in our optimism, we bought a four-bedroom house in Dublin to fill with babies – and waited. And waited. Finally we went in search of medical advice.

Surgery showed my fallopian tubes were so warped and twisted that I was unlikely to conceive naturally. I type in the test results matter-of-factly now, but I'll never forget the shock of that medical pronouncement, how it curdled in my mouth. Still, we were young and the world was ours. We refused to surrender hope – modern medicine would solve our problems.

We had a referral to the HARI unit, the fertility clinic at Dublin's Rotunda Hospital. There, I was told I had a one in three chance of success with IVF. Experts now estimate the chances are between one in four and one in five, but I was relatively young and healthy, a non-smoker, with no history of infertility in the family. I should have been a contender. So we handed over our money in the blind expectation that a baby was the inevitable corollary.

It would simply be a matter of time. That one in three statistic only applied to other women. Naturally I was going to be one of the lucky ones. 'A one in three chance of pregnancy,' that's what the doctors said. You don't hear that slippery word 'chance' when you're desperate to be a mother – you hear nothing but the lush sound of 'pregnancy'.

Looking back, I can see I was hopelessly unprepared for the reality of what IVF treatment involves – for the way it invades your life and colours your relationship with your partner, as well as eroding your sense of self-worth. I simply assumed I'd be able for whatever the process entailed.

And so began the treatment. Like every other woman undergoing IVF, I was pumped full of drugs to suppress my menstrual cycle and send me into a fake menopause. Then my system was flooded with a barrage of different drugs to stimulate my ovaries into overdrive – they swelled up to the size of small oranges and became ultra-sensitive.

Instead of producing one egg, as is normal in the menstrual cycle, I produced up to ten. These were extracted under anaesthetic and fertilised with my husband's sperm – in a Petri dish in a laboratory, as it happens. I've always found it odd that neither my husband nor I were present when conception occurred. Three embryos were returned to my womb a few days later. Then it was a case of going away, resting and hoping for the best. 'I'm hatching my embryos,' I used to tell myself.

I hoped, God knows I hoped. I planned too. Perhaps I was foolhardy in my planning, tempting fate, but I convinced myself that positive thinking was the way forward. I chose names for them, considered godparents, worked out their star signs, designed a nursery, bought baby clothes. Spinning my web. There was a family christening robe I used to take out and stroke, imagining dimpled baby hands at the end of its sleeves, tiny pink toes kicking beneath its hem.

I'd talk to my babies in the womb, urging them to cling on to life, reassuring them, bathing them in love, promising if they could overcome this first hurdle of implanting successfully inside me, we'd all have a wonderful life together. I was consumed by the intensity of my longing to hear a child call me by that most undervalued of names, 'Mum'.

But I miscarried all three embryos after a few weeks. They were never more than pinpricks of life, but they were my babies – and I was devastated.

During this period, all my friends and relatives seemed to be getting pregnant. The phone would ring, an excited voice would say 'guess what?' and I would feel as though a giant fist was slowly, inexorably squeezing my heart. I tried hard not to spoil their moments. I hope I didn't. I did my best to say all the congratulatory things – and then I locked myself in the bathroom and howled.

The staff at the Rotunda were nurturing – I remember the kind faces of every nurse and doctor who treated me – and they tried to manage my expectations, but I didn't want to listen. I was incapable of it.

Already at this stage the pressure was starting to send shockwaves through our marriage, but still we pressed on.

I was a woman driven, my desire to reproduce overwhelming and the consequences irrelevant. Anyway, I was convinced that everything would be set to rights by the birth of a baby. Self-deluding? Possibly, but that's part of the primal instinct. I was caught tight in the grip of a biological imperative over which I had no control.

With the benefit of that fool's wisdom, hindsight, I believe my husband and I needed counselling at every stage of the process. There was one brief session before we were allowed to proceed to our second attempt, but I found it perfunctory. I guess we could have asked for more, but we hadn't the wit to do it – we just assumed we could manage. As you do. At least nowadays the medical professionals have learned how crucial counselling is for couples embarking on fertility treatment.

IVF has a huge psychological and physical impact. I was awash with hormones as a result of the cocktail of drugs I was given and they played havoc with everything from my sleeping pattern to my emotions. I burst into tears at the drop of a hat, feeling disproportionately distressed by trivial incidents.

I remember being incensed with my husband when we went to the Rotunda for our embryos to be returned to my body during the second cycle. He dropped me off and drove off to park, but took ages finding a space. Our names were called twice and still he hadn't arrived. I was becoming increasingly agitated, convinced I was going to miss my turn and my embryos wouldn't be implanted. Finally, he strolled in with a newspaper under his arm and – poor man – I tore strips off him. He'd just wanted something to read to pass the time. But in my tunnel vision trap, it seemed to me that if he'd taken time to go in search of a newsagent, then he wasn't treating this with the urgency it deserved.

Communication was splintering between us, but still we persevered – the IVF whirligig had a momentum of its own. That second attempt ended in failure too.

And so we pressed on with our third and – we were agreed – final IVF cycle. After this egg extraction I remember weeping inconsolably because 'only' seven eggs had been harvested instead of ten as previously. To me, it was a sign my fertility levels were plummeting, a menacing omen for the outcome of that attempt. My husband was embarrassed by my tears outside the operating theatre and tried to hustle me away, which prompted additional feelings of resentment. I felt utterly alone.

I don't suppose he understood quite how disturbed I was becoming and how the drugs, the hospital visits, the blood-taking and above all the strain of wishing for the near-impossible were taking their toll.

Men urgently need counselling when their partners undergo IVF. A man ought to be taken aside and have it spelled out to him that a woman can be transformed by the treatment into a pre-menstrual, post-menopausal monster. If he loves her and wants to support her through the ordeal, he'll have to learn to bite his lip and accept he'll be treading on eggshells around her. I know it's difficult, because while women become completely blinkered, men are sidelined by the IVF process. 'A walking sperm bank' is how many of them refer to themselves. Yes, with more than a trace of bitterness. Couples must take a long, honest look at their relationship before considering IVF. If there are any cracks, fertility treatment has the potential to turn them into chasms.

For some people, the urge to reproduce becomes a driving compulsion which incinerates their life, and I was one of those women. It's overpowering, a force of nature. If someone had offered me a deal and said I'd lose my husband, my home, my health and my career, but I'd hold a baby of my own in my arms, I'd have said fine, show me where to sign up. I'd have had no difficulty with a Faustian pact.

And so we had our third throw of the dice, a path we'd been down before, and yet it remained unfamiliar terrain to us. We didn't know what lay at the end of the road. We had our hopes for the journey's end, of course, but we'd learned the hard way that hopes offered no guarantees.

I took to talking to my embryos during this incubation period. I'd stroke my stomach and whisper to them. 'Stay with me…I need your help. You've got to want this too. Do it for me. Please.'

I was bargaining with my unborn children. They were no more than a few cells – so rudimentary they weren't even at the foetus stage yet – but they were real to me. They were my babies. I willed them to implant, bathing them in love, pleading with them – as though it was a question of choice on their part whether to stay or go. Whether to opt for me as their mother. Or not.

By this stage, I had driven my body to its most far-flung parameters. Perhaps even beyond them. It wasn't just my drug-rattled body which had been sacrificed. I had also forfeited control over my emotions, my mental health and my self-esteem to this yearning. To this baby hunger which burrowed into every cell of my body and wound its demands around my yearning heart.

Our marriage, I knew, was barely stable by now, pummelled by the impact of successive IVF treatments – and by the demoralising aftermath of failure. Assisted reproduction is a cornucopia of possibilities. But it has a shadow side, too, and neither my husband nor I were prepared for it. For the blows to us as a couple, or to our perceptions of one another – which started to waver the further into this hopeful-fearful world we ventured.

We split up almost immediately after the third failed attempt. I had neither the courage nor the capacity for a fourth try – some grain of the survival instinct warned it would harm me to press on; that if the physical ordeal didn't kill me, the emotional fall-out would push me over the edge.

That's when I was at my lowest ebb in life: childless, despite everything, and now loveless as well. Perhaps there wasn't enough love between us to begin with. For my own part, I believe that when my husband looked at me then, he saw the misery of three failed IVF attempts, and when I looked at him I saw the same. And the ache was too intense. We were unable to comfort one another, each one a daily reminder of what we had been through – what we had put each other through. A reminder, I suppose, of broken dreams. We should have had the courage to dream new dreams, but it seemed easier to walk away. Easy was a beguiling option after those punishing years.

It was five years before I was able to write about my baby hunger years. Instead I bundled them into a twilight corner of my consciousness and, while they shaped me, perhaps tempered me, I tried my damnedest not to think about them. But then I relented.

What persuaded me was a growing unease with the way assisted reproduction is perceived as the great panacea, the magical remedy to solve every childbearing problem. I heard other women talk about delaying motherhood until after their careers were established, suitable homes bought and furnished, joking about fertility treatment picking up the slack. Alarm bells rang immediately for me.

Subconsciously, women tend to regard IVF and similar procedures as their safety net.

Yet it doesn't matter how much money, effort or emotional investment you put into it, or the level of angst you go through. It's still a lottery. It works for some people, I'm glad to say, but they're in the minority.

Most of us fail. There. I've said it. The trouble is we only hear about the success stories, those miracle babies, while the couples who submit to the process without that longed-for happy ending lock their sorrow into their hearts. It's not discussed because the wound remains raw. These people feel marginalised, their future seems bleak, while all around them, society plays happy families.

In the early years afterwards, my life was such a burden to me that I tried to escape it by inventing other lives, escaping into imaginary worlds. That's when I started writing fiction and it taught me to harness my distress and tap into it when necessary. After a time, I discovered something which seemed to ease the shadows: I realised that shade allows you to appreciate the light, and the experience of pain helps you value the joy.

Little by little, I learned to do something regarded as old-fashioned now: I counted my blessings. It was something my mother advised me to do, the soundest advice she gave me in a lifetime of wise counsel. With her help I remembered I am an aunt and a godmother – there are ways to have children in your life if you choose to accept that consolation.

Sometimes I think if the IVF option had never existed, I might have come to terms with infertility sooner. Then again, at least I know I gave it my best shot. My mother used to say, trying to offer comfort, that everything happens for a reason. I could not believe this. To me, there is no reason for infertility, it's simply unfair. But life is unfair, though it also has the capacity to smile on you.

Yes, joy has come my way from seeing my novels published. They have taken the place of my children – and as compensations go, they rank as special. But would I swap them for a baby? In a heartbeat.

Martina Reilly is the author of four teenage books (as Martina Murphy), including *Dirt Tracks*, which won a Bisto Merit Award. In 2004, it was adapted for the stage and read by Barnstorm at the Kilkenny Arts Festival. As Martina Reilly, she has written many bestselling novels: *Flipside*, *The Onion Girl*, *Is this Love?*, *Something Borrowed*, *Wedded Blitz*, *Wish Upon a Star* and *All I Want is You*. Her burning ambition is to write sitcom and in her spare time she freelances for the *Evening Herald*, teaches drama and co-manages her son's under-nine soccer team.

Parenting Survival Guide –
Your Questions Answered and Your Answers Questioned

Martina Reilly

You have just discovered that you are pregnant – do you:
A. Read all the parenting books you can get your hands on – after all, so many children go off the rails nowadays. As well as reading, you start watching your diet to make sure it has the right balance of protein, carbohydrates and fat. A correct diet in pregnancy helps the baby develop a healthy birth weight. And a healthy birth weight can help towards your baby's intelligence. When you've finished your daily quota of books, you either go for a walk or attend yoga classes. It's important to keep fit for the birth, which will, of course, be 100 per cent natural. What can be more natural than being underwater with dolphins?
B. See the pregnancy as a perfect excuse to eat for two.
C. Run out and buy another testing kit; those other six must have something wrong with them. There is no way you'd know what to do with a baby.

Your birth plan does not go to plan – do you:

A. Say you are not paying damages for that dolphin you kicked. How were you to know that the whole thing would be so excruciating? No one told you that, did they? And how come there was no way they could give you an underwater epidural? What sort of a health service is this!

B. Look at your lovely baby and think it was worth it. But you won't be doing it again in a hurry.

C. Sleep and cry.

Your baby is crying a lot at night – do you:

A. Read a book on the subject which advises you to go in after five minutes of continuous crying. This will let baby know you are there if he needs you. If baby continues to cry, walk out and go in after ten minutes and then again after twenty and so on. Read another book that tells you to make sure baby is not hungry or wet or colicky. But not to, under any circumstances, bring baby into your bed, as that just sets the wrong habits from day one. And who is *that* going to benefit, eh?

B. Bring the baby into your bed and snuggle up to him. God, he smells gorgeous.

C. Start crying yourself.

Your baby refuses to move from the breast to the bottle – do you:

A. Keep on breastfeeding until your child's fourth class teacher says it's just not appropriate for the child any more and that the other kids are teasing him. You ask your child's teacher if he or she has children and if so, wouldn't they like to do the best for their child and did nobody ever tell them that BREAST IS BEST.

B. Breastfeeding? What on earth would you want to do that for?

C. Start putting sugar on the top of the feeding bottles and vinegar on your nipples. OK, so you don't, but you'd like to. Instead you just cry.

Your baby takes his first steps and promptly falls and bangs his head – do you:

A. Marvel at how intelligent he is, walking at ten months, two weeks and three days. Then examine him closely – you've read everything about concussion when you did the first aid course during pregnancy. Look at his eyes, check that there is a bump on his head. If not, don't panic. Bring him to the doctor, insist on skipping the queue, this is an emergency. Describe the accident in as much detail as you can and if you don't get satisfaction from your GP, bring him to the hospital and insist that they observe him for at least twenty-four hours.

B. Shove a packet of cold peas on his bump and give him an ice-pop.

C. Comfort him while wondering if things will get more fraught now that he can walk.

It's baby's first birthday – do you:

A. Explain to him that he is now twelve months old, that's 365 days, or in a leap year, 364 days old. Can he count up that far? Well, with his abacus, he'll be able to do just that. And with his brand new birthday present of a set of inter-active encyclopaedias, he'll be able to look up just what exactly is meant by leap year and when he can talk, he'll be able to tell everyone what it means and how it came about.

B. Have a big party for the extended family.

C. Think joyfully that it's only four more years until baby is off to school.

Your baby is off to school – do you:

A. Wonder why on earth your child is starting with all the other five-year-olds. After all, he can count up to 365 and can use a computer. He also knows about recycling and global warming and can recite quite lengthy poems with some dramatic flair.

B. Tell your child that he'll be brilliant and make loads of friends before coming home and wondering what to do with all that free time. Oh, you know – you'll have a good cry.

C. Heave a sigh of relief that someone else will be responsible for him for a few hours.

There are a number of after-school activities on offer – do you:

A. At five? Are you joking? Five years old is too late. Your child has been 'in' things since he was three. He's been doing speech and drama since he could talk and dance since he could walk. He does football now, but only with his safety apparatus in place and he knows exactly what to do if he or any of his team-mates should swallow their tongues.

B. He's decided that he's not bothered, so you don't bother either.

C. You wonder if you should – would not doing it make you a stingy mother? Is he missing out on something by not doing the activities? But he says he misses you when he's at school and that makes you feel quite motherly, actually.

Your child is really sick for the first time – do you:

A. Call four or five doctors for their opinions – after all, your child is SICK! You knew he was because he expressed no interest in his seventh birthday present of an atlas and a set of flags. Spend days nursing him back to health but at no time spoil him because that's not good for children.

B. Cuddle him, tell him funny stories about when you were sick, promise to buy him the toy of his dreams if he gets better quickly. Worry in case he won't get better even though you know it's not too serious.

C. As you nurse him, you feel that at last you're getting the hang of this 'mammy' thing. You know you love him because you're worried and you know he loves you because he calls out for you all the time. Where did you go so right?

Your child is in his end of term show, but he only has one line – do you:

A. Think that there has been a mistake. Your child has been doing drama since he was two. His teacher is the best in the country. You explain this nicely to the teacher. He explains just as nicely back that your child has one line and that is it. You suddenly remember that on the night of the concert you have an urgent appointment – your child is actually starring in a dance show. Sorry, he can't make the end of term concert.

B. You go over and over his line with him so that everyone will hear it. Privately you wish that he had a bigger part so that he'd be on stage longer. Who wants to go somewhere to look at other people's kids?

C. Think of how brave he is to stand up on stage and say a line.

Your child misbehaves while out in public – do you:

A. Your child never misbehaves. You have adapted your parenting style to suit your child. Your child understands the concept of star charts and is presently trying to acquire stars so he can get the astronomy wall chart to hang on his ceiling. If your child does throw a bit of a wobbler, you discuss it calmly, telling the child that such behaviour is not acceptable.

B. Shout at him to cop on. Grab him by the arm and tell him that he's grounded.

C. Die.

Your child says he's bored – do you:

A. Tell him not to be so ridiculous. Ask him if he knows how lucky he is to be in drama, dance, soccer, football, judo, antique appreciation, art, swimming and music. How can he possibly be bored?

B. Ask him if he'd like to join an after-school activity.

C. Wonder what you can do to keep him occupied. Maybe he'd like to fix the hairdryer. Or is that dangerous? Oh, you know, you'll enrol him in an after-school activity.

Your child has got into trouble for misbehaving in class – do you:

A. Sorry. No way. Mistake. Your child knows the rules. He did not say maths were stupid, he loves maths. And if he did by chance say it, which he didn't, it was probably just because he was bored. After all, you taught him calculus when he was ten and he loved it.

B. Agree privately with him that maths is a bit stupid but tell him that it's wrong to say so in class.

C. Wonder if you're raising a psychopath. After all, you didn't exactly bond with him in the first few weeks.

Your child wants the latest pair of 'in' trainers — they cost over €100 — do you:
A. Educate him on the slave labour trade. Point out to him the places on his electronic atlas where those trainers were probably made and the conditions that those poor children have to work in. Tell him that he should know better than to want trainers, as he should have a social conscience at this stage. Inform him that as a member of the parents committee, you are going to introduce an anti-trainer wearing policy in his school.
B. Buy him the trainers. He never asks for much anyway. Tell him that the next time he's buying his own.
C. Tell him you'll get him the trainers if he stops telling the teacher that he hates maths.

Your child wants to go out to the local club with his mates — do you:
A. Your child's friends do not go to clubs. His friends have all been hand-picked by you and come from good families with the same values as your own. You've rung around the other parents and you've all agreed that discos are not suitable places for sixteen-year-olds.
B. You ask if you can go too.
C. His mates scare you a little and quite frankly your son is taller than you now, so you suppose you should let him go.

Your child has come home and you can smell drink from his breath – do you:

A. Question your child on whether he thought it was a good idea to get drunk. Well, that's what it says to do in all the books you've read. If he is cheeky (which he shouldn't be) and says 'yes', you show him the stuff you've borrowed from the library about liver disease and liver cancer. Well, you'll show it to him anyway. Also, ask his school if you can have an alcoholic in to talk to your son's class about his or her experiences in a frightening, horrific and graphic way.

B. Shout at him about what a fool he was to pay that much for a pint.

C. Wonder if you're rearing an alcoholic.

Your child is doing his Leaving Certificate and you want to help him study – do you:

A. Clear out a room in the house and paint it a colour conducive to studying. Put up wall charts depicting the pivotal moments in history, the various facts about different countries, the chart of scientific elements, the most frequently misspelled English words, the most frequently used Irish, French and German words, the birth dates of all the famous artists and their masterpieces. When he is not studying, have a tape playing constantly giving hints and tips for doing the papers. Make him high-energy food, ply him with nourishing hot drinks and ban his girlfriend (if he has one) from the house.

B. Ask him what he'd like you to do to help and hope he says nothing, as you were a complete thick in school.

C. Drop gentle hints about doing a little work for the Leaving Cert. Try to get him to watch programmes about people who messed up their lives due to lack of motivation.

Keep your fingers crossed while wondering if you've raised a thick.

Your child is off to college – do you:
A. Make sure you let all the neighbours know how well he did in his exams. Check out where he'll be staying and make sure that he has nice roommates. Ply him with plenty of 'brain' food to put in his fridge and then leave him to it for the first time in his life. Come home and bawl your eyes out.
B. Feel so proud you could burst. College! Wow! You can't wait to hear of all the fun he's going to have. Wave him off, then come home and bawl your eyes out.
C. Rejoice that your child is not a psychopath or an alcoholic or a thick, but instead he's a well-adjusted, well-educated young man. You are so proud of him that you bawl your eyes out.

Summary:
So you see, no matter how you parent, it all ends up the same. Setting them on the road to life in whatever way you can so that you can cry and sniffle at the start of their big journeys.
Good luck!

Alison Walsh is a freelance editor and journalist. She worked as a book editor for many years in London and Dublin before leaving in 2005 to spend more time with her family. In between studying for a degree in sock sorting, worrying and shouting, she contributes to the *Sunday Independent* and works with a number of writers as an editor.

Things I Know Now That I Didn't Know Then

Alison Walsh

Before I had children, I thought that they were a bit of a lifestyle item, the kind of thing that would make me look like one of the cast members of *Cold Feet*. A cute, tousle-haired urchin from a Boden catalogue, complete with golden curls and fairy wings. He/she would be looked at adoringly from time to time before nodding off obligingly, or going to play in the garden, leaving me free to do all the things I really should be doing.

Not that, until the ripe old age of thirty, I would have dreamed of putting this theory to the test. God no, when all I had had to do was smile at one occasionally in what I hoped was an unthreatening fashion in order to prove that I was officially Good With Children, and continue on with my degree-level cappuccino-drinking and paper-reading. I was also able to devote myself entirely to developing my 'career', which mainly involved trying to circumvent my boss's loathing of Post-its by bulk buying my own hot pink ones and festooning every communication with the things, and staring out of my office window at the man in the building opposite who used to strip off to wash himself in the sink every afternoon at four o'clock precisely.

So when the time came and everyone seemed to be having babies, I found myself having to make various interested-sounding noises as I was regaled with tales of sleepless nights and 'colic', whatever that was. One colleague would mutter darkly about how drinking Murphy's stout was the only thing which got her through breastfeeding, therefore allowing me to deduce that it could be fairly uncomfortable, although I couldn't quite work out why – not that I gave a rat's ass, quite frankly. I also knew that it made you senile because of the regular calls from Boots in Hammersmith to say she'd left a bundle of paperwork behind in the baby section, whereupon I would trudge down to retrieve them, feeling a mixture of mild disdain and pity that the simple matter of having a baby could have turned her into such a dork.

How I laugh now, ten years later, with three children under my belt, mild incontinence and piles that would put any granny to shame. I, too, have left items behind in major department stores – hell, I once left the baby in the car outside the shop while I dashed in to get a pint of milk – with the engine running, and the keys still in the ignition. I might as well have hung a sign around his neck: 'KIDNAP ME'. I have endured the mortification of having left my breast pump behind in the office canteen fridge over the weekend, which must have given the cleaners something to ponder.

Now all my bits hang low and I wee every time I sneeze; I will never have a decent night's sleep again – *ever* – that is, until I am sixty-five and the kids have left home, when I will promptly suffer the sleeplessness of old age; and sex will never again mean just that – things will take a nosedive, and no, that isn't a new and intriguing sexual position. But on balance m'lud, it's been worth it.

So, how have I metamorphosed from career-driven, self-obsessed young woman to Dalai Lama of motherhood in just ten short years? To be honest, His Holiness has probably made less of a meal of being leader of one of the world's great religions than I have of being a mother of three, but still, the few gems I hope to share with you now might save you the same lengthy learning curve. As initiation into the world of the mother is akin to joining the Masons, *because no one ever talks about it*, hopefully the following introduction to the essential Laws of Motherhood will give you a head start.

The First Law of Motherhood is that childbirth is a painful but relatively straightforward process. As my only experience of childbirth, until that of my son, was Del Boy and Raquel giving birth to Damien in *Only Fools and Horses*, I associated childbirth with a lot of shouting and pushing in a slightly hilarious fashion. The baby always emerged in the end, didn't he/she? And anyway, a friend had told me that if my waters broke in Marks & Spencer, I'd get a free shopping voucher, so that was okay then.

Little did I know that the myths around childbirth swirl around the subject like the mists around Everest, only more opaque. Appropriated by the twin camps of the medical profession and by unreconstructed hippies, women like poor little thirty-two-year-old me are left bewilderingly somewhere in between. As a first-timer, I was too chicken to give birth at home in one of those nice birthing pools – this was Islington, after all – but neither did I want a spotty student doctor to stick a vacuum cleaner up my backside, but it seemed that the choices in labour were stark. Either I could avail of a fully medicalised number, sampling all of the items on the menu from weekly scans, being induced, having an epidural, etc., as all of this stuff is the only way to ward off the chances of something really bad happening; or I could have my baby by swinging upside down from a tree in the Amazon basin chanting Maya incantations and chewing the bark of the ola-ola tree.

Like all my friends at my first antenatal class in Hackney, I waded through the morass of dubious and helpful information. I did my breathing and my pelvic floor exercises and panted a bit to prepare for the second stage of labour, about which I was buggered if I had a clue. I prepared a birth plan, full of what I now consider to be hilarious statements like 'I don't want to avail of any pain relief', when in fact I ended up threatening a midwife with death unless she gave me an epidural – NOW – and 'I would like to avoid an episiotomy' – who the hell wouldn't? I filled a bag with tiny vests and nappies, unable to believe that I would give birth to something that small (as it happened, I didn't, as my son was too big for all the babygros and I had to give them to the teenager in the bed next door to me with her tiny five-pounder). I bought a new car with enough room for shedloads of baby paraphernalia and a buggy which folded into about twenty different positions and also doubled as a space shuttle. I even contemplated moving house in case the baby wouldn't like the décor in my flat.

And of course, despite all my fretting, all of this stuff was fairly pointless. The first sign that things were not going to go entirely according to plan was the hastening of my son's arrival into the world when I fell outside Pizza Express in Islington. My waters then broke on the bathroom floor, so the M&S spree was now sadly out of the question, and I went into labour that night. For the next forty-eight hours, through a miasma of pain, I had to endure serial comments about the grazes on my knees – 'Oh, they look painful,' mentioned one midwife in a sympathetic tone to which I replied that the pain was secondary to the agony of childbirth: at least that was the jist of my argument uttered through clenched teeth and howls of pain accompanied by a dash of profanity.

After the requisite two days of agony, I was cheerfully told that my labour was well progressed; in fact, it was nearly over. Well, hurray for me, I thought to myself, as I was called upon to 'bear down, dear,' which I would have done, had I been able to summon the energy after the previous days' activity. When I was finally delivered of my firstborn, as my midwife made lunch arrangements out the window with a friend, I reflected on how it had been the singularly most unpleasant forty-eight hours of my life, in spite of a late burst of energy provided by an epidural, the devil's own anaesthetic, which, although it allowed me to actually deliver my son, would, according to some, turn him into a drug addict in later life.

Even though, unlike my friends in my antenatal group, I was spared the indignity of having to rest my bottom on an airline neck cushion for the next three weeks, it didn't get any better afterwards. MI5 interrogators could learn a thing or two from midwives eager to ascertain whether there has been a 'bowel movement since baby?' and badgering me about contraception relentlessly, as if it hadn't occurred to them how I'd got to the age of thirty-two without producing a baby. In any case, I was eager to reassure them that as, after that experience, I would never be having sex again – EVER – they had little to worry about.

My purpose here is not to give you yet another gruesome portrait of childbirth, but simply to point out that the taking over of your body by a tiny little invader is the first life-changing staging post on the road to becoming a mother. Which brings me to the Second Law of Motherhood, the myth that the minute you set eyes on your little bundle of joy you will fall instantly in love with him or her. Confessing that you didn't is akin to saying that you actually like eating small babies. Yet, as a first-time mum, I made what my granny would refer to as a 'holy show' of myself.

From the moment he was born, my son looked at me very crossly and cried in a way which implied that it was somehow all my fault, leaving me feeling confused, anxious and a bit resentful; after all, I was the loving mother, ready with an endless supply of milk, fresh nappies, lots of chat and nice walks to the park – so why didn't he fall obligingly into line and not cry, or turn a lurid shade of yellow, or refuse to feed? After bouts of painful mastitis while trying to get the hang of breastfeeding, interspersed with colic (his) and depression (mine), I was, quite frankly, a basket case, unable to do anything but wander up and down Essex Road pushing the buggy and eyeing up various cafés into which I could dash the minute he fell asleep, like Tom Hanks in that desert island movie when he finally escapes in the life raft – I looked pretty much like him after a few nights awake on the trot clearing up vomit.

The only thing that saved me was the solidarity of my friends in my antenatal class, who rallied around and kept me buoyed up with invitations to John Lewis's baby department and the local park, where we would all sit in the little café under the dripping trees and share our general bewilderment at the metamorphosis which had occurred in our sheltered little lives.

It took my kindly and sympathetic health visitor to sort me out. 'Of course it's a shock, dear,' she pointed out to me, trying to avoid being sprayed by my son's pee as she placed him in the weighing scales. 'You women aren't exactly prepared for it these days, are you?' I wondered what she meant for a while before understanding that of course, with our extended single lives and our distance from families and from siblings with children, and our rabid insistence on controlling the universe, no wonder we find it hard to adjust.

In my case, my only previous role models had been my own mother – whose good example I singularly failed to emulate in my short career as an au-pair/babysitter, when I got one of my charge's heads stuck in railings and allowed another to bounce off the pavement in her pram because I had forgotten to apply the brake – and the Virgin Mary, whose all-round perfection had been fairly drilled into us in school. Both women had been excellent, but sadly hadn't provided any practical tips on raising a child, or none that I would accept anyway: as a twenty-first-century mum, there was no way I was going to let my child cry 'to air his lungs' or put him in his pram under a tree in the garden all day, as my mother advocated. And admittedly, Holy Mary was probably setting the bar a bit high.

Still, I'm ashamed to admit just how much it took for me to grow up and accept responsibility for another human being. My lack of maturity when faced with first-time motherhood is something I find hard to discuss with others, who, it seemed, had made the transition with ease, while I behaved like I had a walk-on part in *Anna Karenina*. And when I look at my eldest, my most anxious, turbulent child, I wonder if some of his worry and emotional see-sawing isn't down to his formative experiences as the guinea pig for a struggling new mother, trying so hard to be a mixture of Butlin's redcoat, Annabel Karmel and Penelope Leach that I forgot just to leave the poor child alone.

Once I'd embraced motherhood, though, which only took about seven years once my skills had improved on my second and third children, I found myself succumbing to the inevitable and finding how much I enjoyed the shift in perspective that being a mother entailed. I no longer bothered about small things, like whether I'd had an optimum amount of sleep, or what I looked like, or where exactly I was 'going' in life. I'm calmer, certainly, and less neurotically self-obsessed. However, lest you think you are in for unwarranted smugness about how motherhood has Officially Changed Me for the Better, I can assure you that my children can provoke in me the kind of murderous, irrational rage that I worry for my own safety, not to mind theirs. And sometimes in the endless cycle of classes/doctor appointments, school cake sales, swimming lessons, etc., I feel the dead hand of routine weighing me down, often accompanied by a boredom so profound I think I will be found slumped in a corner, the remote control clutched in my hand – death by *Ready, Steady, Cook*.

And despite the fact that, sometimes, I really do wish I had a couple of miniatures of vodka clinking away in my handbag to swig furtively while pushing Junior on the swing or to aid me in supervising my eldest son's maths homework, most of the time I feel proud that I've managed to pull it off after such inauspicious beginnings and that all my children have more or less survived the process.

What I suppose surprised me most of all about becoming a mother, and what I find hard to accept because I can't control it, is the Third Law of Motherhood, the inevitable, but nonetheless irritating, change in status that results from having a child. This I shall call the That You Will Never Again Be Waylaid by Charity Muggers law.

Now, you might think that not being pestered by someone wearing a day-glo orange bib and an enthusiastic smile on his/her face is one of the singular benefits of motherhood, but when you can't get a desperate drama student with a sales target to attempt to extract €10 a month from you simply because you are pushing a buggy up the Rathmines Road, you know you've become officially invisible. And then there's the dubious stereotyping of mothers: as a stay-at-home mother you are a brain-dead yuppie with a lifetime's membership of The Westwood, or the alternative, a Career Bitch who would happily leave her children gaffer taped to their beds with a note to the cleaning lady to feed them rather than miss a board meeting. You are either a MILF (Mummy I'd Like to F***!), a Yummy Mummy, a 'homemaker' with a snot-stained T-shirt and dishevelled hair and a permanently glazed look on your face, or a red-taloned workaholic with a roster of nannies whose children are always last to be picked up from school.

Following my encounters with the hairdresser who persisted in giving me the same lank, lacklustre 'do' every time I went to him, a frumpy haircut because I was a 'mum' and not a sexy single girl going out to Dundrum in my Ugg boots and Abercrombie & Fitch tracksuit; or the girl in the office who invited everyone to her party except me – 'Oh, I didn't think you'd be interested in a *party*' (now that you are a MUM with an unfortunate dress sense, a brain the size of a pea and who could bore for Ireland on the subject of your children) – I now appreciate just how invisible mothers can become. Sure, political steps can be taken to recognise the status of mothers in society, but this doesn't change people's attitudes. The only thing we can do is take comfort in the long-term goal of raising the next generation, satisfied that in ten or twenty years' time, after all the piano lessons, the rugby camps and the educational holidays in Italy, our kids will be in therapy, having first shoved us into a retirement home.

So there we have it. And whether you view the above as a handy little primer or simply too much information, it is useful to remember that no amount of advance preparation will ensure that you have the perfect birth, or that you'll take to breastfeeding like a duck to water, love your baby's every poo and barf, or relish the kind of responsibility that, were you to give it much thought, would make running Virgin Enterprises a doddle.

The raising of another human being to avoid them becoming a drug addict/member of a religious sect/accountant/priest/ice skater – whatever takes your fancy – is no small matter, which just goes to show that there is some reason why no one talks about this stuff. If we did, no one would have a child ever again. So perhaps the trick is not to subject motherhood, like everything else, to the kind of twenty-first-century neurosis in which I have just indulged. Perhaps we should ignore our fretting, learn a thing or two from our ancestors – and simply get on with it.

Born in Vermont and raised in Baltimore, Maryland, Kate Holmquist followed her heart to Ireland in the 1980s. She is a high-profile *Irish Times* journalist who is highly regarded for her sensitive and nuanced writing on a range of issues. She lives in Dubiin with her husband, journalist, broadcaster and author, Ferdia MacAnna, and their three children. She is the author of a memoir, *A Good Daughter*, and a novel, *The Glass Room*.

A Good Daughter
Kate Holmquist

As my mother's death approached, I began to panic. When she died, I would not know how to mourn. Where were the women who would wash the body and lay it out for the family to sit with and pray for throughout that first night of death? Where were the women whose keening would give us permission to cry? All I would be offered would be Valium and comfort from people who would be afraid to catch my eye but would try to make me laugh, meaning well.

I began to realise that all my life I had been protected from death, yet it had been with me all the time. Death was removed from life and neatly packaged in white hospital rooms. We kept the bodies safely away from us, cloaked in the pretentious decor of the coffin and the funeral home in order that we might remain protected. I had been so much a part of this communal deception that even in the seconds before Mom's last breath, I still wouldn't know what death was. Until my mother died, I would have not a hint of how the loss would make me feel.

As she clung to her last hours of life, I asked myself: what is it like to die? What transformation takes place?

Are you watching over me, Mother? Or are you dust?

I remembered her telling me, when I was a child, that her own parents visited us from time to time, in their way. They were spirits, she said, who could pass through us unnoticed and observe our lives.

'One of them may be sitting in that chair right now watching us, but we will never know,' she told me.

She described for me the death of her father, the Swedish pastor, whose spirit was seen by her mother to rise up from his body. This I took as solid evidence, although later, when I started questioning the existence of God, I wondered if it was merely a soothing fantasy imagined by my distraught grandmother to ease her anguish at her husband's passing.

My mother was a long time dying, but it was only in those final hours that I began to lose strength. During her final two weeks, she slipped in and out of a deep, coma-like sleep. As the end approached, her sleeps grew longer and deeper. During the final days, we tried to rouse her from unconsciousness, terrified that she would never awaken.

My father called her name, 'Ardis, Ardis.' She responded to his voice and when she opened her eyes, her face took on a beatific expression, like an infant staring into the eyes of its mother.

My father called me in to see. She looked into his eyes with a pure and forgiving love as though they had never argued or disappointed each other, their loose ends instantly resolved.

I continued to clutch my unfinished business to my heart, aching to tell her what I had always been afraid to say. *Please understand, Mother, what he did to me I could not stop.*

It sent me on a journey to places I wish I had never gone. I know I disappointed and frightened you. I am sorry, most heartily sorry.

A day or two before she died, we had been unable to awaken her for nearly twenty-four hours. In terror and despair, I knelt by her bed and cautiously lay my head beside her breast, careful not to hurt her.

'I love you, Mom,' I told her, believing that she did not hear and wondering if this would be the last time I would say those words while she lived.

Every time, as death approached, was the last time: the last time she would hear me say I loved her, the last time I would kiss her cheek, the last time I would bathe her, the last time I would feel warmth in her hand, the last time I would hear her voice.

Then, for the first time, I said what I had been afraid to say for so long.

'Mom, I don't want you to die.'

It was the first time that I had despaired in her presence. It was the first time I had surrendered my role as the strong nurse who could deal with anything. It was the first time I had admitted in her presence that she was going to die. I had tried to remain inscrutable against death because I had been afraid to let her see my pain, believing that it would ease her anguish to see me behaving stoically. It was foolish of me to hide my feelings.

If I were dying, I realise now, I would want to see the painful tears of loss on the faces of those I loved. Did I deprive her of my grief? (I seem to have no shortage of memories that evoke the most excruciating guilt.)

With my knees on the floor and my arms around my mother, I breathed in the smell of her like the tired child that I was.

All my regrets about my relationship with her and about my own behaviour crowded into my head. Why hadn't we been able to talk? Why, always, was there a distance between us, a fear of candour? I could not tell her the truth about my life for fear that I would make her miserable. And the things that did come out of my mother's deep-rooted and repressed anger, near the end, came too late to be resolved. I felt powerless to heal her and overwhelmed by the tragedy of her life.

She was dying too young. She felt cheated and angry. My contribution to her unfinished life had been enormous. I was an extension of her. She would live on in me and yet she detested my moral choices. Later I would understand my mistakes, but I would never have the chance to explain to her why I made the decisions that had upset her. Children rebel. That's healthy. With maturity, they usually reconcile with their parents, and while the generations may continue to disagree, they may at least reach some understanding of why they are different. My mother and I never had that chance. She was denied the fulfilment of seeing her daughter blossom. With her death, I lost my chance of ever becoming the prodigal daughter.

I realised all this a decade after her death. But as I leaned against her death bed that day, I was confused and remorseful.

I wanted to be her daughter again. I realised too late that I needed to rely on her support and comfort. I wanted her to know how much I hurt, but cloaked in the darkness of her final slumber, it seemed that she would never know.

Then, gently, I was roused from my dark contemplation by her hand lightly stroking my head, comforting me. She delicately caressed the nape of my neck with her cool fingers in the same movement she used to lull me to sleep when I was a child.

She still loved me. Perhaps, even, she forgave me. No longer the wayward twenty-three-year-old daughter, I was miraculously the child again in the embrace of its mother. I felt momentarily purified by her touch, as by a blessing.

Raising herself out of her coma was the first of many ways my mother would make herself felt to me during the mourning years.

Her death opened a door to the spiritual world that exists parallel to our own. I was surprised, and yet not, when my mother's father appeared to her in her bedroom shortly before she died. I did not see him myself, but I have no doubt that he was there. I was sitting beside her bed, trying to drip some water into her dry, cankered mouth from the tiny eye-dropper. She was drifting in and out of a profound sleep. She lay back on the pillow, exhausted, with her eyes half-opened.

Suddenly she became alert. Her face brightened and was animated with happiness. Her gaze was directed towards the end of her bed. The expression of sheer joy in her face was utterly hopeful and innocent, again like a child's.

'Daddy,' she said.

Her voice was raspy, but the word was clear enough.

I looked at the end of the bed, at the chest of drawers against the opposite wall, at the ceiling, at the floor, but this mundane scene offered no evidence. I looked back at my mother's expectant face and into her eyes, which were bright after having appeared milky and dead over the previous days.

'What do you see?' I asked.

'Who is it?' asked my father. He was smiling and seemed not at all surprised by what was happening.

She ignored us. We watched her face.

'Daddy,' she said again.

From that moment on, I felt him with us. So I stopped expecting to see him like some Hollywood ghost and looked instead into my heart, where I could see, quite clearly, my grandfather who had died before I was born.

The way my mother timed her death was the second sign that during her final lapse into coma, she remained aware of us. The day before she died, her breathing suddenly became laboured and blocked due to a build-up of fluid in her lungs.

'The death rattle,' my father said.

The words were brutal, but there was no other description for that terrifying, gurgling, wheezing, clattering noise made by her breathing. For the first time in my life, I became frightened of my mother. Death had invisibly infiltrated our house and it was hanging over her bed like a guillotine ready to cut her off from life. In my eyes it had changed her from a gently woman into a Medusa. Several times a day she needed to be washed and her sheets and nightgown changed. I began to touch her with a new terror because I expected her body to undergo some monstrous transformation wrought by death, which could come at any moment. I was frightened at the prospect of how she might look in death's embrace.

The trauma I had experienced of being unable to effectively control her pain had made me feel even more helpless against death. When the death rattle began, my panic increased with her every strangled breath. We had wanted her to die at home, but when my father suggested that we call an ambulance to take her to hospital, I agreed. If I had possessed faith in my own ability to care for her as she passed away, we would have kept her in her own bed at home, but we were worn down by our anguish, and hers. We had struggled to negotiate a battlefield of emotions in a losing war.

As soon as the paramedics arrived, I was sorry that we had called them. Instead of offering her hospice and a gentle death, they immediately started to intervene. I rode with her in the back of the ambulance down Route 6 to the hospital in Hyannis, twenty miles away. The ambulance roared down the centre of the highway, scattering cars to either side, while a paramedic worked on my mother, forcing a tube down her throat to clear her lungs. She writhed in protest. It was torture for her to have the metal-tipped plastic tube shoved down her raw throat which had been rotted by cancer. It was torture to watch.

'Do you have to do that?' I shouted above the siren.

'She's in a critical condition,' the ambulance man shouted back at me accusingly.

'She has cancer. We know she is dying,' I said.

'It's our duty to do everything for her that we can,' he replied coldly, as though I wanted her to die.

Hadn't we been doing everything for her that we could? In the emergency room, we waited with my mother for a long time. She was lying on an uncomfortable trolley. Being moved by the paramedics from her bed at home to a stretcher and now onto the trolley had obviously twisted her cancerous abdomen in some way that caused her enormous pain. For the first time during her illness, she moaned and cried in her agony. We kept trying to get someone's attention. I don't know why, but I had brought the morphine and the needle in my purse. I wanted to use it.

A young intern finally came to examine her and he ordered that she be X-rayed.

'Why?' we asked.

'Hospital procedure,' was the reply.

My father and I sat helplessly in the hallway outside the room in which she was to be X-rayed. Then the real hell began. We heard my mother screaming in pain as they moved her from the trolley to the X-ray table. She wept desperately.

'I have the morphine in my bag,' I said to my father.

'Maybe we should give her an overdose,' he said. Euthanasia had never occurred to me. Now it seemed the only way to stop the hospital torture. We hadn't the courage.

Finally, after a few hours spent diagnosing the obvious, the doctors admitted my mother to a quiet, private room. A nurse injected her with something for pain, which we were grateful for (and I'm sure my mother was too), but when the death rattle began again, the nurse insisted on suctioning the fluid out with a tube stuck down my mother's raw throat. My mother's eyes were wide with an animal panic and fear as she fought the nurse.

'Do they have to do that to her?' my brother asked. 'She hates it.'

'It's hurting her,' I said to the nurse.

It had to be done. It was hospital procedure.

Finally, they left us alone with her. We silently sat around her bed until evening. I silently prayed for that eleventh hour miracle.

We did not know how long she would last and thought that it might be a few days, so we decided to sit with her in shifts. My father and Stephen would remain with her until four o'clock in the morning and then Mark and I would relieve them. At home that night, neither Mark nor I could sleep. I wrote in my diary that night of my overwhelming desire to have a child. Giving life, carrying it within me, was the only anecdote to the dance with death that I had been through with my mother. I believed that giving birth would heal me by balancing death in my life. Only birth could fill the deficit of strength and hope and desire that death had caused.

Mark and I returned to the hospital and sat with my mother through the morning while my father and Stephen went home for a rest. I watched idiotic game shows on a tiny television that hung from a crane over my mother's bed. Mark didn't watch them and I was aware that watching TV might be disrespectful, but I needed to numb my mind and, I suppose, I was a coward.

As my mother lay comatose, she soiled the sheets several times. Each time, I helped the nurse to clean her and to change the sheets. Mid-morning, a new shift of nurses came on with a different attitude about this. After my mother again soiled herself, I pressed the button which signalled the nurses' station that we needed help. An older nurse arrived, a redhead with a hard face. I asked her if she would please help me clean my mother and change the sheets.

'We like to wait and clean them when they're gone,' she said.

Then she left the room.

Her callousness knocked me cold for a few moments, then I became enraged. I demanded to see someone from hospital administration and then complained to them at the disgusting and insensitive way the nurse had responded to our request.

I was in tears, and maybe as I was railing against the nurse's behaviour, I was really protesting against death.

The administration sent a nurse to remain with us full time.

I told her what had happened. My brother and I were enraged.

'You must be very careful what you say in front of your mother,' she said quietly. 'It is possible that she can still hear us. We think hearing is the last to go.'

Again, I felt deflated. I had failed once more. Nobody tells you anything about death, I thought. For every person, must there be this wicked game of search and discovery? When you are caring for someone you love who is dying, do you have to learn from your mistakes? There isn't enough time to make mistakes. These errors leave lasting scars.

After the nurse told us that, Mark and I started talking to our mother, telling her how much we loved her. Telling her that we didn't want to lose her, but that we would be okay.

My brother held her hand gently. He and my mother had been so close and much more intimate than she and I had been in our constant struggle to understand each other.

Late morning, the nurse took my mother's blood pressure, which was dropping rapidly.

'It'll be soon now,' she said. 'I think you should call your father.'

I phoned him and we waited for him to arrive. My mother's eyes were wide open and unblinking.

'Her eyes must hurt. They must be dry,' I said to the nurse.

She put a square of damp gauze over each eye to keep them moist. It also protected us from having to watch those horror-struck eyes.

While we waited for my father and Steve to arrive, I had an overwhelming need to see the babies in the hospital nursery, thinking naïvely that I could use the sight of life to counterbalance death. I was being melodramatic again. When I found the nursery, there was only one infant there and its skull, its two legs and its two arms were in casts. So much for my attempt to orchestrate a happy ending, I thought.

I returned to my mother's room, but I must have been away longer than I had thought. Mark was waiting for me in the hallway. He and Stephen had been looking for me. My mother was about to leave us any minute and they were afraid I would miss her death. We went into the room and circled her bed, holding hands: my father, his mother, my two brothers and myself. While my father prayed aloud, I closed my eyes and wept. Then one of my brothers whispered my name and I opened my eyes and looked at my mother. She was heaving her last sigh. Her chest was slowly sinking into the bed, expelling more air than I thought possible.

Whoosh-sh-sh-sh, her breath went, so quietly. Her body gently pushed life out. And that was it. She simply stopped breathing. It was finished.

She had waited for me, I was certain. So that we would all be together around her when she left us. That was the second sign for me that there was something beyond death. Perhaps the separation between her body and her soul had already begun and she was able to consciously let go.

I hoped that the timing of her death meant that she had

finally accepted that she was going to die and that her death was not merely the arbitrarily timed breakdown of her central nervous system, rotted away by cancer.

As we stood around her body, I was afraid to look at her staring eyes, now dead and still hidden by the two white patches of gauze which I had kept moistened throughout the morning. Maybe we all were. I do not know how long we stood around the bed, for time had stopped. I was holding her tapered hand, finer and more elegant than my chubby paw, and trying to memorise the way it looked. I catalogued the almond-shaped fingernails, the faint lines across the back of her hand, which was still brown from the weeks she'd spent sitting in the sun before she died. Her hand was bare, youthful. It hadn't dawned on me yet that she was without her wedding ring.

Holding her hand, I felt the life drain out of her so quickly, much faster than I would have imagined. Within minutes, she was being transformed from my mother into a corpse. The skin on her thin, sun-speckled arm suddenly lost its tautness and became flaccid. Her entire body seemed to shrink a few inches, sinking lower into the bed as her life force drifted away. The body was just a body. Without its life pulse, it wasn't my mother any more.

I tried to see her spirit rise, but I could not. All I felt was emptiness, a loss more profound than I had thought possible, and I could think of nothing but her permanent absence from my life.

I looked up and saw my father weeping and Stephen trying to comfort him. I don't remember that my brothers and I cried.

I don't remember us ever crying in front of each other after she died. Each of us had our private grief and we never shared our feelings together. Our joint loss was intuitive and bound us together. Although I cannot speak for them, I know that from that moment on, I remained arrested by the trauma of her death for many years to come.

We left her in the hands of the nurses. It wasn't satisfactory at all. The tradition of family members bathing the body and dressing it in its shroud died out long ago. Still, I wanted to do this for her. This was the body that had given me life and, to me, it was still sacred. People have told me since that cleansing one's own dead is a beautiful and powerfully therapeutic experience. But then, I only knew this as an outdated, possibly barbaric custom. Death would be taken out of our hands and the rituals would be performed by people who were paid to do it, professionals with no emotional stake in the process. At the time, I felt intuitively that having cared for her intimately for months, I was not properly finishing my duties by leaving her in the hands of others. I dared not speak about the handling of her corpse for fear that it would simply be seen as another sign of my eccentricity. We left her in the hands of the nurses. My father said that the hospital staff would handle her with respect, although after the performance of that unfeeling nurse earlier in the day, I doubted it. I kept my thoughts to myself. After we left her room and had closed the door, Stephen went back alone. He wanted a solitary moment with her, I guessed. I admired his courage.

I have never asked him what he did when he went back, but I have wondered whether or not he did what I hadn't the courage to do, which was to remove the squares of white gauze and, tenderly, close her eyes. Someday, perhaps, I will ask him.

We drove home along Route 6, the same road on which the ambulance had raced less than twenty-four hours earlier to bring my mother to the hospital. I watched the people passing by in their fast cars and I felt, again, a distance from the world as though I was not a body at all but a mere soul. How could the world go on as before when we had just lost our mother? How could people look at us and talk to us as though nothing had happened?

We passed a skid mark where my mother and I had nearly been killed the summer previously. She had been driving when an enormous truck travelling in the opposite direction crossed the double yellow line and came bearing down on us, head on.

My mother froze. The truck was coming at us at sixty miles per hour at least. I shouted to her, 'Turn it to the right,' then I reached over and grabbed the steering wheel, pulling us into the ditch just in time. We weren't out of danger yet – we were headed straight for a metal roadside barrier and my mother managed to steer us clear; I don't know how. Behind us, cars crashed together with the splintering, crushing sound of metal and glass. We sat shaking, knowing that we had come within seconds of certain death. My mother began to weep, which was understandable after such a shock. When we got home, however, her crying only worsened. I had never seen her so despairing. It was as though we had really been killed and we had become ghosts, mourning ourselves. It was not until the moment that we passed the same place on the road, an hour or two after she died, that I fully understood her pain the previous summer. She had been mourning her own death. Death had reached out and touched her and reminded her that she should have been taken already. I didn't understand then that the doctor had already given her a death sentence. I didn't know that she was truly keening for herself.

Her pain filled me that first night of her death. I was too numb to feel my own.

I fell asleep with the help of half a Valium tablet that night and the next. I felt empty and exhausted and bruised. I was filled with her absence. On the third night, after her funeral, my mother made her presence felt to me again. I half-awoke, deeply aware of her presence. I began to feel myself floating, surrounded by a warmth that was precisely the same temperature as my body. It is difficult to describe the sensation, which was like nothing I had ever felt before or have felt since. It must have been what a foetus feels like, floating in the womb. I felt completely calm and at peace and I had the sensation of my body being completely supported on all sides by a firm pressure, as though suspended in a viscous fluid. I felt like I was being completely embraced in every molecule of my physical and spiritual self by some benevolent energy.

There were two beds in my bedroom and I was sleeping in one, my mother's youngest sister, Helen, in the other. Suddenly, my aunt rose and kneeled on her bed, holding her arms out towards something above my body and shouting my mother's name. My aunt had not seen my mother in years because she lived far away and she had flown to the Cape for my mother's funeral the day after she died. She shouted my mother's name in agony. It sounded as if she was trying to stop my mother from walking off the edge of a cliff.

The next morning, I realised that I had experienced my mother's final goodbye during the night. The feeling of being suspended in warmth was simple to explain. My mother had bathed me in pure love. I thought of the stories I had heard told by people who were revived after being clinically dead. Their stories were always the same. On the brink of crossing to the land of the dead, they had been greeted by a being of light which emanated pure love and offered to escort them to the next dimension.

Are you there, Mother, a being of light, waiting for me?

My father said that it was possible that the dead experienced the trauma of separation as keenly as the living. Maybe that explained the unsettling feeling my brothers and I had all that summer of my mother's presence. We kept expecting her to walk into the room at any moment. When the telephone rang, we expected it to be her. Once, my brother thought he saw her looking in on us through the glass door to the patio.

'It will get better with time,' an old friend of my mother's told me at her funeral. It does not get better. I still ache for her. I needed her when I was lost and had no one to turn to. I needed her the day my husband was diagnosed as having cancer. I needed her when I got pregnant and lost the baby.

I couldn't cry at her funeral. I can cry now. Sometimes I think that I have spent the last decade trying to remain in control and that I am only beginning to mourn.

I have learned that death is not a single moment. It is ongoing and exists in the eternal present where love also remains rooted, long after lovers have parted. The pain of my mother's death is always fresh when I remember how much I need her.

There have been so many things I have wanted to talk to her about. Sometimes, when something wonderful or terrible has happened, I have said to myself, 'I must phone Mom and tell her.' There is a part of me where she is not dead. Sometimes, in my imagination, we have conversations. I have asked her, When you lost your first pregnancy, Mother, did you become anxious and depressed for months, like I did? Did you blame yourself too?

We never had a chance to have those womanly conversations, those hours spent at the kitchen table ruminating ruthlessly over the details, analysing and embroidering upon events and emotions, stitching them together into a patchwork quilt of patterns that make sense. Other women have served in her place, offering love and talk, but you know what they say about a mother's love. It is irreplaceable.

The fourth sign of her presence, after death, came during the quiet, dark summer nights after the funeral, when my father, my brothers and I were sitting in the living room in Chatham with the windows and doors open. After nightfall, one of us noticed the singing of a lone bird.

It seemed to be coming from a tree near the kitchen door. None of us could identify the type of bird (we were city people). Its song was sad and distinctive and it continued always in the black of night, all summer long, coming from the same place. We could never see it, only hear it, and it never sang during the day. One of my aunts said that when the birds sing at night, it is a sign that Armageddon is near. But we heard only one bird and we believed it was my mother.

Clare Dowling is originally from Kilkenny. She trained as an actress before writing her first play, which was produced at the Project Theatre in Dublin. She wrote five more stage plays, some short films, a children's book and a magazine article about what Boyzone wanted for Christmas when times were tough. Eventually she landed a regular job as a scriptwriter for Ireland's top soap, *Fair City*, for which she still writes. She also writes novels and is published in Ireland, the UK and abroad. Her latest book is *No Strings Attached*. She lives in Dublin with her husband, Stewart, and kids, Sean and Ella.

Kids to Go
Clare Dowling

It starts pretty much the minute you leave your own drive-
way. 'Are we there yet?' And your heart sinks. Because
'there' is a three-hour drive away, followed by an overnight
ferry, then another three-hour drive on a strange motorway
on the wrong side of the road. The trip will be broken by
at least seventeen loo stops. Pitched battles involving food
and toys will break out every half hour in the back of the
car/ferry, along with cries of 'He bit off my ear, Mum.' If
there's a baby on board, a small pile of dirty nappies will
accumulate in the boot of the car until the stench becomes
overwhelming. And playing in the background will be 'The
Wheels on the Bus' on a continuous loop, wrecking your
head. Then, as the heat and the tension and the smells
mount, the adults will start fighting over the map, and the
kids will look on in a kind of terrified fascination as the
name-calling starts, and for once it doesn't involve them.
At the end of all this torture is not a five-star luxury hotel
with world-class spa, but a glorified caravan in a campsite
overrun by other people's children, where the highlight of
each day is the under-nine's disco and, if you're lucky, a
stiff gin and tonic by the toddler's pool.

Let us be honest here. There's not a mother in the whole country who hasn't been scarred by the annual summer holiday. Or indeed any holiday at all. Christmas offers up its own horrors. This year I decided that I couldn't face into two and a half weeks at home, with the weather so bad that I couldn't even put them outside and shut the door on them, and the whole family would take a 'mini-break' (how I despise that phrase) in a cottage in Clifden. More importantly, after all the Santa excess, I was determined to show them there was life outside wrapping paper. I felt an obligation to make them stand on something green as a change from the city tarmac. We would go and be among the mountains, I decreed. Heedless of the howls of outrage, I loaded up the boot and headed west. That weekend, the country experienced its worst storms for fifteen years and the roof of the cottage held on by only a thread. And the television had no channels except for TG4. I tried to convince the kids that it might be an opportunity for them to brush up on their Irish. They looked at me in baleful incomprehension before going back to beating the heads off each other as it blew a gale force wind outside. Should we have stayed put at home? Probably. Definitely.

The thing is, I actually look forward to getting away with the kids. No sooner have I unpacked the debris of the previous disastrous excursion than I'm already thinking of where we might go next. In theory I love the idea of spending all that time with my children, unburdened by timetables or worries over what to cook for tea. We would all eat chips! To hell with it, I'd be magnanimous and let them have Coke as well. And so I begin to build a rosy little picture in my head. I would show them new places. Teach them skills like horse riding and kayaking. We would lie on the beach into the late evening with our toes wiggling in the still-warm sand and I would gently bore them with stories about my own childhood. In short, new bonds would be forged between mother and children in those two magical weeks, so much so that we would never exchange a cross word again and that they would wait on me hand and foot in my old age.

And that, of course, is half the problem: the air of expectation that's built up over months, even whole seasons, in advance. As with Christmas, we go into the annual holiday with unrealistic expectations of family bliss. Those two weeks would make up for all the bad behaviour and bouts of poor parenting that go on throughout the rest of the year. The kids would be angels. I, in turn, would stop nagging them to do their homework, and generally ruining their lives. By about February, when the days are still dark and the moods at an all-time low, someone will witlessly ask, 'Where are we going on holiday this year?' and we'll all stampede down to the travel agents as though it holds the answer to all our prayers. 'I'll be really, really good this year, Mum,' my son will fervently promise as he drools over pictures of Disneyland (no chance whatsoever) and sunny beaches in Spain (some chance). And so we book, in foolish anticipation that this year will be different; this year we'll all behave like the kind of mothers and offspring that we'd really like to be, at least for two weeks. Now it's just a matter of packing.

Ah, the packing. That's when my holiday halo suffers its first slip. And it's not as though there's anybody to help. Packing is firmly a mother's job, and there's no point pretending otherwise. When we gave birth, we apparently had to acquire the ability to compile lists. Further, to break down any such list into sub-lists, usually one for each person in the house. Depending on the age and gender of the person, the list should be tailored to individual requirements, and include such items as 'Extra Underpants', 'Gameboy' and 'Cuddly Rabbit'. From bitter experience, I've removed 'Contraception' from the list, as the holiday itself is usually adequate protection. Then there are the clothes. Before anything can be packed, it first has to be washed and ironed. Then hidden away for the three weeks preceding the holiday so that it doesn't have to be washed again. My kids usually spend most of every July in big thick winter jumpers because everything else is in the wash/iron/pack cycle. The list will also include such diverse items as a medical kit, toys, Dozol, crayons and more toys. If you're going on a self-catering holiday, God help you, the list will be ten times as long and even less glamorous. First up is a set of sharp knives – for cooking, primarily. You can be sure that no matter how many stars your holiday cottage has, the only knife in the whole place will be a stub of a thing that doesn't make a dent in the butter, never mind prepare a dinner for a whole family. Packing for the self-catering holiday requires hidden resources of strength and determination and acres of boot space, and by the time you've ticked off pot scrubs, Oxo cubes, salt and cereal, you'll be on the point of collapse. Forget the lovely two-piece you got in Marks & Spencer with the matching sarong – you'll be too exhausted to wear it. For those mothers who have had to clear desks at work on top of it all, Valium helps.

But the kids will love it, right? Even if you haven't the energy left to swat a fly, you know that it'll all be worth it when the sleeping beauties in the back of the car (departure time is usually 5 a.m.) open their eyes and find that they're at the ferry terminal at Rosslare Harbour. You're giving them the stuff of memories. Wait till they're adults themselves, poring fondly over their childhood holiday snaps. You're a good mother, if a bit short-tempered that particular morning, and have already lost control of the folding map. But wait. In the intervening months since the last family holiday, you've forgotten that peculiar things happen to children who are Out of Their Routine. You notice it first in their face. They're unusually flushed, and it's not just from four hours asleep with their heads bent at the wrong angle. They start to ricochet around the car like ping pong balls and their voices grow loud. And fractious. Far from happily playing Travel Scrabble like they promised, they burst uncontrollably into tears every five minutes. Now, add two weeks' worth of late nights, heat rashes and stomach upsets, multiply it by however many children you have and set the whole thing hundreds of miles away from the comfort of your own house. The truth is, when released from the shackles of routine, perfectly nice children turn into monsters. Or quivering wrecks. 'I want to go home,' my daughter sobbed pitifully into my shoulder in West Cork last year five minutes after we arrived. I wanted to go home too, but we were supposed to be having a brilliant time, and so I spent an hour coaxing her into staying. 'All right,' she grudgingly agreed. 'Did you bring my Cuddly Rabbit?' I looked at my husband. Oh, f**k.

I try to remember back to my own childhood holidays, and things seemed much simpler. But maybe that was because nobody ever flew anywhere, certainly not for a foreign holiday, and things were generally confined to a week in a caravan in Tramore. My main memories are of eating delicious egg sandwiches on the roadside on the way down, and then roaming around the caravan park with my siblings like gypsies. We would spend our entire time on the beach, happily building sandcastles or swimming for hours on end. The sun would generally shine ten hours a day, and it didn't rain at all on any of those holidays, not even once, over the course of eighteen years. Which is rubbish, of course. I'm sure there were wet days and bad moods and that at some point every one of us wanted to go home. But of some memories I am sure: my own mother, patiently hand-washing mountains of sandy clothes, and having to prepare three square meals a day in a tiny caravan kitchen. Probably smiling all the time. I must try harder.

Like lots of mums who end up spending vast tracts of time with their kids without any of the usual amusements, I've learned a few hard lessons on the way. For instance, there's no sense in taking toddlers or babies on city breaks of any kind, or adventure holidays or to hotels. Stick to the beach, preferably in your own country, and you'll enjoy each other an awful lot more. I've also tried to stop expecting every minute of it to be great and to appreciate the edited highlights, such as the time my son caught his first crab (and then nearly died of fright). Or the look on my daughter's face when she saw the sea for the first time. There were nice family meals together, even if they were followed by an afternoon of bickering. Each holiday offers up at least several fabulous, memorable moments that I didn't quite manage to catch on camera but I can tell them about in later years, hopefully before I go senile. Don't ever say I didn't take you anywhere or show you anything, I'll say to them piously. They will owe their sense of adventure and love of travelling entirely to me. In fact, if they don't turn out to be perfectly rounded, sophisticated, multi-cultured human beings with tons of air miles, I'll be sorely disappointed.

I've got the brochures for next year already.

Jacinta McDevitt lives in Malahide, Co. Dublin. She has written four books, *Sign's On*, *Handle with Care*, *Excess Baggage* and *Write a Book in a Year: Writing Workshop & Workbook*. She is one of the Irish writers in the *Thirty and Fabulous* short story collection by Poolbeg. She also gives writing workshops. She has two children, Alan and Lucy.

Alannah, a Leanbh
Jacinta McDevitt

In order to get any job, you have to go through years of studying, or so my mother told me. I have always thought it odd that the exception to this rule is for the most precious, responsible job of all. For the job of mother, there is no need for exams or submitting a thesis or dissertation. For most of us, all it takes is one good night, a nine-month wait and *voilá*, you're a mother! Then you're left to your own devices to make as good a fist of it as you can. It's all trial and error.

If you're lucky enough to have a good mother or a good mother-in-law to hand or at the end of a phone, you're on a winner. After that, it's a matter of doing your very best all the time and hoping that your best is good enough most of the time. I'm still hoping my particular best is good enough and I have been the best mother I can be now for thirty years.

I have absolutely loved every single moment of being a mother. It has been such a joy and a privilege. It has been the best of times. It has been the worst of times. Times I have rejoiced with them. Times I have cried with them. I have loved it all. Loved it more than anything else.

I am a mother of Alan and Lucy. I am a grandmother to Alannah. I am mother-in-law to Maire. I am soon to be mother-in-law to Conor. That's a lot of mothering!

And all I know about mothering I have learned from my own mother. A great mother. A great teacher. For that and more besides, I will always be grateful to her. She is now a great-grandmother. She is giving me master classes in the art of being a good grandmother. I am hanging on her every word.

'Cuddle her, love her, spoil her, then parcel her up and send her home!'

It's the sending little Alannah home part that I am struggling with. It's getting harder, not easier, as time goes on.

So because I'm new to the job of grandmother and this is a very special book, this piece is for my new little granddaughter, Alannah.

Darling little Alannah,

Welcome to you. Welcome to the world. Welcome to our little family. All six pounds of you. All seventeen inches of you. Tiny hands. Tiny toes. Tiny little mouth. Big bright eyes.

How can anyone so small bring such joy? And what joy you have brought. How can anyone so beautiful bring such wonderful turmoil? A house once pristine and beautifully minimalist. A house with a place for everything and everything in its place. A home of leather recliners and plasma screens has now become a safe haven of baby smells and chuckles. Book of firsts. Daily diary. Teddy bears and rattlers. Toys and sounds of lullabye-byes.

Photographs. Baby wipes. Tiny baby outfits for a tiny baby. Winnie the Pooh and Tigger. Beatrix Potter and Dr Seuss. Oh, the wonder of it all. The wonder of you. And to you, everything is such a wonder.

New Year's Day. Your mammy and daddy told me that you would be born on New Year's Day. Start your new life at the start of the new year. And silly ol' me, I believed them. I was so delighted. I was charmed with the idea of you.

But I should have known you'd never wait until New Year's Day. I should have known better. You'd never miss out on Christmas. Not this Christmas. I should have known Christmas would always be special for you. It's special for your mammy and all of us. Yes, Alannah, I should have known you'd arrive early. I should have guessed you just couldn't wait to see us all!

So, on 18 December 2006 you made your grand entrance into this world. Came into our family and our hearts with great aplomb. A mad dash across Ireland to be born. Doonbeg to Limerick to Dublin to Holles Street. At the same time, I made a mad dash across America. Houston, Newark, Dublin. You arrived just ahead of me. Just in time to get a letter off to Santa. Just in time for jingle bells and putting up the Christmas tree. A real one, of course. Just in time for us to add you to our Christmas lists and excitement. A festive time to arrive. But whenever you arrived, it would have been a celebration.

But I have a bone to pick with you, Alannah. Just before I left for America, I rubbed your mammy's tummy and told you not to move until I arrived home. I even promised you a lovely surprise from America. But did you listen to your ol' Gran? No you did not. Now, Alannah, I hope that is not a sign of things to come! In fairness to you, I suppose you did wait until you knew I was on my way home. So I suppose you get off on a technicality. But only just, and only once. And nine months is a long time for you to be hanging around waiting to be born. It was no picnic for the rest of us waiting for you.

Nine months is an eternity of anticipation. I know, because I have done it twice before. Once for your dad. Once for your Auntie Lucy. This time, for me there was no morning sickness. No swollen belly. No backache. But I hung onto every bit of news from your mammy. Her visits to the doctor. You doing summersaults. Kicking. Growing. Getting ready. Your mammy and daddy minding you and you not even born yet. I have to say, the pregnancy I had with you was far more nerve wracking than the other two! My nerves were gone by the time you were born.

And long before you were born, I wondered what you would be. A little boy or a little girl? I knew you'd be a bundle of such joy for all of us, particularly for me, your ol' Gran. But secretly, and this is just between the two of us, I guessed you were a little girl. I was thinking pink and frilly things. Bonnets and booties. Ribbons and curls. Buttons and bows.

Oh, Alannah, when you were born you were cute as a button. Big, big eyes. All gums. Your daddy's dimple. I thought we'd have to have the smiles surgically removed from your mam and dad. They were delighted with their tiny morsel. The little woman. So little that none of the clothes they had bought for you fitted you. You had to get another lot of new clothes. A whole new wardrobe, in fact. And immediately I knew we'd click. You were a woman after my own heart. I like your style. A special outfit for

Christmas, with matching hat. Baby's first Christmas. Baby's first Levis, all the way from America. Tiny ones for a tiny person.

You were tiny to me. So tiny beside your big dad. So petite like your mam. You had the most extraordinary fingers. Long and thin. You moved them so gracefully. Pointed them. Showing them off. Hypnotising and mesmerising us. We all fell under your spell.

And I was lost for words. Me, who could talk for Ireland. Me, who writes books with over 250,000 words in them. Imagine it. When words are your chosen tool of craft, it is an extraordinary thing not to have any. When you deal in chapter and verse and there is none to describe how you're feeling, it's strange. But I did lots of crying to make up for it. It was my release. Me and your Auntie Lucy took to crying buckets of tears every time we drove home from seeing you.

'I think she loved the hat I bought her and the little bear, she loved the bear. Did you see her looking at me, did you see her?'

'Oh, yes, I think she was thrilled with her Gap outfit. I must get her another pair of bootees. Those ones looked so cute on her. She was looking at me too when I was holding her.'

'Did you ever see anything like her? I know she's tiny, but I honestly think she recognised us. She's just magnificent.'

'Magnificent.'

And then we'd relax into silence and have another little cry. See what you reduced us to, Alannah? Alannah, we had another little cry when we heard your name. Your mammy thought of it. After your daddy, she said.

So, Alannah. I have known you now for seven weeks and you are such a lovely little person. You have a ready smile and still as gummy as you were, but not quite as tiny. You are thriving. You have your mammy and daddy in the palm of your tiny little hand and they are loving every minute of it. The rest of us are besotted by you. I know you and I are going to be great pals. We are already. I love singing to you and you are such a great audience; not once in the seven weeks have you asked me to be quiet. You listen wide eyed when Auntie Lucy reads to you. *Guess How Much I Love You.* You hang onto Brian's every word, even when he tells you to have a little doze.

You are a very lucky little girl. Lucky to be born to two parents who adore you, grandmothers who cherish you, great-grandparents who relish in you, aunties and uncles great and otherwise who delight in you, little cousins who are charmed with you and me and Brian who do all of the above and more besides.

It's unique for a granny to be given a chance to talk about being a granny. So for grannies everywhere, I want to say what a very special thrill it is to just be a granny.

It's unique for a granny to be given a chance to give a grandchild advice that is written down, so I have to be careful what I say to you. I have to choose carefully what I think are pearls of wisdom. I have to take time to make sure they are the right words. And you too, Alannah, take time – there's no rush to grow up. Let's all enjoy you now when you've just started to smile and chatter to yourself. Let's not look to see when you'll sit up or when you'll walk, there's time enough to enjoy those things when they happen. Let's just treasure this moment. This special moment, because we won't get this one again.

All I can say, Alannah, is be yourself. Compete with no one but yourself. Be kind always. Grab happiness and never let it go. Know how much you are loved and rejoice in it. Treasure the moments.

Love the bones of you, always, Alannah

Your ol' Gran
Cindy XXX

PS. I'm not a bit upset that you made me a granny at fifty! I know everyone said I would be a hip granny and like you to call me by my name. They were wrong. It's a joy, a privilege and a wonderful pleasure to be your Gran and for you to always call me Gran.

Lucinda Jacob is a children's writer/illustrator. In addition to her poetry, she writes story and picture books, writes for TV and radio and reviews for specialist magazines. She also leads creative workshops for schoolchildren and is a textile artist.

Octopus Mother: An Action Rhyme

Lucinda Jacob

I really should be an octopus,
I need eight arms at least,
Two to hug my husband,
One to cook up a feast,

Two to cuddle you children,
One to clean your clothes,
Two to drive you safely,
One for a dribbly nose.

I've got to nine already
But I still need to walk the dog,
I'll fit in work somehow, and phew!
My legs take us out for a jog.

I'll need an arm to paint a picture,
The same one could write a book,
Like every mother I know
I've eight arms at least – just look!

Denise Deegan began her career as a nurse at St Vincent's Hospital, Dublin. She spent much of her time there on the respiratory ward, where she nursed and grew to know many cystic fibrosis sufferers. She has fond memories of that time and the numerous patients who touched her heart with their courage, optimism and humour. Denise would like to dedicate this story to Patricia Kavanagh, whose character always towered above her illness. It was Patricia who created a nickname for Denise that stuck with her until she left nursing. (Sorry, it's a secret!) Her fourth novel, *Do You Want What I Want?*, has just been published by Penguin Ireland.

Who Is Going to Look After It?

Denise Deegan

The last thing you think about when buying your first family pet is the day it's going to die. More common are concerns like 'who's going to look after it', 'what happens when we go on holidays', or in the case of a rodent, 'what'll I do if it escapes from its cage?'

I don't remember the exact moment I promised my daughter a hamster, but I know I was feeling sorry for her. She'd been craving a pet for too long and I had refused everything. We don't have room for a dog. Cats scratch. You can't hug goldfish. Rabbits wreck the garden. By the time we'd got to hamsters, I'd been broken down. Weren't they those cute things in *The Wind in the Willows*?

At the pet shop, I realised my mistake – not just that I had misjudged what a hamster was, but that I had promised my little girl one and brought her to buy it on the day of her birthday. We stood side by side, looking into a hamster cage. In my mind, I saw a mouse. My daughter tells me I screamed. I know I didn't because I remember how hard it was not to. I will admit to silent hand flapping and walking very quickly to the other end of the shop. From where I'd abandoned her, my dark-haired angel looked at me with big blue eyes. And I knew what she was thinking: *It's my birthday. You promised.* That she didn't say this made it worse.

Then I did a terrible thing. I suggested she might prefer something from the toy shop next door. She said nothing. Her eyes did the talking. Surprise. Disappointment. And finally resignation. In silence, she followed me from the pet shop. Which made me feel terrible. If only she'd argue.

In the toy shop, she made straight for the soft toy section. There, she picked out the biggest cuddly dog she could find. And my heart melted. I couldn't do it. I couldn't let her settle for something she couldn't feed, talk to or love – without pretending.

'Let's go back,' I said.

She looked up, suddenly hopeful. Then her expression changed, as though it had just occurred to her that I might reconsider once faced with the rodent again. Well, that settled it – as far as I was concerned, there would be no backtracking, no wriggling out of this. We were getting a hamster.

As the pet shop loomed, I wondered how I might fool myself into believing that something that had made me want to scream minutes earlier was, in reality, something very precious, something good for my child, the jewel in the crown of the animal kingdom. Or at the very least, tolerable.

The bell over the door pinged, announcing our return. The shop assistants glanced in our direction, then away again. They'd experienced us before. Clearly they hadn't been impressed. Keen to prove to my daughter that I now meant business, I asked the least lethargic of the two if he had any other type of hamster. I waited for the words, 'How many types of *hamster* do you think there are, lady?'

Instead, he started walking. We exchanged hopeful glances, then hurried after him, narrowly avoiding collision when he stopped at a Perspex container that we had looked into earlier and thought empty. Now, in at the back, underneath a mound of bedding, was the faintest sign of fluff. Disturbed, the fluff woke and revealed itself. I stared. Could there really be such a thing as a hamster so covered in hair that it does not resemble a rodent? Could there really be a solution to the mother/daughter/birthday crisis? Could there be a God?

Money changed hands. As did the hamster and all the paraphernalia that goes with one. We were given a few lethargic tips on caring for it. (I made sure my daughter was listening.) Then, on our way out, the issue of choosing a name occurred to me. How could we if we didn't know whether it was male or female?

I stopped. Turned. And asked.

There was a silence. The shop assistants looked at each other.

'Male,' one said.

I recognised a shot in the dark when I saw it. But didn't care. We had only one hamster, so babies would never be an issue. Didn't matter if it was a boy or girl. We had a gender. We could name it. This took place as soon as we were in the car. I was quite keen on something ironic, the way one might call a goldfish 'Jaws'.

'Hammy,' my daughter said with a single, very definite nod.

It wasn't original, but it was what she wanted. Who was I to argue?

'Hammy Concannon,' she confirmed.

I noted that, already, he was part of the family.

At first, my daughter was so caught up in the novelty of looking after a pet that she didn't notice that I was not exactly what you'd call 'getting involved'. In time, though, the penny seemed to drop and she began to seek proof of my love for Hammy Concannon.

'D'you want to hold him?' she would ask, raising him up to me in her cupped hands.

Absolutely not, I'd think. But because I didn't want to hurt her feelings by rebuffing Hammy, I'd say, 'I'll give him a little rub.'

She had no idea how big a deal that was for me. It meant coming out of denial, admitting that this was more than a ball of fluff. Underneath all that crisis-solving hair lay a rodent, a rodent my fingers could feel. There are things you do for your kids. Things you would never do for anyone else. Stroking hamsters became one for me. Out of necessity, I developed a technique – superficial stroking that appeared to be much more. To the onlooker, I was getting right in there, into the spirit of hamster.

In time, I grew very fond of Hammy Concannon, so long as he was on the other side of the bars. It was not unusual to find me there, chatting to him when my daughter was asleep or away and I thought he looked lonely. We had many adventures – including my personal favourite, Hammymania, which involved SuperHams (contained in a small box) sliding down a diagonally suspended rope, James Bond style.

Hammy Concannon began to embark on outdoor adventures, and on these occasions, he became Indiana Hams. Our neighbourhood green became a jungle as he nosed his way, fearless, through stalks of grass that towered over him. Once he got lost. Which caused panic, tears and the formation of a search party.

He became a bit of a star, actually. Visiting kids loved him. The fridge was regularly raided for raw carrots and broccoli. Children who were normally only happy in front of a computer (my son especially) got that bit closer to nature. And nurture.

Sometimes I found myself asking what the hell I was doing, like the time Hammy developed an eye infection and I spent a week trying to negotiate eye drops into his tiny black eyes while my daughter held him. Or the time I realised I had become indignant on his behalf when I heard that some vets weren't 'hamster friendly'.

The average life of a hamster is two years. I should have noted that. I should have been prepared. I should have dropped hints. Prepared my daughter. But this whole pet experience was new to me. Or at least that's my excuse.

We had almost two Hammy-filled years. Then one day, we sensed a change. He was weak and wouldn't eat or drink. When he walked, he wobbled. It was a Sunday. I promised the vet first thing next morning. My daughter asked me if he'd die. I said I didn't know. Because I kind of suspected he might. I think we both did.

In the morning, I told her that we shouldn't disturb him, just bring him to the vet. I didn't want to hurt him, I said. In reality, I was afraid that the worst had happened and I didn't want to be the one to find out. So to the vet we went, where we learned that Hammy Concannon had curled up and gone to sleep. And wouldn't be waking up any time soon.

'He didn't feel any pain,' my seven-year-old son told his older sister. She hugged me tight. And cried. I thought about how much she had loved him and how this was her first experience of death. Then, softie that I am, I was crying too, embarrassing, given that it was probably a first for the vet – a grown woman, crying over a hamster.

Driving home, my baby held onto the cage that housed the little dead friend she had mothered, confided in, doted on. Loved. I wished I had a guide to tell me the best way to help her deal with this, her first experience of death. I had no guide. Only instinct. Which I decided to trust.

We got home. Standing in the hallway, I was surprised when she told me she wanted to bury him straight away.

'OK,' I said, while worrying that maybe we were being a bit premature. Out we went to the shed to get the necessary burial tools. That's when it dawned on me that she was right. Action was what we needed. We didn't have to look at each other. We didn't have to talk. The physical activity of digging avoided all that. And it felt like we were helping him. Doing something for him even though he was dead.

Hammy Concannon was buried with everything he might need in the 'afterlife', including his favourite foods, even one cereal he didn't like – in case he changed his mind. My daughter chose a smooth charcoal stone instead of a cross.

'I'm not religious,' she explained. 'And neither was Hammy.'

She carved an inscription on the stone: RIP. Hammy Concannon. Loved pet. Then she lit a candle and said goodbye. She told him she loved him. She wasn't crying. But I was a mess. We came inside. I sat her on my lap, held her. The same brother who told her that Hammy hadn't felt any pain piped up, 'Queen ants live ten times longer than hamsters.' I shook my head to tip him off that maybe that wasn't the best conversational tack to take. Death was new to them. I don't think they knew what to say. Neither, of course, did I.

I was surprised then, in the days that followed, by my little girl's words of wisdom.

'I'd like him to have lived longer, but not in pain.'

'I want to forget him, but I don't.'

'I don't want another hamster. I want Hammy to be the only one. I wouldn't be able to love another hamster as much. Maybe I'll get a different pet. But in a few months.'

When, in the middle of something, she'd remember he was gone, her eyes would water. I'd tell her that I'd be her hamster, to squeeze me really tightly and see if she could make me burp. A week later, she drew him. We got photos of him developed. Where his cage was is now covered with cuddly toys. And there is a place on the wall in honour of Hammy where his picture and photos are displayed.

We have goldfish now, Christmas presents from Granny. Blinky and Speedy. No offence to the fish population, but they're just not the same. I know we need a dog. We've needed one from the beginning. And I *have* promised one. Just as soon as we get a bigger house/I've the time and many other excuses. It will happen, though. Just as soon as I'm dragged to a pet shop on someone's birthday.

A version of this piece first appeared in The Irish Times.

Anne Dunlop is the author of five novels and the mother of four children. She enjoys a challenge, is expert at juggling and is married to a very tolerant husband. Anne has lived in the Middle East and Africa; she currently divides her time between a farm in County Derry and a housing estate in County Kildare.

A Glammy Granny
Anne Dunlop

For a start, she's not called Granny; she's called Glammy, short for Glamorous.

Glammy has just spent her sixty-fifth birthday in Amsterdam smoking dope.

Glammy is rather cross that she had to pay for the flight; she thinks her new bus pass should give her free travel in all EU countries. She also thinks her new senior citizen status should have got her free into the Sex Museum.

Glammy's grandchildren have made her birthday cards with glitter and gel pens. They've bought her suitable birthday presents (suitable for a woman of sixty-five): hyacinth-scented bubble bath and body lotion from Marks & Spencer, a family photograph in a frame that says 'I love my Granny'.

Glammy was still in bed when we delivered them – she'd been out all night clubbing with a bottle of vodka in her handbag. Now she was so hungover and exhausted she couldn't lift her arms and she was afraid to sit up too quickly in case she vomited.

Her grandchildren were kind and concerned.

'Is Glammy sick?'

'Does she have a sore tummy?'

'Would she like some Calpol?'

'Would she like my teddy bear to hug?'

Glammy's eyelids fluttered weakly. 'I'm suffering from low blood pressure. Maybe your mummy could make me a cup of tea? Two teabags, two sugars, soya milk. I read somewhere that cow's milk gives you breast cancer. And darlings, there are crisps in the fruit bowl in the kitchen. Switch on the television if you want.'

Her grandchildren shot out of her bedroom; they raced down the stairs and were gone before spoilsport Mummy could speak up and say, 'Thank you, no, Glammy. Not at ten o'clock in the morning.'

Glammy struggled up into a sitting position. 'You shouldn't frown so much. It's causing a permanent crease between your eyebrows. You're going to need fillers soon. Don't go for collagen – they're old-fashioned. And they're made from an animal – pig, I think – the body sometimes rejects them.'

(I immediately have a picture of Glammy with a snout instead of a nose.)

'The Hydrafill fillers are the latest thing – *and* they're synthetic. Perhaps when you're there you could get some botox to relax the muscles in your forehead? Will I book you an appointment with the botox doctor? There's a waiting list – he only comes once a month.'

The frown between my eyebrows deepens. Where has she acquired this encyclopaedic knowledge of cosmetic surgery? Why has she acquired it?

Glammy has five children, twelve grandchildren and a husband. Every morning she rises at seven and swims with the early birds at the local pool. When she comes home she does an hour of Pilates on the kitchen floor. Every evening she walks two miles round our country road. She drinks hot water with lemon squeezed into it, she eats only fresh fruit and steamed vegetables. Chocolate hasn't passed her lips since she was forty.

She shops in New Look.

She wears bling.

When she drives her black Mercedes sports car, she wears black sunglasses.

She's tanned and blonde and wears size 10 jeans.

Glammy says, 'If you start off good looking, it's harder to let your good looks go as you get older.'

'But you're sixty-five, Mum! You're old! You should be taking it easy in a rocking chair in front of the fire. Where's your knitting, your twin set, your blue rinse?'

'Blue hair? Are you joking?'

It's hard to let go. Sometimes I didn't like her when she was my strict mother who frogmarched me to piano lessons; who sat with me every night, helping me with my homework while simultaneously spoon feeding and distracting my younger brothers and sisters. Explaining equations though she wasn't sure how to do them herself and we had to wait for my more mathematically inclined father to come in from the milking and help us.

Every day she cooked us boring, nutritious meals and polished my shoes for school.

And she insisted that I walk for the school bus, even when it was raining – 'You need the exercise! A healthy body is a healthy mind! Take a change of socks and wear wellies if you're worried about getting your feet wet.' (Wellies? to school? when I was fifteen and desperate for a boyfriend?)

She gave us 100 per cent when we were children and we were like sponges – the more she gave, the more we expected her to give. We never thought of her as a person in her own right. I have no vivid recollections of how she looked or what she wore and there are hardly any photographs of her because she was always the one behind the camera, taking photographs of us.

We were a gang – Mum and her kids – because Daddy was always farming, and though I had two grannies like everyone else, one was a mad old witch who lived at the end of a long lane; she drank gin, kept cats and couldn't have picked me out of a line-up. The other, though serene and lovely (her shoes always matched her handbag and she came bearing gifts), had died young.

My mother was our whole world, our unchanging picture. Her most memorable dictates have become a private language among my brothers and sisters and me.

'It's not the *first* wee bun that makes you fat!'

'Once a nice girl gets a *reputation*, she can never get a man to marry her.'

And her favourite, the one she always used when I failed another piano exam: 'You're never a loser till you stop trying.'

I may not remember exactly how she looked, but I remember that she was always there for me. Bossy and kind, she's in every memory I have of my childhood. On the days I felt discouraged – with a spotty chin and no boyfriend – she advised me to keep my eyes firmly fixed on the bend in the road.

'It's not going to be like this forever,' she told me. 'Everything has its season. This too will pass.'

I didn't realise it at the time that she was also speaking about herself.

When she had us reared and we left her nest for the bright lights of adulthood, Glammy decided she needed a career. My siblings and I were unanimously unsupportive. We didn't like the idea of our mother going out to work. We wanted her to stay exactly where she'd always been – chained to the family sink.

'It's hardly worth your while getting a job, Mum. In a couple of years you'll be sixty and they'll pension you off!'

'That's why I have to get a career. I want to work for myself. I hope to still be earning my own money when I'm eighty!'

'If you're bored at home, why don't you become a childminder? Get a couple of little children into the house during the day to keep you company.'

I still remember her chilling response to that suggestion. 'I've had my day of rearing children,' she said.

Glammy took night classes and learned to be a photographer.

'But she's hopeless at taking photographs! All those photographs she took of us as children – she always cut off the top of our heads!'

Once she'd learned her trade, she became the assistant of an assistant to an old boyfriend of mine – a boy who ten years before she'd caustically dismissed as 'not good enough' to marry me. Now Derek was her ticket to a glamorous new career. At photo shoots, she silently adjusted the lighting and watched and listened while Derek (who was always charming) coaxed relaxed smiles from hatchet-faced politicians and flirted with highly strung society brides.

Soon her new career began to seep into her private life – she bought and read the magazines which featured Derek's photographs and we watched with amusement, then bemusement, and finally a little grudging pride as she metamorphosed from a middle-aged farmer's wife with Empty Nest Syndrome into a hot chick who shot (cameras) from the hip and was frequently mistaken for my older sister.

Glammy especially enjoyed taking photographs at weddings – in particular, she empathised with nervous mothers-of-the-bride who felt self-conscious and over-dressed in uncomfortable high-heeled shoes and make-up.

'It's such a lie that the camera never lies,' she reassured them with the same bossy, kind confidence that had swept me through acne and A Levels. 'Now we've gone digital, I can airbrush the ugliest duckling and make her into a beautiful swan!'

Quickly and effortlessly she became famous in the fluffy world of wedding photography. Her brisk, sensible advice – 'Make sure you wear waterproof mascara. I always recommend Max Factor's Aqua Lash. I wore it when my own daughters got married, and I cried buckets I was so relieved that they'd finally found men prepared to marry them!' – was quoted in glossy bridal magazines the length and breadth of Ireland.

It was inevitable that she'd open her own business – Glammy Photography – on her sixtieth birthday. Now every weekend is fully booked with weddings and when she visits her grandchildren it's always a flying visit to give them birthday cards bulging with money and bicycles and expensive school shoes and the latest kids' movies on DVD.

'But Mum—'

'Oh, don't be such a spoilsport! I wanted to buy you all

these nice things when you were a child but I never had any money – any spare money I had was spent on your piano lessons.' (The only reason I got my first teaching job ahead of a hundred other applicants was because I could play the piano.)

'But Mum—'

'I've been so looking forward to becoming a grandmother! All of the pride and joy but none of the responsibility.'

Glammy's life has become an equation I am struggling to understand.

Subtract the demands of grown-up children and the opinions of others.

'My days of conforming to a traditional stereotype are over; I will never have to set a good example to impressionable minds again!'

Add new money and like-minded friends.

'There were thirty of us went out together last night to celebrate my birthday. We hired a minibus to take us to The Rainbow's End. Thirty respectable, decent women with good jobs and tolerant husbands keeping the bed warm for us at home.'

Equals a new confidence.

Last week she was smoking dope in a coffee shop in Amsterdam, last night she was dancing round her handbag in The Rainbow's End. Next week?

'Since I'm not yet in a bath chair with a blue rinse, I'm going to see Dido in concert. I know you were never any good at maths at school, but even you must realise that when you're sixty-five, there's not a lot of good years left.'

There are days when I'm discouraged with the demands of full-time motherhood. There are days when no one will eat the boring nutritious meals I've stood cooking and my children fight like savages when I'm struggling to help them with their homework. There are evenings, after they've gone to bed, when I'm almost too tired to polish their shoes for school.

There are days when I'm sitting in a steamed-up car with freezing feet outside their piano lessons and I wish I had a life to call my own.

'You should learn to knit,' Glammy advises. 'I used to knit when I was waiting for you.' (Which I suppose explains why she won't knit now.)

'Sometimes I wish you'd help me,' I said, for I never stop hoping that she'll eventually soften into a traditional grandmother stereotype. She dismisses these moments of weakness with a wave of her well-manicured hand.

'You don't need me to rear your children for you! I taught you how to do it when you were growing up. Now it's your turn. And if you're a good girl, when you're sixty-five, I'll take you to Amsterdam to smoke dope for your birthday present.'

Mary Bond spent her Dublin childhood scribbling in notebooks, often under the school desk. Early motherhood temporarily deferred her writing dreams, but in time she dusted off the typewriter and began writing articles, poems and short stories. Now that her children are grown up, her husband has taken up golf and Mary has a shiny new laptop. In addition to working as a Training Officer, she has had two novels published by Tivoli, *Absolutely Love* and *All Things Perfect*. She is currently working on her third novel, *If I Can't Have You*.

Most Mothers Are Made, Not Born

Mary Bond

The midwife wasn't impressed.

'You've hours and hours to go,' she cheerfully asserted as she patted my tummy, her words alone compounding my agony.

I knew otherwise. I was about to give birth, quite soon, or explode in the process. She bundled my clothes into a clear plastic bag, thrust them at my husband and robustly sent him on his way. In those days, daddies weren't encouraged to hang around, let alone be present at the birth. They certainly couldn't take up space in the then sacrosanct corridors of the hospital at the ungodly hour of eleven o'clock at night.

He'd no option but to kiss me goodbye and he left me feeling bereft.

The midwife marched me towards the enema room. Or rather, she marched and I slowly shuffled, impeded by the excruciating activity taking place in my body, never mind the thoughts of what was to come.

We'd arrived at the hospital courtesy of a stranger, who

came to the rescue when our car was off the road, all our immediate neighbours were – most unusually – out for the night, and I found myself, suddenly, unexpectedly and three weeks too soon, thrust into the height of labour. For fifteen long minutes my husband had watched me yelping with pain and clutching my tummy in stunned disbelief before he tore out into the night-time streets and began knocking on doors in our housing estate. Eventually a friend of ours who lived a couple of streets away roused her neighbour from his pre-bedtime television slumber in order to do ambulance duty.

My two sleeping children were whisked out of cots, swaddled in blankets and thrown into the back seat of the car along with their frantic daddy. In the front passenger seat, I gritted my teeth and tried to stifle my groans as the kind stranger tore down the Naas Road. Every rattle of the car sent renewed shock waves through my delicate abdomen, so much so that one contraction painfully grinded into another. Having flung the children in to their startled grandparents, we finally halted in a screech of brakes at the hospital, and with all the finesse of Rambo springing into action, my husband commandeered a wheelchair to rush me straight to the delivery unit.

That was when the midwife brightly announced that I'd still a long way to go and she dispensed with the wheelchair and sent my husband packing.

He was no sooner back at the door of my parents' house – some ten minutes later for him, and a lifetime later for me – when the hospital phoned to announce the safe arrival of our baby daughter. As it had taken me approximately two days to deliver our first two offspring, no one in the house believed him.

And that was how I found myself sitting in a hospital bed on a late November night, slightly shocked and sore, yet happily clutching my tiny, pink-bonneted bundle of joy. She was perfect in every way, despite her early and rushed appearance.

That was where I found myself at twenty-four years of age. With three children (babies, really) under the age of four, my little family was now complete. It was 1979 and it still seems like yesterday.

Life was very different then. Starting with maternity hospitals, there were no thrilling pregnancy scans, no pain-blocking epidurals, no brow-mopping husbands or partners and no birthing pools. Soothing whale music hadn't been invented. It was strictly a lie-on-your-back, ungainly legs-in-stirrups performance (after the rigours of the tortuous enema, and having the delicate nub of all your agony scrupulously shaved to within a millimetre), with all this riveting action captured in the relentless glare of mega-wattage spotlights.

No wonder I was glad, if a little shocked, that my daughter had been born in a hurry.

At home, there was no such thing as the luxury of a phone. (Thus the panic-stricken husband and startled grandparents.) In new Dublin housing estates, it took about four or five years for land lines to be installed. Yes, *years*. Then it cost nothing short of a king's ransom to be connected. The very concept of a mobile phone was absolutely laughable.

There were no computers. No surfing the net. No gossipy or advisory morning television shows. No convenient cartoon videos, never mind DVDs. No Pampers, McDonald's, Argos or Smyths.

No microwaves. No M50. No DART. The list is endless. So how did we survive?

Quite well, actually. It might have been the cusp of the lean, grey Eighties, but following my daughter's birth, I spent almost a week in a spotlessly clean, pleasant hospital ward under the vigilant care of Matron and her efficient team of nurses. Visiting hours were strictly adhered to. Our meals were prompt and hot and nourishing. Every night, our lovely new babies were fed and looked after in the nursery unit so that all the new mums would get a well-deserved good night's sleep. On Saturday night we all sat back in our beds, babies safely consigned to the nursery, and watched the *Late Late Show*. And Matron most benignly relaxed her rules to allow one tardy and apologetic husband to ignore usual visiting hours and bring in fish and chips for everyone in our postnatal ward.

It was bliss.

On Monday morning I said goodbye to the new friends I'd made and I brought my baby daughter home, feeling as though I'd been on holidays. Three-year-old big sister was delighted with the new addition. My son, still a toothless, crawling baby at thirteen months, looked curiously at this tiny infant who was suddenly usurping his pram. Within a month, he was running around and feeding himself, and he'd also managed to produce a row of pearly white teeth. There must be a lesson there somewhere.

Better again, they were then, and still are, all the best of friends.

The next few years were busy – in fact, they were hectic – but they were fun. I might have been up to my eyes in double rounds of cloth nappies and laundry, not to mention bottle feeds and constant cleaning and wiping, while my portable typewriter along with my writing dreams gathered dust in a corner of the wardrobe, but they were great days also. The landscape of my children's childhood is something special that's always recalled with fond memory.

I didn't have to juggle breakneck timetables or worry about getting big sister out to playschool and collecting her again in between baby's feeds, for playschools were few and far between, and children mostly played at home. And in those early Eighties, we managed quite well without microwaves and McDonald's and morning television. We seemed to have one decent summer after another and there were winters with enormous blankets of crisp, exciting snow. We lived in a neighbourhood where every house had children the same age as mine and the primary school was within easy walking distance of all of them. Tight housing densities was something else that hadn't been invented and every house had decent-sized front and back gardens that were perfect for little ones' supervised play. There was a large neighbourhood green with inviting trees and bushes that called out for climbing and football and sports days, where our children safely and happily ran and skipped and played to their heart's content.

If you had to bring a child to the hospital or clinic, there were plenty of willing mothers around to keep an eye on your other offspring. And always plenty of mothers with time to chat and swap nuggets of advice. I made friends then that I still rejoice in now. The 1980s were hard times on the one hand, but we had a wealth of riches on our doorstep and, indeed, in our own home.

Yet for all the differences in lifestyles between then and now, some things never change. A lot of what I experienced as a new mum is equally as relevant for new mums in today's world. Advances in modern technology and affluent lifestyles have no bearing on the condition of the human heart, and certainly not when it comes to finding your identity as a mother.

The nature of motherhood, like life itself, is wondrous, joyous, crazy and quite incomprehensible. It's not about ergonomic baby equipment, state-of-the-art sterilisers and child-friendly television on tap, never mind exciting innovations in disposable nappies and training pants. You won't pick it up from surfing the net for mother-related topics, or shopping in Smyths, or bringing baby home from the hospital in the latest SUV. And to a large degree, despite welcome advances in antenatal care and birthing procedures, instant bonding is a starry illusion. I expect my daughters, when the time comes, will have the same hopes and dreams, the same fears and anxieties as I did when I was rearing my young family.

For example, one night when I was still tying to find my way around the unfamiliar landscape of being a mum of three, I tucked the toddlers into bed, the baby into the cot and came downstairs to answer the hall door. The woman in the porch held up a sponsorship card.

'Is your mammy in?' she asked. With a casual wave of her card, she dismissed the tenuous strands of my fledgling identity and I felt as though the ground had been swept from under me. My children were my whole life. I thought I was doing a brilliant job, yet this good lady collecting for charity didn't think I even *looked* like a mother.

'*I am the mammy,*' I timidly replied, feeling all at once vulnerable and defensive and slightly outraged, and wondering what else I had to do to earn my stripes and join the club. Surely three small children were proof enough that I was a real, live mum? Why didn't I look the part? Was I falling down somewhere? Surely motherhood itself is tribal and instantly recognisable? After all, becoming a mother is a perfectly natural experience.

Or is it?

Eventually, when the nappies were finally off the agenda, the pram consigned to the attic and the three small children running under my feet turned into quite pleasant and independent school kids, I found time to blow the dust off the portable typewriter, buy a new ribbon and start to write. Naturally, I wrote about what was closest to my heart – the goings on in my family and experiences of child rearing, and I had several articles published in the *Evening Press*.

Maybe the woman in the porch that night struck a raw nerve; maybe having babies in quick succession is a little overwhelming for the human psyche; perhaps having babies at all is such a tremendous upheaval that it invokes a confidence crisis, for the incident stayed in my mind for quite a while. And when I penned an article about my experiences called *Most Mothers Are Made, Not Born,* this is what I wrote:

> Contrary to popular expectations, maternal instincts don't strike as a lightning bolt when you first hold your baby in your arms. In fact, in the weeks following childbirth your incipient feelings of exhilaration and relief are more likely to give way slowly but surely to a condition of numbed fatigue.

Your days are a non-stop round of early-morning disturbances and late-night feeds, a routine which induces chronic exhaustion. All the outwards signs of becoming a mum are evident. The house is chock-a-block with baby equipment. The clothesline is weighed down with miniature vests, lacy cardigans and towelling bibs. Visit the supermarket and your shopping trolley is bulging with baby requisites. People stop you in the street to gaze at and admire this tiny scrap of humanity who is consuming all your energy.

Yet in spite of this visible evidence, deep down inside you may not feel like a real mum. Your new role in life is unfamiliar. It chafes at the edges like an ill-fitting shoe. You almost feel you are acting a part in an unknown play and you haven't yet learned the script. You look at other mums and they seem so relaxed and confident that you feel like a complete fraud. Your baby is a stranger to you, and you wonder if you will ever develop a genuine mothering instinct.

Although there are reams of advice available in the best-intentioned baby books, maternal instincts cannot be taught. They are acquired over a period of time. Becoming a mum is a slow, ongoing process. Eventually there comes a time when you realise that the ill-fitting shoe has by degrees transformed itself into a comfortable slipper. Motherhood has crept up on you unawares and become an integral part of your life.

For maternal instinct is fashioned, you see, in the cold chill of the night as you spend long hours keeping vigil over your sick child. It is a process which takes shape as you delight in your child's small triumphs and accomplishments. It is an awareness which produces stomach-churning anxiety should your child be hurt in any way.

Maternal instinct helps you to plan your shopping trip into town so as to incorporate as many loos as possible at regular intervals on your itinerary. When you enter your favourite department store, it guides you unerringly towards the children's section first. It is an attitude that thrives as you wait patiently at the end of a long queue at the parent–teacher meeting. It is a state of mind that keeps you sitting up until three in the morning as you struggle, bleary-eyed, to complete a bunny rabbit costume for the school play. It is a perpetual condition that encourages you to give up your Saturday night out in order to pay for music tuition.

Developing maternal instinct can be an aggravating, frustrating process, but when you cannot close a cabinet door on your best china dinner service because the space inside is jammed with a collection of home-made greeting cards decorated with matchstick mums and misshapen hearts and kisses, you know it's all worthwhile.

Now, looking back, I wouldn't change a thing. How lucky – how *blessed* – was I.

Tara Heavey was born in London and moved to Ireland at the age of eleven. She read modern English and History at Trinity College, Dublin before studying law and practising as a solicitor for five years. She lives in County Kilkenny with her partner and two children. Her novels so far are *A Brush with Love*, *Eating Peaches* and *Making It Up as I Go Along*.

Feeding Time at the OK Corral

Tara Heavey

I'd rather work in Gordon Ramsey's kitchen than cook dinner for the kids. Some nights. Most nights. Take last weekend's infamous 'chicken ball extravaganza'.

The chicken balls were made in strict accordance with the instructions of a certain famous child food expert. Accompanied by such assurances as 'your toddler is going to love them' and 'guaranteed to become a family favourite'.

Not my family.

First of all, my wondrous offerings resembled 'splodges' rather than the tightly compacted 'balls' I had been led to envisage. With a sense of foreboding, I placed the morsels upon each plate – red car plate for him, to distract, yellow Winnie the Pooh for her, to tempt. What follows is a true story. Although names have been changed to protect the identities of two not-so-innocent children. (I am tempted to sign this piece 'Anonymous'.)

Number one child – let's call him Heronymous (rhymes with anonymous), who had in fact helped assemble the chicken splodges and was more than partly responsible for them becoming splodges rather than balls – because that's what you're supposed to do, isn't it? Let the little blighters help with the food preparation so they'll eat the bloody food.

The conversation went something along these lines.

Heronymous (whiny tone): I don't like chicken balls.

Mother: But you haven't even tried them.

H: They're yucky.

M: How do you know if you haven't even tried?

H: I don't want them.

M: Just have a little taste.

H: No.

M: Please.

H: I want Seven-Wup.

M (kneeling on kitchen floor, knees sticking to remnants of chicken splodges that didn't make it to the pan): Please.

Whereupon H bashes down remaining – for that, read all – balls with fork until they are reduced to unappetising, never-to-be-eaten-except-by-dog mush.

And in the pink corner, child number two, who for the purposes of this story shall be known as Cadence. Cadence has yet to develop sufficient verbal skills to communicate her needs/likes/dislikes at the dinner table, other than to scream such orders as 'nana' (banana), 'ogi' (yoghurt) and 'dinky' (drink). With trepidation, I placed three chicken balls beside her modest mound of noodles, taking care not to overload the plate and overwhelm her, as advised by all leading child nutrition experts. I proceeded to watch her out of my bloodshot eye.

Cadence picks up first chicken ball daintily between thumb and forefinger, examines it in minute detail. Lobs it onto floor. Splat!

Picks up second chicken ball daintily between thumb and forefinger, examines it in minute detail. Fires it directly onto floor. Splat.

Picks up third chicken ball...splat.

Dog wolfs down all three chicken balls. Thinks all his birthdays have come at once.

Mother sobs uncontrollably while attempting to make dinner for self and life partner, which is late due to lengthy assemblage of chicken balls.

Life partner paces around kitchen, sighing and rolling his eyes, muttering such helpful nuggets of wisdom as 'I told you so.'

Mother contemplates alternate use of chicken balls as missiles.

Consider the scene: life partner and mother sit down for simple tagliatelli dish.

Heronymous: I want 'glitelli.

Cadence climbs on top of table and grabs handfull of tagliatelli from each plate and stuffs it into her gob.

Mother and life partner finish dinner in record time. Life partner takes ulcer medication and mother races back to kitchen to prepare more pasta for children who are now crying with hunger because:

(a) Chicken splodges inedible.

(b) Noodles could not be eaten either due to contamination by said chicken splodges or because heartless parents wolfed down own dinner in front of starving children.

(c) Children's dinner now an hour later than usual due

to hours of preparation necessitated by chicken splodges.

Unfortunately, it takes ten to twelve minutes for pasta to cook. A lot can happen in ten to twelve minutes. A toddler can climb on top of the dining room table and sob uncontrollably (she gets it from her mother). A lot can be said too. Such as 'I'm hungwy' x 100 and 'I want Seven-Wup' x 200. Nervous breakdowns can occur.

Conclusion:

(a)   Approximately half of the pasta was consumed.

(b)   The dog ate well that night.

(c)   We had fish fingers the next day.

So what is the moral of this tale? That the longer it takes to prepare a dish for your children, the quicker it lands on the floor?

That the sole purpose of a child care guru is to make you feel inadequate?

Yes and yes. But for me, the kernel is that motherhood, food and guilt are inextricably linked.

Until recently, I've spent my whole life – quite successfully, it has to be said – not being able to cook. A domestic trogladyte rather than a domestic goddess. And in a funny way, I was almost proud of this. I thought that it marked me out as a modern, career woman type. Then I had kids. And the feeding began. Breastfeeding, to be exact. I thought this would be the easy part, as there was no cooking involved. But I wasn't prepared for the pain which tore me apart from the inside. Deep, excruciating and more exhausing than preparing a dinner party for ten. How could something so gorgeous, so wholesome, so bond-enhancing be so hard and hurt so much? As if God had decided that childbirth itself wasn't painful enough. It took me the best part of two weeks to break through that particular pain barrier. Looking back, it was worth it – if only to avoid several months of making up bottles, which was far too much like cooking for my taste. And I couldn't have given up. Imagine the guilt.

Then one day, having finally got the hang of it, I was sitting in the conservatory, son latched on, both of us basking in the sunlight, when I had a sudden and dreadful thought. Was I really meant to provide breakfast, lunch and dinner, seven days a week, for the next twenty-odd years for this child? The horrifying and resounding answer – yes! I couldn't even comfort myself with the thought that I'd be cooking for myself anyhow. I wouldn't. I would have been eating sandwiches, cereal, TV dinners and takeaways. This wasn't what I'd signed up for. I had signed up for the cuddly, dimply, gurgly baby who would love his mammy forever. Not a being for whom I would have to cook, iron and clean up after forever. Because you don't think about that pre-pregnancy. You just want a baby. Consumed by baby hunger, you forge right ahead, more than happy to let Mother Nature trick you. Afterwards, you're grateful she did. You just wish she could have shown you the slightly bigger picture.

Next came the solids. And what a terrifying prospect that was. So terrifying that my son ate nothing but baby rice for three weeks. It was only then that I felt ready to steam all those vegetables and freeze them in dozens of ice cube containers. Asking myself was this really why I'd spent all those years studying dementedly and trampling over the broken bodies of my work colleagues. Through a curious series of fateful twists and turns, I had somehow ended up in my kitchen, mid-afternoon on a Wednesday, defrosting square green cubes of brocolli while Joe Duffy listeners complained angrily and my baby cried tunefully in the background. Meanwhile, said baby, who had yet to master the requisite verbal skills to say 'that's yucky', still managed to convey his meaning through a combination of facial contortions and spits.

And nothing much has changed. I'm still trying to get him to eat his greens. I must admit to reaching an all-time low the other day when I told him that 'eating cabbage makes your hair grow curly'. Shockingly, this did not induce him to eat his cabbage. It did, however, transport me back in time to a place where cabbage was bottle green and stringy and curly hair was a desirable commodity (pre-hair straighteners).

The date: 1976.

The place: The canteen, All Saints Junior School, Upper Norwood, London.

You see, I spent my childhood in England and was therefore the lucky recipient of (cue drumroll) school dinners. This is why I speak knowledgably when I speak of cabbage. And splodge.

The mashed potato, which was served most days – chips on Friday – was a lumpy, bumpy, tasteless, grey-white mound redeemed by neither milk, salt nor butter. They would dole it up with an ice-cream scoop – which didn't fool anybody – and slap it onto your plate, where it would sit dolefully beside the stinking, dark-green, ubiquitious, suspicious-looking cabbage. And that's where I heard it. From well-meaning, mostly Irish dinner ladies: 'Eat up your cabbage, it'll make your hair grow curly.' And 'No dessert until you've eaten all your cabbage.' But I was the most cunning of them all. I would lift up the pastry lid on my square of meat pie, stuff in as much cabbage as I could, replace the lid and squash the whole thing down as flat as possible (now that's what I call hidden vegetables), thus leaving me free to wolf down my spotted dick or jam roly poly with custard.

The point I was trying to make before I got carried away by reminiscences was that when it came to fussy eaters, they didn't come much worse than me. If it wasn't sweet, I wasn't interested and no one was going to persuade me otherwise. So really, the difficulties I have in getting my children to eat what I want them to eat is just a case of what goes around come around. A tasty karmic stew (now that's *really* yucky). I tear my hair out in worry and frustration, just as my mother tore hers out before me and just as my daughter might tear her tresses out in years to come. Just carrying on a great family tradition. I take comfort in the fact. I was a fussy eater and look at me now – enthusiastic eater and fine heifer of a woman.

But I can't entirely shake off that guilt. The same kind of guilt that makes the mother of a grown-up, overweight son insist on making him a fry-up every time he comes to visit. I understand that now. Food for the stomach equals food for the soul. 'Eat this, I made it especially for you' means I love you. And I continue to love my children, even as they continue to turn their noses up at my home-made banana muffins. And I live in hope that one day they will stop throwing their food around the dining room. Only to possibly take it up again when they are teenagers. But how do you reason with a little person who, having insisted on having tomato ketchup on everything, including ice cream, for two whole years decides overnight that ketchup is the work of the devil?

The answer is, you don't. Don't even try. Buy your prepackaged food if that's the only thing they'll eat. Ignore the experts who show you how to construct a Bob the Builder figurine with the aid of carrots, cauliflower and spinach. Comfort yourself with the thought that your children are far too intelligent to fall for such a dumb trick. Her own children must be numbskulls. Because when you get right down to it, it's all a load of chicken balls.

Morag Prunty has written four novels under her own name but her latest book, *Recipes for a Perfect Marriage*, was written under the name Kate Kerrigan. It has been translated into fifteen languages, was shortlisted for the Foster Grant Romantic Novel of the Year Award and film rights have been sold to Augustine Films. A new Kate Kerrigan novel, *The Miracle of Grace*, has just been published. Morag lives in County Mayo with her husband and son and is writes a weekly column for *The Sunday Tribune*.

Precious Time
Morag Prunty

Motherhood sucks you into a bizarre time zone. It seems inconceivable to me that Leo didn't exist six years ago. And yet while I'm dropping him off to school, getting ready for his fifth birthday party, bemoaning the speed with which his life is passing me by, a small part of me is still standing, shocked, with the white stick in my hand, the thick blue line hollering at me – 'you are so, so pregnant' – wondering how I could have not noticed I had missed a period even though we were trying for a baby.

I had just got back from Mayo, where I had been holed up, on my own, finishing a book in my mother's cottage. I had eaten nothing but salmon and spinach for two weeks and had been feeling nauseous every morning. A heavy smoker, I remember thinking it was the fags and vaguely thinking I should give them up. In the second week I bumped into an ex-boyfriend in the local town who had recently had a child. I told him I was thrilled for him – then I went back to the empty cottage and bawled my eyes out for no reason. I took the next train home, marched in to my husband and before I had even taken my coat off announced to him that, after a year of trying, I had decided that enough was enough and he had to go and get himself tested. He reacted, as any man would, by saying that there was nothing wrong with his sperm, thank you very much. When I flipped my lid altogether he tried to calm me down by saying that it didn't matter to him if we couldn't have children as long as we had each other. This sent me entirely over the edge and I suspect we didn't speak for days, never mind try to rectify our childless state.

It was a pregnant friend who finally sussed me out. I was standing in her back garden, sheltering from the rain under my parka hood, smoking a fag. 'These things are killing me,' I shouted into her kitchen. 'I'm bloody exhausted all the time.' 'You're pregnant,' she said. I bought a test on the way home without telling my husband. The next morning I peed my blue line. 'We'll have to get a four door,' my husband said. I could see he was thrilled. Nothing wrong with my sperm, his smile said, like every father in history before him. Although it was surely tempered with an unspoken 'Phew!'

Nine months. It's not long when you are writing a book, or building a house or doing virtually anything except for incubating a human being. Then nine months seems like an age. And the thing they don't tell you is it's not nine months, really – it's forty weeks, which seems a lot, lot longer than four times nine, which is thirty-six. I decided that I was going to relax during my pregnancy. Pamper myself. Enjoy my last nine months of single life by not working and treating myself with facials and pedicures and blow-drys – and lots and lots of daytime TV accompanied by takeaway food and Butler's chocolates. And I did. But when I think back on that time, I am shocked to remember that we also found, purchased and moved into a new house. While pregnant, I launched my first book and did a press tour of the UK and Ireland. We went on holiday to Italy and I also visited New York for the first time and went up the Twin Towers. Just before my son was born, the Twin Towers fell. I was walking along Dublin's Grafton Street when a friend called to tell me about the dramatic attack. Leo had been less than three months inside me when I had sat in its top bar with my flavoured water and looked out at the dizzying New York skyline. It was like being in a film, the shimmering, glittering glamour of it felt familiar but distant – like a dream. Inside me, my son was still a theory; I was carrying a dream so big I didn't dare presume it would come through for me. Months later he was a weighty, kicking, certain lump in my sack of a stomach and the place where we had enjoyed our 'first date' was shockingly destroyed. So many people died and I was about to give birth.

Several people asked me at that time how I felt about bringing a child into the world given what had happened, and I remember thinking it was a strange question because it felt like my son was already with me. Once I got the all-clear of the first scan, Leo was born for me. I was in my mid-thirties and offered tests to see if he was Downs Syndrome. I didn't care. I didn't even want to think about it. I went private so that I could have lots of scans. But I never wanted them to count fingers to see if everything was 'OK'. I just wanted to have a look at him. Say hello through the scanner. He was alive and he was mine and that was as OK as it got. That's the time difference between men and women. We become intimate with our babies months before they are born. Even if you are married to a tree-hugging, hand-holding, birthing expert of a man (which, thank God, I am not), your joined bodies means you have already met before they leave your body.

My husband walked in on me one day late in the pregnancy while I was getting dressed. After I had abandoned my fashionable frilly pregnancy thongs, I was careful to spare him the shock of my enormous passion-killers. He stopped short at the door and I grabbed at the duvet to cover myself like a surprised virgin. We laughed – but not before I thought I saw a moment of fear flash across his face. Supposing there's nothing in there. Supposing the woman I married is just morphing into a giant egg. Or worse. Maybe it's not a baby, but some kind of dreadful alien thing. For first-time fathers, the physiology of a pregnant woman must be frightening. My husband did an excellent job in reassuring me that I was still attractive and that he found my pregnancy inspiring. He felt my tummy for kicks, but every time he wrapped his arms around me, our son fell still and silent. He was delighted to have such power, but I think a little, secret part of him thought I might be somehow making the whole thing up. I knew the difference the moment our son was born. He came by Caesarean section so that one moment he was inside me and the next he was suddenly aloft in front of us, screaming. A quiet, understated man, my husband let out an emotional yell. A perfect mixture of joy and shock. I was feeling, 'At last, he's here,' but his father was still taking in his existence.

By far the most terrifying way that time has played with me is the speed at which my son is growing up. The first Christmas after he was born, I asked my husband to buy me a digital video camera so we could record our son's life, every step of the way. A year later I was pretending that I couldn't use the thing. I bemoaned the waste of money, the passing of unrecorded events, the christening, birthdays all not on camera. The reality is more painful than just fecklessness. It is that recording my son's journey through life is too painful because the passing of each stage means letting go. Recording his life just reminds me that it is passing, and that one day I will have to let him go. And despite how much I love him, how precious our time together is, while he is doing his growing, I am writing and cleaning the house and doing other things. I have these fantasies about the two of us picking blackberries and setting up camp in the garden, but they go the same way as my fantasies to eat healthily and exercise daily – they turn into occasional photo opportunities rather than a way of life. When I make an hour to play, he is stuck into *Scooby Doo*. When he wants attention, I'm mid chapter. So most of the time Leo has his fun while I do the washing up, and I have my fun after he has gone to bed.

Although I work from home and have more time to spend with him than most mothers, my hours with Leo always seem to turn into something else. Reading becomes an educational exercise, walks get set at my own brisk pace until I get irritated with him lagging behind, or time gets eaten up with practical stuff, feeding, bathing. My mother just seems to relax with him and chat. I hear them in the other room while I fuss over some pointless, thankless task and I wonder why I am allowing myself to miss out.

When I do set aside specific time to do things with him, I feel distracted and slightly anxious. I watch him stick melting, pulverised Smarties into his birthday cake icing and I think, 'No! You're ruining it!' I set up camp in the back garden, then get stressed out when he brings a worm into my Cath Kidston tent. I do two rounds of hide and seek and I'm thinking, 'I must go inside now and finish sorting the cutlery.' It comes from the same school of compulsion as eating that doughnut I don't really want or buying ridiculous things that don't fit me in designer sales – it's vaguely self-destructive but not bad enough to take seriously. Something I do to keep my guilt at a manageable level; an inherently female thing. (You rarely hear men worry that they're not good fathers. Yet we women constantly doubt our ability to mother.) Or perhaps it is the dreadful truth that I take the people I love most for granted, so that I think I have all the time in the world to play hide and seek and only one precious hour this week in which to organise my knives and forks.

The reality is that my simple mother–son relationship is as susceptible as any intimate relationship to love's fuzzy, messy complications.

When he was a few weeks old, a besotted aunt said to me, 'I don't know how you get any work done. Do you not just want to sit and stare at him all day?' And I did spend many hours just sitting and staring and indulging in the 'I can't believe you belong to me!' reality of a newborn. I had waited a few years for him, but in the moment he was born, I realised I had waited all my life. As Leo started to grow – develop a personality, a will – I realised he didn't belong to me at all. He is separate person, and one day he will grow up and leave me. The more time I spend with my son, the more I can see this happening; this wanting to hold on tight to him, never being able to let him go. Every day he says or does something that makes him more remarkable, more adorable to me, so that the more time I spend with him, the bigger the love gets and so does the pain of letting him go. Perhaps it is fear and not fecklessness that stops me from spending more quality time with my son. Leo is happy and protected in my company; he knows I will always be here for him. But the terror of loving somebody and fearing they will leave you is more prevalent in my son than in my husband. If I'm lucky, there's a chance that the old man will hang around for keeps – but Leo will *definitely* leave me. It's my responsibility to make sure that he does; that he grows up independent and makes it in the world on his own. I'll make that happen for him, I just don't know if I'll ever be mature enough to accept it. So I ration the amount of fun we have to protect myself, and to a certain extent, him. Mummy's boys are attractive to nobody except their mothers, and he needs to make childhood memories with his friends, his father, his cousins as well as icing buns with me. Or perhaps while he is still young enough for it not to matter that I'm his mum, I will take my four-year-old camping, exploring, to the bouncy castle park, wherever he wants and I will try to have fun. Not for his sake, but for mine. After all, I only have another ten or twelve years, tops, before he leaves home. And ten years, that's nothing, right?

Tracy Culleton has written three bestselling novels: *Looking Good*, *Loving Lucy* and *More than Friends*. She's also an Emotional Freedom Technique practitioner, specialising in using it for peak performance and personal development, as well as in healing traumas and phobias. She currently lives in Carlow but is planning to move to Cloughjordan, to Ireland's first eco-village (www.thevillage.ie). She is married to Peter and is mother (and teacher!) to Tadhg. Her website is www.tracyculleton.com.

Too Cool for School
Tracy Culleton

As the school bus pulls away from its stop outside our house, whisking the other children off to school, my eleven-year-old son Tadhg is probably still in his pyjamas, eating his breakfast and watching television. And we don't mind in the slightest.

Because, you see, Tadhg is one of an estimated 2,000 Irish children who are home schooled (or home educated, as we prefer to call it), so he's not going to be on that school bus anyway.

You're probably wondering – most people do – why on earth we've decided to do such a seemingly strange thing.

People come to home education for different reasons. Some are forced into it by circumstances. For example, if their children are desperately unhappy in school, because of bullying or other issues, then the parents have to seek other options. Other parents choose it from the beginning and their children never go to school. They are people who have heard about home education along the way and they like what it offers.

We fall into the latter category. Our experience with parenting had made it seem a very natural choice because we had been lucky enough to be exposed to the concept of attachment parenting.

I remember, long before I ever had my baby, reading that babies take about six weeks to even realise they're born. (Now how they figure that out, I've no idea!) But it seemed to me that for that six weeks, it would be good to hold the baby close, as he was used to being close to me as mother anyway, while he adjusted to this new world. (I'm saying 'he' because it's a son I have.)

Then again, before I was ever pregnant, I saw and, intrigued, bought a book called *Three in a Bed* by Deborah Jackson. It was making the argument that human babies are designed to sleep with their parents, not alone in cots, and the argument seemed compelling to me. (Note: Absolutely *do not* do this without further research, as there are safety precautions you need to take to do this.)

Then, at last and to our great joy, I conceived our son. In the latter months of my pregnancy, I attended La Leche League meetings. La Leche League is the foremost organisation for supporting breastfeeding mothers. Since I knew I wanted to breastfeed, I joined this organisation to learn as much as I could, and that's in the top three best decisions I ever made.

Apart from much-needed help and support for breastfeeding, I learned that La Leche League encouraged things like co-sleeping and being with your baby. They even had a name for it: attachment parenting.

This made huge sense to me and my husband, and so that's what we did when Tadhg was born. He slept with us (again, we took due precautions) from birth, we carried him in a sling, he was long-term breastfed. Because this is all so contrary to the way most of society does things, it can seem a bit strange to other people.

But it's not by any stretch a clingy, co-dependent kind of parenting. For a start, it's going back to the way humans have parented for millennia – we evolved this way, and it's only in comparatively recent times that things have been different. Attachment parenting is about meeting all the child's needs – and only he knows what he needs. It's very baby-led in that way. In breastfeeding, the mother can never tell how much milk the baby had, but the baby knows when he has had enough. Her job is to make breastfeeding available when he needs it.

Likewise, attachment-parented babies are the best judge of when they've had enough of mother. I remember Tadhg, aged four months, decided that he had had enough of the sling. (This is most unusual; most babies love them well into the toddler years. Not all the time, of course, but when they choose.) He arched his back and made himself rigid when I tried to put him in. And of course, I didn't insist; I acknowledged that he wanted more independence than that. Although he was sitting up by then, he was too small just to have the freedom of the floor, so we got him a baby nest and he loved that for the two months it took before, aged six months, he started crawling. And then there was no stopping him!

Attachment parenting is about meeting the baby's needs, not the parents'. Those who promote attachment parenting say it makes for very secure, well-bonded babies and children. And that is certainly our experience.

Another advantage of being members of La Leche League was that we met people who were home educating, and thus knew that it was a valid option. We also liked how happy, bright, articulate, knowledgeable and contented the home-educated children were, and how close the families were. We decided we'd like some of that please.

Mind you, it was a *huge* decision. A rather scary leap into the unknown. But still, the advantages outweighed our doubts, and we were willing to do it despite our fears.

It's a way of life with great flexibility – we're not tied to a school timetable in any way. We can take the morning off if it's a nice day and go for a bike ride instead of doing our homework (or can we call that PE, and have it as part of our schooling?). We can – and do – go on holiday off-peak with no problems.

Because home education is so efficient (the work is pitched at the child's level to stretch him without overwhelming him, and there's no time wasted enforcing discipline or administrative tasks), it doesn't take very long – a couple of hours a day at most – leaving us all with lots of free time.

In school, the curriculum has to be one-size-fits-all and children have to fit into it. This causes problems because some children are slower than that and need remedial help, and others are quicker than that and get bored. The solution is for teachers to give extra work, but in speaking to friends and reading parenting forums, it's clear that the children resent the extra work and feel it's a sort of punishment.

One of the biggest gifts of home education is that the children continue to love learning. Pre-school children are insatiable in their desire to know about the world, as anybody who has been followed around by a toddler incessantly asking 'Why?' will attest! Home-educated children never lose that, so their questions are a curriculum all by themselves.

We also feel that the school curriculum is very narrowly targeted. The respected Harvard professor Howard Gardner has identified multiple intelligences, and we all have greater or lesser amounts of each one, rather than somebody being definitively intelligent or not. These intelligences are linguistic (good with words, e.g. writers), logical/mathematical (good with maths), kinaesthetic (good with your body, e.g. athletes), interpersonal (getting on well with people, e.g. politicians and diplomats), visual/spatial (e.g. artists and architects), naturalistic (good with nature, e.g. gardeners) and intrapersonal (good at knowing yourself).

My understanding is that the school system only values the first two intelligences (linguistic and mathematical). Other skills such as music, art and PE are very much the poor relations. This is fine for people whose skills are linguistic and mathematical (ironically, that would be me!), but it isn't so good for the others.

Other reasons to home educate are that our children miss out on bullying and peer pressure. Not that this is our reason to home educate – I think that would be very fear-based reasoning. But it's surely a perk. And it's a big perk – bullying is a huge issue, both in terms of numbers and impact, and I think our society isn't facing up to that. Likewise, peer pressure is a big issue. Schools encourage conformity (they have to in order to operate successfully); children who are somehow *different* are the ones who are picked on for bullying – it's not surprising that it's hard to stand up against the crowd. One very obvious trait of home-educated children is that they're quite happy to be different. If you don't like it, that's your problem, is their attitude.

The big question about home education is *socialisation*. It's the question everybody asks us. Our answer is this: inherent in that question is the assumption that school is a wonderful place for socialisation, and I would question how true that is. My memory of school is that they tried to stop me socialising – I would have chatted and socialised all day if I was let, but school demanded silence except for limited prescribed periods. Also – again talking about bullying and peer pressure – I would question the calibre of a lot of the socialisation.

Now of course children make friends at school; it would be ridiculous to suggest otherwise. But it's because that's where they meet other children; it's not anything intrinsic about school. And home-educated children meet other children too, and make friends with them: other children in the home-education community, neighbours and children from extracurricular activities.

It seems to me that home-educated children have excellent social skills. Because they're living life in the world, rather than in a school, they're going lots of places and meeting lots of people and are well able to talk to anybody. In my experience, a defining trait of home-educated children is how articulate they are.

So how does home education work in practice?

Home education is not school at home (which is why we prefer the phrase home education to home schooling). We don't sit at desks from 9:30 till 3:00. We don't have timetables and subjects and breaks and tests and so on.

For us, each day is different, but usually Tadhg switches off the telly after his breakfast, washes and dresses and then does his list of daily jobs. Once he's finished those, and if we have no other plans for the day, he'll spend about an hour and a half to two hours doing homework. We do a lot of maths because we both love that, we read factual books (such as Dorling Kindersley and Usborne) and good-quality fiction, we research things on the internet and we chat about life, the universe and everything.

However, the homework goes out the window if we do have something on, so there's many the weekday that we'll do nothing formal at all. Yet we'll often do educational stuff at evenings and weekends. Even last Christmas Day we watched a programme about maths and numbers. This is no hardship for Tadhg, as education and learning are fun for him.

After his homework, his day is pretty much his own. But learning doesn't stop with the formal stuff. We play educational games such as Scrabble, Monopoly and Discovering Europe and we have various maths games which he adores.

We watch a lot of documentaries and there's usually lots of spin-off from those. For example, we recently watched Michael Palin's *Pole to Pole* and *Around the World in Eighty Days*. We watched both of those with an atlas to hand and spoke a little bit about each country that Michael visited. We had these on DVDs from the library, and one night Tadhg went to bed begging us, 'Please don't watch any more without me, I want to see it all.'

At another stage, as Michael was on a ship going across the Pacific, he asked, 'But how does navigation work?' We didn't know – so we went on the internet and we all found out – it's fascinating, actually. (All home-educating parents would say that they have learned so much through this journey; it's one of the perks!)

We have an education infrastructure: our house is filled with books and magazines, art materials, educational software, educational DVDs and of course the internet, which is an absolutely magical resource. Of course, so do lots of houses where the children go to school – but we have so much time to avail of these resources. I imagine it's the rare child who, after school and after homework, has the energy to pursue knowledge for the interest of it. And of those children who do pursue knowledge for its own sake, they would do so well being home educated and having so much time to learn.

Home-educated children tend to have quite broad general knowledge, but it could be about anything. Tadhg was speaking of the irrigation models in ancient Mesopotamia the other day but doesn't know all the rivers of Ireland. He carefully (and, truth be told, the tiniest bit patronisingly!) told me why a plastic bottle compresses if you drink out of it without letting air in, but he doesn't know any poems off by heart.

It distresses me somewhat when people say, 'I admire you so much, you're so wonderful to do home education.' It distresses me because that perpetuates the myth that it's difficult and only special people can do it. It's not true. I only have a mediocre Leaving Cert to my name (school didn't suit me at all) and I'm home educating, and I passed the inspection by the state authorities, so I must be doing it okay!

I would much rather that people know that it's possible for almost everybody to do. In fact, I'm stating that categorically right now – if you're reading this, you're competent to home educate. Home education isn't nearly as much about teaching as it is about answering questions and finding resources (and with the internet, that's a doddle).

I'm often asked, What about secondary school? What about exams?

We're not planning to send Tadhg to secondary school. Of course, if he shows a desire to go, then that would be different, but so far he's happy to be home educated and would hate to go to school.

Having said all that, home-educated children can join the school system at any time. They tend to fit in well when they do, although they typically have two main challenges. The first is that they're just not used to the sheer amount of handwriting required, and that can take a while for them to adapt to. Also, because they love learning, and because they want to learn, they get frustrated with the time wasted by the teachers having to discipline other students and the slow pace at which everything moves.

There are several ways to get a third-level education without having been to school, and that's the route many home-educated children take.

For now, he's home with me. And it can be quite chaotic. There are usually books everywhere and art projects on the go, not to mention science experiments. To be honest, this can get frustrating, but it's just the way it is. I laugh hollowly when people say, 'You must be so organised to home educate.'

The hardest part of home education is the self-doubt. For all that I've written, and I know it all to be true – we are sailing against mainstream beliefs. We are assailed by well-meaning people telling us we're ruining our child's life. It can be hard to keep the faith sometimes. Also, children learn the same way they grow – i.e. one day at a time, imperceptibly – and sometimes it's easy to believe they're learning nothing. That's where the home-education community comes in. We've all taken turns at wailing at each other, 'He/she/they are learning nothing,' and our friends gently point out all that the children have learned.

The other hardest part (oh yes, there are two) is the constant pull on my time. I know that every working mother feels this, that only my details are different. But it's hugely challenging to make sure that everybody's needs get met. However, Tadhg is eleven at this time of writing in early 2007, and it will only be a very few short years before he's much more responsible for his own learning. My job will be reduced to resource-finder and chauffeur. So this is a temporary situation.

But it's worth it, for me and hundreds of other parents. The most wonderful part of home educating is that we're so close as a family (and all home-educating families would say that – those with bigger families report that siblings tend to get on better too). It was as exciting for me to witness his first reading as his first steps. It's a gift to share the journey with him. This, of course, is not to say that schooling families aren't close. It's just that we home educators have so much more time together to grow a relationship, and the time together is much less pressurised.

As we curl up together on the sofa on a stormy day with wind-driven rain beating against the windows, reading in front of a fire while everybody else is out at school and work, I know it's worthwhile. When we're playing on a beach on a sunny day in May with our home-educating friends, while other children are stuck in classrooms, I know it's worthwhile. When his face lights up as he makes a connection between two pieces of information, I know it's worthwhile.

For us, and for all the home educators I know, it's not about 'hothousing' our children to get their degree by age fourteen or whatever. It's about getting an equivalent education to a traditional one, but in a more relaxed way. Because the pupil–teacher ratio (even in the largest family) is so small, and because what they're learning is always pitched at their abilities and usually at their interests, they learn very efficiently, which leaves lots of time for play and exploration and discovering who they are.

And maybe that, at the end of the day, is what it's all about.

Sharon Owens, born in Omagh in 1968, is a writer and an artist. A lifelong bookworm, Sharon began writing romantic fiction in 2003 and her first novel, *The Teahouse on Mulberry Street*, has since been published around the world, followed by *The Ballroom on Magnolia Street* and *The Tavern on Maple Street*, also published worldwide. Her fourth novel, *The Trouble with Weddings*, has recently been published. Sharon lives in Belfast with her husband and daughter.

The Birth Experience
Sharon Owens

Friday night, 28 May 1993.

I was eight months pregnant.

A new-build semi on the outskirts of Belfast, still smelling of dust and plaster – we'd only moved in six weeks earlier. We'd no furniture except for a small sofa-bed and a portable TV (we were temporarily sleeping in the living room), but my husband Dermot and I had lots of grand plans for our first proper home together.

Meanwhile, we were celebrating my twenty-fifth birthday with two cups of tea, a giant cheese and tomato pizza and two enormous slices of carrot cake – our once-hectic social life on the Belfast rock scene having disappeared entirely under the financial constraints of our first mortgage and related expenses. But I remember feeling almost euphoric that evening because eight months of near-constant all-day 'morning' sickness had ended abruptly the day before and I was able to eat all my favourite foods again. Hence the carrot cake and pizza feast. I was eager to regain the 30 lb I'd lost after so much time subsisting on cups of sugary tea, salt and vinegar crisps and fresh strawberries. And that week I'd barely escaped having to have a blood transfusion for a very low blood count.

Hooray!

And then I got a pain.

'You won't believe this,' I said, slowly to Dermot. He was yawning and starting to look around for the duvet. 'But I think the labour just started.'

'Don't even *joke* about it,' he said, kicking off his shoes. 'You've only eaten too much pizza. I told you not to have that last slice!'

There was still a month to go until my due date. And he'd had no proper sleep all week, what with sitting exams for a masters degree in IT that he was taking during night classes after work. 'I've never been this tired in my whole entire life,' he added. 'I'm going to sleep all day tomorrow.'

Famous last words.

'Yeah, it's probably the food,' I agreed and we settled down companionably under the quilt to finish our tea and watch *Friends* and *Frasier*. And then I got another pain, a very big stabbing one. Like period cramps, only much stronger. It also felt strangely cold in my 'baby bump', like I'd put on a pair of jeans that'd been in the freezer. A dragging sensation – and I knew for certain that Alice was on her way. (We already knew we were having a girl.) I suppose she was feeling rather squashed in there and impatient to see the outside world. Sometimes I could see her heels pressing out and skidding across the skin on the inside of my abdomen. Some of my friends thought this spectacle was absolutely terrifying, but I thought it was beautiful to behold. And not at all painful, just tingly and exciting.

'No,' I said. 'It's definitely time.'

Oh jeepers, the scrambles of the two of us then as we panicked with light switches and plates and cups and a bag for the hospital full of breast pads and nappies. Hearts in our mouths, we set off in our battered red Peugeot 205. All the door handles had been broken by would-be car thieves – the one and only drawback from our days living in the action-packed student quarter of Belfast. I was wearing a black trench coat and Doc Marten boots over my pink pyjamas. At this point I realised I'd forgotten to buy new slippers for the hospital. Normally I go about the house in bare feet and only ever use slippers for special occasions. There was a traffic jam on the Ormeau Road, needless to say. It was totally gridlocked. We joked about me giving birth in the car and then naming our daughter 'Peugeot'. Mobile phones hadn't been invented in 1993, or at least we didn't have one. I tried desperately to stay calm and think ahead, to concentrate on our precious baby and not on the next few hours, on the delivery itself.

Midnight saw me safely ensconced in the hushed atmosphere of the maternity unit, puffing merrily away on gas and air. Painkilling injections and an epidural had failed to numb the labour pains, which were coming hard and fast. (Having an epidural isn't quite so bad in reality, even though the idea of drugs being injected directly into your spinal column does seem a little brutal in theory.) Anyway, those dastardly labour pains were something else. Somehow, I thought they'd be spaced about fifteen minutes apart and I'd have time to apply some fresh make-up or polish off a few rounds of nourishing tea and toast in between contractions. But no, one pain was just subsiding as the next one took off and it suddenly dawned on me that that's why they tell you to practise panting in the antenatal classes: because otherwise you'd forget to breathe at all. The other women in the maternity unit that night had all been there before and knew the routine. One woman had just calmly pushed out her *seventh* child and was chatting casually to the rest of us about how dull apple pie tastes without fresh cream on it. Minutes later she strolled outside for a cigarette as a midwife heated some formula milk for the new arrival.

'I can't breastfeed,' she explained defiantly. 'I'm back at work on Thursday.'

Show off, I thought resentfully.

I was shown into a private room and examined. Despite some monumental abdominal rumblings, my waters still hadn't broken, so a kindly midwife broke them for me with a crochet hook, or something remarkably similar looking. It's mildly embarrassing to find a strange woman's hand rooting around inside your vagina on a Friday night. Or maybe it isn't, depending on your point of view. A rush of warm water immediately flowed out.

'There you are now,' she said cheerfully. 'That'll speed things up.'

'Oh good,' I said brightly, feeling very sorry for myself. I'd almost forgotten what was about to happen.

'Bloody hell and blimey Charlie,' I said some time later as the sun rose behind flimsy floral curtains. My sweat-soaked pyjamas were replaced with a green paper dress and I was examined again. 'If men had to go through this carry-on, there'd be no such thing as overpopulation. Or war. I'll tell you that for nothing.'

And so on.

Honestly, what a stupid way to bring children into the world. Dermot was ashen-faced and rather traumatised. I think it was worse for him, not being able to do anything to help me. He's a very helpful person by nature.

'I'm so sorry,' he kept saying. 'And we haven't even got the upstairs carpeted yet. Or bought a car seat. Or a new car, for that matter. Or ordered home-heating oil for the tank. I thought there'd be more time, you see?'

(He's practical too.)

We'd been living on the breadline since the pregnancy began in order to save enough money for a private consultant to be present at the birth. I'm a Smiths fan of twenty years' standing and a fervent socialist to boot, but I'm also a confirmed pessimist. And the pessimist in me won out with regards to the delivery. I feared all sorts of things would go wrong and I wanted an expert on standby. Which was why we hadn't got around to replacing our ancient car. It'd recently been valued at £10 (yes, ten pounds) and so we hadn't bothered getting the locks fixed. However, because I'd gone into labour a month early, my lovely consultant, Jim, was still sunning himself in the Maldives, and so another one was being sought urgently and summoned from his bed on the upmarket Malone Road, no doubt. To come and attend to a paranoid Smiths fan in Doc Marten boots.

Well, money talks.

'I'm sorry,' Dermot said, yet again.

'Ah, it's not your fault, love. It's his fault, him up there!' I replied, jabbing a finger at the ceiling. For a moment, my poor husband thought I meant another man was the father of our precious baby, but then he understood I meant God. 'You'd think someone who could make a whole entire universe on his own could have hit on a smarter way for mammals to reproduce, wouldn't you? Ridiculous! If only we could lay little eggs and keep them in a safe place for a while. Actually, I could murder some scrambled eggs on toast right now, I'm bloody well *starving*.'

'Can she have some food?' Dermot asked anxiously. Anxious to flee to the safety of some far-off canteen with a very long queue, I teased him.

But, no. The midwife said sorry, I couldn't have any food just in case I needed an operation. Drat and double drat. I promised myself all kinds of treats as the labour went on and on, gathering force with each contraction. Chocolate squares, roast chicken, egg mayonnaise, cheese toasties with HP sauce…

Six o'clock in the morning and still nothing doing delivery wise. The pains were galloping along, overlapping each other (or so it seemed to me). I was only half-conscious after hyperventilating on the gas and air. It's a very disorientating activity, overbreathing. I thought I was lying at the bottom of a swimming pool and thinking to myself, I don't remember asking for a water birth. Perhaps private patients get a water birth thrown in for the price?

'Oh dear, what's this? You're fully dilated, Mrs Owens, but the baby is transverse,' the midwife said quickly. 'Transverse, I said! Can you hear me, Mrs Owens?'

Mrs Owens was Dermot's mother.

I thought to myself, what's Dermot's mother doing here? She lives miles away on the north coast. (We were less than a year married and I was still getting used to my new title.)

'Wake up, honey. The baby is transverse.' Poor Dermot. He was ageing before my eyes like something out of *Star Trek*. I think his hair turned grey that night; he's not very keen on hospitals.

'Jesus Christ, what are you playing at?' I wept. I thought the baby was hurt in some way, folded in half maybe? 'What's transverse mean?' I shouted to no one in particular. I feared that plate of scrambled eggs was getting further and further away from me.

'Nothing to fret about, don't worry.' The midwife again. 'She's on her side, that's all. She's not head first any more. It's a big baby, isn't it? I suppose she's moved onto her side for comfort. Look now, there's a little hand out waving hello to us. Look!'

I peered down between my knees.

A tiny pure-white hand was curling and uncurling its perfect fingers, from the scene of the crime, as it were. It looked like a calm little hand and I thought to myself, This baby takes after her father. He's very calm, most of the time. Unlike me. I go to pieces if the phone rings after nine o'clock at night, thinking someone's been killed in a car accident.

The midwife bolted from the room.

'What'll happen now?' I asked Dermot bleakly, fearing forceps and scissors were on their way. I think my cervix had snapped shut at the very idea of further intervention. And then I looked again at that little hand and wanted so much to see my baby's face. I was afraid to move a muscle in case I hurt her. I was afraid to cry. I was afraid to breathe.

'Oh, doctor says a Caesarean, immediately,' the midwife said, running back from the nurses' station with two co-workers in tow. 'Chop chop, look lively!' Epidural tubes were removed at lightning speed and my trolley bed was pushed out of the room at ninety miles an hour.

'No time to get you ready,' the midwife said to Dermot.

'Wait here.'

We held hands for a second as the lift doors opened.

A bit of 'site preparation' followed in the lift going down to theatre. The midwife was shaving off my what we nowadays refer to as a lady-garden. And dousing me with iodine, or something similar. Or maybe she'd just spilled a mug of black coffee over me in all the confusion. Again, not something I'd recommend as a way of passing a Friday night, but it takes all sorts.

Theatre was very quiet. There were faint humming noises, dimmed lights, metallic sounds. The consultant appeared from a side room, gowned-up, masked-up and magnificently composed. Regal as anything with a plummy voice, a healthy tanned complexion and lovely shoes. Why are all consultants tall and handsome? A swift introduction followed, a consent form for me to sign and then I was having the blessed anaesthetic injected into the back of my hand.

'Count down from ten.'

'Ten, nine, thank God for drugs,' were my last words that night. I was high as a kite. I'd forgotten all about my birthday.

Some time later, the sun was shining into a small quiet room with peppermint-green walls. There was a picture of a bowl of pink roses hanging on the wall in front of me. I could feel no pain at all. I was just incredibly sleepy and tired as anything. At first I thought I was all alone in the room and then I saw my beloved husband sitting by the window, cradling our newborn daughter in his arms.

'Hi there,' I said. 'Well, I made a right bags of that. As per! What's she like?'

'She's beautiful,' he said. 'Absolutely beautiful. She's got blue eyes.'

'Did she make it out all right?' I said.

'Yes, she did,' he told me, already looking the consummate parent, supporting the baby's neck properly and everything. 'She's so big, no wonder you had such a time of it. Nine pounds, almost! And you eating next to nothing for months, it's a miracle! And the tallest baby they've had in here for years and years, they said. Maybe ever! Wait till you see her legs! I don't think any of the clothes we bought are going to fit her.'

They didn't.

Not even her cosy white padded travelling suit.

We had to take her home from the hospital four days later in a blanket. Dermot had bought a car seat and spent hours checking it was fitted correctly – so much time checking, in fact, that he'd forgotten to buy a bigger-size travelling suit for the baby. I was off the morphine by then and allowed to eat solids again, thank goodness. One more day of hunger and I'd have snuck out of the hospital in my bare feet and taken a branch of Burger King hostage. I was quite stiff and not allowed to bend over unless absolutely necessary. I'd had a couple of 'assisted baths', which basically meant I'd stood up in a bath and been sponged down by a nursing assistant called Muriel. I didn't mind. By that stage, I'd no reserves of embarrassment left. I knew the staff had seen it all before and I marvelled at their strength and kindness and wondered why we admire celebrities so much when medical staff are the true heroes of this topsy-turvy existence we call modern life.

We named our daughter Alice because I wanted a name that started with the letter A. The first letter of the alphabet. And Alice seemed to suit her, a timeless and elegant name. My general health was on its knees and I often fell asleep standing at the kitchen sink, but I knew I'd get better with a few good meals inside me.

And not one moment of baby blues at the time or in the thirteen years since. In fact, everything about my life-before-Alice simply faded away and was replaced with a massive tidal wave of love. Which came in handy at times, because she didn't sleep through the night until she was four years old. Alice is choosing subjects soon for her GCSEs and is very good at writing poems and telling jokes and showing me how to use these latest hi-tech mobile phones. She's already five feet six inches tall and eager to learn to drive. She gives me fashion advice and does the grocery shopping online.

She's amazing.

My advice to mothers-to-be is get plenty of sleep while you can and buy some comfy slippers for the hospital. Everything else will happen anyway.

Mary Malone was born in Cork. At eighteen she moved to Dublin to join the Civil Service, where she met her husband, Pat. They returned to live in Cork in 1999 with their sons, David and Mark, and built the home of their dreams in Templemartin, near Bandon. Mary works in the Central Statistics Office and is also a novelist and a freelance journalist. Her first novel, *Love Match*, was launched in 2006 and her second novel, *All You Need Is Love*, has just been published. She is currently writing her third novel. Mary's website is www.marymalone.ie.

0–19: One Mum's Diary
Mary Malone

Being a mum, as I'm sure most mums will agree, is a poorly paid job, has really long hours, lacks any definite parameters and is full of unexpected surprises and shocks. Yet it's undoubtedly the most satisfying and rewarding position in life and generally, unless experienced first hand, its unconditional love is impossible to comprehend.

Most mums need little persuasion to talk about their kids and I'm no different. Sharing some of the ups and downs, tears and laughter that I've experienced as a mum gives me immense pleasure. While my sons, David (nineteen) and Mark (fifteen), are well-balanced young adults now and I'm finally relaxing in the knowledge that I've brought them this far without any major catastrophe, I often wonder whether parenting would be easier if children arrived into the world with an instruction manual (and perhaps a danger sign over their heads)!

Over the last two decades, my children have brought the best and possibly the worst out in me. In no other aspect of my life have I experienced the same depth of love, protection, pride, frustration or anxiety. So if you have a few moments to spare, I'd like to invite you on a short trip down memory lane as I recall some of the more memorable moments of these precious years.

Early October 1987

Idyllic honeymoon on foreign shores fantasising about our glorious future, looking forward to a few magical years on our own before the pitter-patter of tiny feet…famous last words!

Late October 1987

Something's amiss. My period's late. 'It must be the stress of the wedding,' I console myself, ignoring the little voice in my head screaming, 'YOU'RE PREGNANT!'

November 1987

Still no arrival, despite ten-minute visits to the loo. Nothing for it but to call in the expert – a visit to my mother in Cork is urgently required.

Oh dear, the knowing sympathetic look on her face is enough as she instructs me to go straight to my GP when I get back to Dublin (no reliable home pregnancy kits then).

Our kindly GP listens to my tale of woe, hands me a container and orders me to the tiny bathroom.

Worst fears are confirmed later in the evening (I had to wait five hours for the result). Hubby and I huddle in the telephone box, waiting patiently with baited breath for the doctor to answer her phone. 'Congratulations, you're going to be a mum,' she says brightly. 'Come in to see me in a few weeks!'

I faint with shock.

Christmas 1987

Still reeling, cannot get used to the idea that my life is over. I'm already bloating, am constantly exhausted, have no interest in socialising and am terrified of what lies ahead. A honeymoon baby. How romantic! Everyone else thinks our news is fantastic. Why can't I?

February 1988

Feeling a little better. Energetic again. And then my turning point, I feel movement. I'm terrified once more. The baby is alive inside me. More tears.

May 1988

Soaring temperatures, glorious sunshine. I'm too hot. I'm huge. I've nothing to wear. I talk to the baby when nobody's around. I'm convinced it's a girl. No. It's definitely a boy. I'm curious. What will he/she look like? What will I do if my baby doesn't like me?

23 June 1988

Due date arrives. Cases packed for weeks. Why isn't anything happening? How long more must I wait? I DON'T WANT TO BE PREGNANT ANY MORE!

12:10 p.m., 5 July 1988

It's a boy! 'Congratulations, Mammy.'

Mammy? Is the midwife talking to me?

I look into a red, wizened, familiar little face. Oh my God, I'M IN LOVE. Then suddenly it hits me. Oh the poor baby – he looks horribly like me!

'David,' we both say. Hubby and I are instantly smitten. We've never seen a baby quite so gorgeous in our whole lives and we can't believe that together we've made him. He's a miracle. Our miracle.

And then our little miracle screams in my arms. We look at each other. We don't know what to do.

Hubby suddenly remembers he needs to make phone calls and tell everybody about our little David. He leaves me alone with a crying baby.

I don't know what to do. I cry too.

Cork, August 1988
It's such a good idea staying with my mother. Gorgeous dinners placed before us. 'You need your strength,' she says, taking our handsome, gurgling baby from my arms, leaving hubby and I to finally eat an uninterrupted meal.

We smile at each other and then glance adoringly at a contented David. All thoughts of those first few weeks at home with a screaming baby a distant memory. He's angelic now.

Things are so much easier when we have help and advice from someone who knows what she's doing (unlike us, who are still reading the book on how to be perfect parents).

Dublin, 5 October 1988
Just as I'm getting confident at being a mum and finally have him in a proper routine, I've no choice but to leave him in the care of my terrific neighbour, Ann, and return to work. He's only three months old and I hate handing him over.

What if he forgets me while I'm at work? What if he can't sleep and he needs me to sing his favourite song?

Guilt: I should be at home with my baby, but we need the money.

Worry: I think I forgot to pack his favourite soother.

Relief: Somebody else is responsible and I can talk to adults and relax.

Weary: I have loads to prepare every evening for the following day.

Adoration: I look at David fast asleep in his cot.

More guilt: I didn't have enough time to play with him before he fell asleep.

July 1991

Life is easier now. David's three. He's walking and talking. I no longer have to follow him around the house and garden coaxing him to eat his dinner. His teething pains are a thing of the past. We have the occasional night out and some of our friends have started having babies too. We're no longer alone on this adventure.

We're so proud of him when he behaves well in public. We try to reason with him when he throws a tantrum in the supermarket. It's because he's three. He'll grow out of it…it's not his fault! But then I worry that he only behaves like this when I take him shopping. Am I a bad mother because I can't diffuse these instances? Is it because I'm working full time?

Everyone's asking when we're going to have company for David. They're telling us we shouldn't leave it much longer.

But the thought of having to go through pregnancy and sleepless nights all over again is daunting.

And then my brother announces he's getting married in May 1992. This decides us. We'll either have our second baby before the wedding or we'll wait until afterwards. It's the push we need.

September 1991

David's enrolled for Montessori school. I hate letting him go. He won't be my little boy any more. He'll grow up overnight. What if the other children pick on him? What if he doesn't make friends? What if he's lonely?

I take time off work. I need to be there for him on his first week in case the school rings for me.

He cries at the door. He holds onto the leg of my jeans and won't let go.

Teacher pulls him gently from me and ushers me away. She shuts the door. I can't see him any more. I cry too.

Every minute is like an hour until it's time to collect him.

He hurries out with another boy. He's smiling. He's happy. Relief.

Why am I still crying? I should be happy now.

Oh dear! I don't need the expert this time. I can guess why I'm all teary-eyed. I'm pregnant!

Christmas 1991

David's first Christmas panto. We're beaming with pride. We record every moment and play it over and over for everybody who calls to visit, dismissing any protests.

This pregnancy flies by. I'm content. I'm looking forward to the event. I know what to do now. It won't take me an hour to dress the baby after every nappy change.

But sometimes I look at David and fret that I won't be able to give him as much attention when I have two children. What if he's jealous? What if he doesn't love his new brother or sister?

9:02 p.m., 28 February 1992
It's a boy! We cry again. He's gorgeous. We can't wait for David to see him. He's excited to have a new brother, thank goodness! All is well. I can't wait to bring the new baby home. David chooses his brother's name: Mark.

Summer 1992
I love having two children. I hate returning to work and opt for part-time hours. It's the best of both worlds, even if we are broke. Huge deliberation whether we should send David to primary school this year or next. Decide against it but spend months agonising over decision.

September 1993
David starts school. All four of us go along on his first morning. He doesn't want to stay in the classroom. Mark doesn't want to leave. Difficult moment. Teacher is kind but firm. I wish I could take him home again. She's too stern.

Summer 1994
Our first family sun holiday. Disaster. Mark spends every waking hour in danger. He's two. He's independent. He won't hold my hand. He sticks his fingers into everything, including filthy drains. He won't eat. He picks up a bug. He's really ill. Hubby wants to take him home. We stick it

out. So busy watching Mark, David gets sunburned. Holidays with small children are frightening. But when we arrive home, we distort the truth and tell everyone we had a great time.

September 1995
David joins a soccer team. What if he's not as good as the others? What if he's left on the sideline? It's cold standing on sidelines every Saturday morning. He says I bought him the wrong boots. Can I get him the ones Eric Cantona wears? Every other player has them.

September 1996
Mark runs into school on his first morning. He doesn't even look back. Now they're both in school, making new friends and dealing with life's little troubles. I miss my babies, my toddlers. Looking at the bigger boys charging around the schoolyard, I fear for my lads. Will they be tough enough? What if they're too tough? I don't want them getting into trouble or making enemies. I want everyone to like them.

February 1997
An anxious teacher meets me at the school gates when I arrive to collect the boys. 'We were trying to contact you...'

I have an immediate rush of guilt: I was shopping and I don't have a mobile phone.

'Mark's had an accident.'

I pale.

'He tripped over the step and hit his ear on the door frame.'

I rush to Temple Street Hospital, heart racing, engine roaring. His ear has slit. The doctors terrify him. He has to have plastic surgery. He's under anaesthetic. We're under a spell, unable to focus on anything, terrified he won't wake up.

Scare over. Thank God he's fine. I need a mobile phone.

Summer 1998

David's team makes the cup final. We buy him the £100 boots. He shoots. He misses. He's devastated. So am I. He won't let us hug him in front of his team-mates. We can't fix it.

We try another sun holiday. It's much better this time. They're a great age. We have a ball spending quality family time together and vow to do it every summer.

August 1999

We decide to move from Dublin to Cork. Boys think it's a great adventure although unsure about leaving their friends. They want a dog. They promise to walk him and feed him. Feeling guilty for uprooting them, we buy them a dog. Within weeks they have new friends in Cork. I'm left walking the dog.

September 2001

David starting secondary school. Huge school. Loads of pupils, loads of teachers. He loves it. I hate it. Very little communication with teachers. He's more independent. Doesn't tell me everything any more. He's a teenager. He has spots and mood swings. More new friends. I don't know their parents. It feels strange not being in full control. I need to trust him. I try, but it's difficult.

September 2002
Constantly driving between two schools. The boys play every sport available. Hectic schedule. I sit in the car for hours, watching and waiting. I hurt when they're disappointed or upset and keep a supply of treats to ease the pain. I burst with pride when they perform well. They're growing. They're taller than me. I can't keep enough food in the fridge. Parenting is exhilarating, exhausting and expensive.

Christmas 2003
David's constantly in the shower and spraying deodorant. He goes to his first disco. His mobile is constantly beeping. Who is he texting? I wish I could read them. I shouldn't.

Millions of teenagers queue up outside disco. Girls half naked, boys agog. He's too young to be going out yet but it's too cruel to keep him home. Everyone else is allowed go, or so I'm told. Panic when I spot lads with beer cans approach from nearby field. More worry. Park nearby and monitor the exit doors until my eyes blur out of focus. He survives it. I discreetly smell his breath. He's okay...this time.

June 2004
David's Junior Certificate exams. He hates studying. I hate nagging. I wish I could do the exams for him. He doesn't worry. I don't stop praying.

Another cup final. A winner this time. We celebrate for days. Exhilarating. Whole family walk tall and proud.

July 2004

David's sixteen. He gets a summer job. First day is a disaster. He's exhausted. He hates it. I fret. I feel sorry for him and want him to stay home. He refuses to quit. He's determined to save up enough money for a motorbike. He's excited. I'm terrified. We argue. He promises to be careful. I give in. How will I know where he is when he has his own transport? I don't sleep for weeks.

September 2004

Mark moves to secondary school. Life should get easier. It doesn't! David has a girlfriend. They're permanently on the phone. His head is in the clouds. He's floating. I hope it doesn't end in tears. It does. His tears. My heart breaks for him. I hate girlfriends! I spoil him until he's happy again. Once more his phone is ringing, who is it this time? Will she break his heart too? He tells me to relax and stop worrying!

Easter 2005

Mark goes to his first disco. Girls wearing shorter skirts, more boys with beer cans. I lecture. We laugh. He tells me to trust him. I try. He survives. So do I. It's slightly easier second time around.

July 2005

David falls in love again – this time with cars. He passes his theory test. Swaps motorbike for Fiat Punto and takes to the road. What if he turns into a boy racer? Girls love boys with cars. I hope they won't distract him from his driving. Worry intensifies, but I've less chauffeuring to do. He worries about alloy wheels and turbo exhausts. I worry about his safety and yet I'm proud of his achievement. Confusing. Mark thinks it's cool to have his brother driving him around. Sweet to see them going off together like two young men. Panic sets in. My sons are growing up. Hubby and I are home alone a lot.

July 2006
Eighteenth birthday. A flashier car. Another football final, another win. Celebrations. David has a few pints of beer with the lads. More worry. Loads of lecturing. Terrified of what this change will bring about. New phase. He deals with it much better than I do. He's an adult while I'm a worrier who needs to let go. I do, a little. Nights out become more frequent. I sleep with one eye and one ear open.

He doesn't come on holidays with us. Going away with one child is different. We miss David, but I'm not sure he misses us! He's still in one piece when we return.

January 2007
Change of heart: he's delighted to come on a short holiday to New York with us. Perhaps being left behind wasn't so cool after all.

Exam year. Pressure on. David in Leaving Cert, Mark in Junior Cert. Lots of worry – for me at least. Boys unperturbed. I'm constantly advising on jobs and courses.

Nudge hubby at Sunday mass when the priest says a special prayer for all students filling in their CAO forms. He forgot to pray for the anxious mothers who invariably complete it for them!

It's been a great two decades. I've loved every mothering moment and thank God every night for blessing me with healthy children and nerves of steel! I've no doubt but there's lots more fun and heartache in the years ahead. I can only imagine what it will be like when they announce they're emigrating or getting married! They'll probably spread their wings much wider than I did. But whatever experiences I've missed out on in life, I'm delighted that the gift of being a mum isn't one of them. Who on earth would I be if I wasn't a mum?

To be continued…

Suzanne Higgins is the bestselling author of *The Will to Win*, *The Power of a Woman* and *The Woman He Loves*. She lives in Dublin with her husband and four young daughters. In a former life she was a 2FM DJ and a televsion presenter.

Mother Was Right
Suzanne Higgins

I remember the utter thrill and surprise at first discovering that I was pregnant. It was incomprehensible how one little bottle of champagne could result in a change so gargantuan. To be honest, having had four adorable little babies, I still think that it's just too big to take in when you first discover you're expecting.

To be pregnant is one thing and to get your head around that is job enough; but the reality that the 'bump' is going to change into a tiny living, breathing, kicking, screaming, demanding tyrant — well, that's another matter altogether.

After a few days of letting it sink in, I told my mother and naturally she, too, was thrilled for me. Something she said that would always stick with me was how my life was never going to be the same again. I remember a slight chill trickling down my spine. What in heaven's name was I letting myself in for? Whatever it was, it didn't really matter because the 'ball was in play', as they say, and pending something going wrong, the baby was coming one way or another.

Yesterday morning when I was thinking about writing some 'mothering experiences' I had no idea what aspect of motherhood I was going to write about, but by lunchtime it came to me – literally, dear reader. It fell, or more accurately, sprayed, into my lap.

How easily are you embarrassed? When we're young, we are all so self-conscious. Hopefully as we age, common sense prevails and we can escape from some of our more egocentric hang-ups, but believe me, nothing beats having a baby for obliterating any remaining vestiges of self-importance. Either you learn to live with embarrassing situations or you die! I don't want to upset my children by naming names, so I'll tell you about 'a friend' and a few of the spectacular stunts her angels have pulled off, and yes, she has survived to tell the story. She may perhaps have a few more grey hairs than she should have and there is no doubt that the waistline would not be quite as elastic if all those babies hadn't come into her life, but I – that is to say, *she* – wouldn't have it any other way.

The scene in the swimming pool. This was one of the first experiences that really embarrassed her. Let's call her Susan. They were on holidays and staying in a lovely hotel. It was the first day and Susan couldn't wait to take the baby into the water. Naturally, she had packed her swimmers nappies as all good mothers do, but it was only when she was putting them on in the changing room that she noticed how they were just a little baggy. (They come in different sizes and such was her enthusiasm Susan had bought large instead of small.) While whooshing the baby up and down in the water at the shallow end, she noticed the child's expression change slightly. It was only moments later that Susan saw the dreaded floating turd. Now as a novelist (yes, can you believe it, she writes too!) Susan has a vivid imagination but she could have sworn that she heard the

Jaws music in her head at just that moment. Could it possibly belong to her baby? Surely not. She desperately looked around the pool. No other babies in the water. She glanced at her child for some help, but only got a post-poo cheesy grin. It had to be hers. Still, it bobbed menacingly close. Susan was appalled. No bigger than a cocktail sausage, for a brief desperate second she wondered if perhaps it *was* a sausage. After all, there were teenage kids in the deep end. They could have been messing about. Another glance and she knew she was dealing with the real deal. Mother and daughter were out of the water in a flash and decided that attack was the best form of defence. She marched up to the lifeguard and informed him that she was appalled to see a poo in the pool. (Obviously if she was the one bringing it to his attention, her baby wasn't the culprit – warped logic of a demented mother.) She knows it was wrong and she's sorry, but Susan just couldn't take the blame for the pool being cleared. To be honest, I think the lifeguard knew that it was the baby's production, but he said nothing. It was just mortifying on an epic scale.

That was nothing, however, to the time that Susan had to go to an incredibly posh dental clinic. This is the kind of place that has *The International Yachter* magazine on its coffee table. The receptionists were all gorgeous, perfect nails as well as perfect teeth. But Susan had the ultimate fashion accessory. She had a two-week-old baby. The newborn was positively edible. Anyway, Susan had to go to this clinic because her teeth always suffer appallingly in pregnancy (another cross to bear). The beauty queens working the phones all oohed and ahhed at the tiny arrival, because let's face it, the whole world loves newborns. Susan was breastfeeding and so the baby went everywhere that

Mum went. Today was no different. As you may know, very young babies can't hold their own heads up, so the mother does this after they've been fed. That way they can burp happily. Susan was doing it like a pro at this stage and so she was surprised when she felt a warm sensation along her leg. (Note to women who haven't had babies – newborns don't poop, they produce something that looks like Dijon mustard – liquidy). To Susan's utter mortification, the baby had done a Dijon and because she was so tiny it had slipped out the side of the nappy and down Mum's only pair of white linen trousers. Then it dripped down into the luxuriant, thick white carpet of the über-sophisticated waiting room. There was nothing that could be done. To even say the word 'babypoo' to the supermodels at reception would have been a crime. To suggest that she needed something to clean one up out of the designer carpet – well, she just couldn't. Susan grabbed *The International Yachter* and casually threw it onto the carpet stain beside her chair. She tried to clean up the trousers in the equally chic bathrooms and then she wrapped her jacket around her waist like a right gombeen. At least that way she wasn't there when they found the mess. She can only imagine the uproar and panic when her sin was discovered. They probably called in an emergency cleaning company.

Now, poops are bad, but give me them any day over barf, because I'm afraid it really does get everywhere, and as for the smell! You'd think that as a mother of four I would have accrued a certain amount of common sense at this stage, and yet still I manage to amaze myself with my utter naïvety.

Another holiday and another story about Susan. This time one of her daughters complained of a bad tummy pain. She and the child wondered if perhaps the girl was hungry. Susan *should* have given her a slice of plain bread or toast, but no, she gave her a chocolate muffin. Then they went swimming. OK, it's really obvious now with blessed hindsight, but it wasn't at the time. That is, until the poor girl brought the whole thing up in the pool. (Actually, it was the same pool – just a different holiday.) There was no side-stepping that one. Everybody within a ten-metre radius knew it was Susan's little darling who was shutting the pool down for the day. That was cripplingly embarrassing. Naturally, the child showered down and perked up instantly, saying that she was much better now and what would they do for the afternoon. Susan suggested hiding in their hotel bedroom.

Compared to the above, I find tantrums a doddle. One of the girls threw an Oscar-winning performance in a shopping centre in Blackrock a few years back. (I think I refused to buy sweets.) I just copied her action for action and then some. Well, she didn't lick it from a stone! I wailed and gnashed my teeth. I cried and stomped my feet. The child was so horrified by my behaviour, she quietened. Easy-peasy.

Yesterday brought my public scenes to a whole new level, however. (OK, I'm giving up the Susan bit for a moment – it's exhausting.) The day started out fine. Admittedly, my baby daughter had been sick at the weekend, but with two days down, I assumed that she was over whatever bug she had picked up. We went to the park and fed the ducks – lovely. We went to the bookshop and bought a book that quacked like the ducks in the park –

really nice – and then we went for a coffee and fruit juice upstairs. If I had thought about it, I would have suggested water, but then again, she had been fine for a couple of days. I had a cappuccino and she an orange juice. To my delight, she downed it almost in one. Obviously the poor girl was thirsty after all that quacking. Then she did something I have never actually seen before. I have heard about it, but never seen it. The orange juice returned with such force and speed that it hit four other tables. There was a lovely elderly couple just finishing their fry (dear God). There were two young girls having coffee and scones and I stopped looking at that stage. Staff appeared from nowhere with mops, cloths and buckets. (I tell you, if you're ever fed up waiting for service, just get a child to— OK, too drastic.) The other patrons and the restaurant staff were all so nice, but as I saw the damage that my darling and I had indirectly caused, I nearly cried. We tried to pay for everybody's food and discomfort, but all refused. (I think they just wanted us gone.) We were covered in recycled orange juice mixed with breakfast cereal. God, it was truly awful and we swept out of the place in a flurry of apologies and promises to pay for any dry cleaning bills. My little girl cried the whole way home in the car and I did my best to cheer her. When she was bathed and changed and gone for a little snooze, I soaked in a bath and tried not to cry too.

That said, dear reader, that was yesterday and today I'm bouncing back. I'm even thinking of dropping in a small potted plant into the coffee shop by way of thanks for their incredible understanding and patience. Every story I've told you is true and these are just the ones I can think of this morning. There are probably loads more of a similar nature and I know it goes on in every house in the country because I remember the time one of my siblings puked into the heater fan of Dad's car. After a few weeks there was no sign of the mess – until you turned on the air con. It was still there when he sold the car.

Like everything in life, however, I have discovered that there is a flip side to my life of 'motherhood mortification'. For the last decade, my girls have embarrassed me, surprised me, humbled me and more or less tamed me, but there is a bonus. As the older ones are getting just a little mature, I've discovered how incredibly easy *they* are to embarrass. It's true, just a slight sway of my hips when a good song comes on and they're dying with shame. The power of this newfound information is yet to be used to its true potential. It's kind of thrilling. I will be able to blackmail them into all sort of household chores and little favours in exchange for not embarrassing them in public. As they get older and more easy to mortify, I realise that this is the beginning of their journey. They will continue to be image conscious and self-aware until they, too, become mothers when their children, in turn, will tame them. That, I suppose, is the circle of life.

So my current belief is that kids ruin the figure, the bank balance, the social life, the romance in your life, your freedom, your car and quite possibly your entire reputation in every good coffee shop and dental clinic in the country, but would I have it any other way? Not on your nanny. Mother was absolutely right. I had no idea what was ahead of me – it was better than I ever could have imagined.

Thanks, Mum. XXX

Kate Thompson is the author of eight bestselling novels. Her number-one bestseller, *The Blue Hour*, was shortlisted for the RNA Parker award. Kate has also been published under the pen name Pixie Pirelli and is the director of Mischief Publishing. Her latest novel, *Love Lies Bleeding*, is an infinitely collectable www first! You can check it out on www.loveliesbleedingthebook.com.

Letting Go
Kate Thompson

From the moment she was held aloft in the delivery room, we knew that our daughter Clara meant business, for at 5:30 a.m. on 3 January 1987, she surveyed her brave new world with an expression of cool detachment as if to say, 'Okay. Now I've finally arrived after those nine endless months, I'm gonna make the most of it. I'm gonna kick some ass.'

My husband Malcolm and I were utterly clueless as parents. We had never held a newborn infant before, let alone bathed one, changed a nappy or tried to ease tiny limbs into the straitjacket confines of a babygro. The screeds of conflicting advice made me weep – literally. Feed on demand. Don't feed on demand. Let her sleep in your bed. Don't let her sleep in your bed. Put her lying on her back. No, no – put her lying on her front. In the end, we decided that we'd muddle through somehow and simply try to rear a happy human being, and a friend for life.

Clara was intrepid. She swam before she crawled; her crawling was more of a prance than a shuffle; and when she finally found her feet, the expression on her face was that of an explorer who'd just discovered a vastly exciting new territory.

As she grew, she terrified me with her audacity. The first time she saw a fire lit in a grate, she greeted it with an intrigued 'Hello!' before tottering towards it with her arms outstretched in welcome. On her first excursion to a playground she gave me a disdainful look when I set her on a baby slide and promptly crossed the tarmac and climbed the steps to the highest one of all. In supermarkets she turned into a miniature commando, deploying evasive action and scooting off any time my back was turned. I would cast around wildly, bowling along the aisles between toiletries and household goods like Jack Nicholson negotiating the maze in *The Shining*, until I found her. Invariably she'd be sitting on the floor, delving into a box of éclairs, chocolate all over her mouth. In an attempt at foiling her, I invested in a pair of 'childproof' reins, but when I strapped them on, she doffed them with the chutzpah of a Houdini.

Any time we went on walks, Clara would set off on her own the moment she was unleashed from the constraints of her car seat, heading straight for the tantalising glimmer of the horizon. She routinely flouted the 'Stranger Danger' rule, engaging men, women and dogs in conversation – she showed scant inclination for social intercourse with other children. Once, on Grafton Street, I rang the changes by slipping away myself, hiding in a shop doorway as an exercise in observation. I watched her toddle along the busy thoroughfare, oblivious to my absence and chatting away happily to anyone who'd listen. I was finally obliged to emerge from my hiding place when a woman whose shoes Clara had been admiring started looking around anxiously for a parent or guardian to make their presence felt. 'I was wondering how long it would take her to notice that I was gone,' I told the astonished woman. 'But it doesn't seem to have fazed her at all.'

That evening, I picked up the phone to my own mother. 'Was I like that?' I asked her.

A little,' she conceded. 'You lived in Cloud Cuckoo Land most of the time.'

'So when do you stop worrying about them?'

'Never,' she said. 'You *never* stop worrying about them.'

The more Clara's independent streak burgeoned, the more Malcolm and I realised it would be wrong not to encourage it. It was time for us to start letting go. When she was twelve we suggested that she do a course in scuba diving so that she could come diving with us on holiday. The first time I sank beneath the murky surface of the Irish Sea with my daughter, I spent the duration of the dive trying vainly to shepherd her – an impossible task. Underwater, Clara was as elusive as Tinkerbell: she sent my heart tattooing at such a rate that I vowed I would never dive with her again.

At the age of fourteen, she made the decision to leave Dublin and become a boarder in Kylemore Abbey, that fabulous Gothic edifice that makes everyone who lays eyes on it think of Hogwarts. There she roamed freely through the wilds of Connemara, climbing mountains, exploring forests, swimming in lakes and giving tourists extremely precise directions as to where to go to find leprechauns.

At eighteen she headed off with the British Schools Expeditionary Society to spend two months in Kwa Zulu Natal, in South Africa. There she slept under skies ablaze with shooting stars, listening to the sound of lions on the prowl through the bush and the coughing of cheetahs. She learned to shoot a gun and to skin and gut an impala. She trekked zebra and acquired all the skills of the game ranger, she climbed high into the Drakkensburg mountains and white-water rafted, she nipped adroitly out of the way of charging hippos and hurled abuse at marauding monkeys.

During those two months – because the only means of communication with the expedition was via satellite phone – we heard nothing from her, apart from a couple of e-mails sent from hill stations. We were learning to let go a little more.

The toughest call came later that year, when Clara announced that it was her intention to go off Inter-railing through Eastern Europe with three girls from the UK whom she'd met on the African expedition. She took her mobile phone with her on this trip, but every mother knows the terror generated by the phone that's out of range, or the dread induced by those automated tones that deliver you straight to voice mail. Most mothers I know have learned to resist the temptation of trying to make contact with their daughters by mobile because if no answer is forthcoming, worst-case scenario inevitably sets in and one's imagination spirals into orbit. Twilight is said to be 'the hour between dog and wolf', but for me it's four o'clock in the morning when your daughter's out clubbing and there's no text message in your inbox. That's when the instinct to make that phone call is at its most dangerously insistent – and that is the phone call you know you really must not make.

Fast forward to the summer of 2006. Clara sets off with the same three girlfriends, this time armed with an itinerary of places to visit in Thailand. Their first destination is Koh Tao, down south. It's a Lotus Land of an island that proves to have the allure of Bali Hi in the movie *South Pacific*, for, a week after arriving in Bangkok, Clara ends up watching from the beach as her girlfriends set sail back northward on the ferry. She has broken the first rule of the backpackers' code: she has abandoned her travelling companions, seduced into staying on the island by her rediscovery of scuba.

Dear God in heaven. My beautiful girl is living alone in a beach hut on an island in the Gulf of Thailand…

I get an e-mail from her. It reads, 'What kind of parents encourage a kid to do something as fascinatingly brill as this?!' And I find myself wondering exactly *what* kind of parents actively encourage such free-spiritedness? Have we in fact been arrantly irresponsible? Have Malcolm and I put our only child in jeopardy by fostering a passion for what is effectively an extreme sport?

But more e-mails follow, breathlessly telling us that she has completed her advanced course, that she has done speciality courses in peak performance buoyancy, deep diving, night diving and underwater photography, and that she intends to return to Koh Tao next summer to undertake a Dive Master course.

Her final e-mail was sent an hour before she was due to leave the island and rejoin her girlfriends in Bangkok: 'Last night we went out on the boat with the sunset and came up under a canopy of stars. I saw a turtle!!! the one thing I hadn't yet seen! we were practically bursting with excitement as we followed it through the water…promise that u will come and visit me here next summer when I do my Dive Master course! then I will be qualified to take you round a dive site. I want to thank u guys again for introducing me to this world which is so unbelievably perfectly me. I have never felt so at home somewhere away from home – diving. I really look forward to seeing u! I have so many stories for u! Love love love. Clara XXX'

It was then we knew that we had done the right thing. We had muddled through nineteen years of parenthood, and somehow managed to rear a happy human being, and a friend for life.

During Clara's last month at Kylemore, when she was sitting her Leaving Cert, I would send her cards on a daily basis, with affirmations on the front. These affirmations took the form of quotes from illustrious personages – such as this from Winston Churchill: *Never, never, never give up.* And from T.S. Eliot – *Only those who risk going too far can possibly find out how far one can go.* And the following, courtesy of Eleanor Roosevelt: *Do the thing you think you cannot do.* My own personal favourite comes from Lewis Carroll's *Alice through the Looking-Glass,* and it goes like this: *Sometimes I've believed as many as six impossible things before breakfast.*

On the day of her final exam, I made Clara promise that she would not look at that day's card until after she'd completed the paper. This is what she found when she opened the envelope: *Twenty years from now you will be more disappointed by the things you didn't do than by the ones you did. So throw off the bowlines. Sail away from the safe harbour. Catch the trade winds in your sails. Explore. Dream. Discover.*

Anon.

Inside the card I had written: *But always remember that the safe harbour is there for you any time you need it.*

I've let her go. My daughter, my baby, my friend, my dive buddy (correction – my dive *master!*) may, as you read this, be perched on a mountain peak in the Himalayas; she may be floating over a coral reef in Egypt; she may be spinning through the air at the end of a bungee cord; she may be sharing a bowl of goat soup in a Jamaican shantytown; she may be huddled in a bivvy bag dreaming of Connemara. But my lovely, liberated girl will live in the safe harbour of my heart forever.

Saffa Musleh lives in Tallaght, Dublin, and this is her first published story. She was the winner of the TV3 Ireland AM/Mothercare competition. She is a nurse who moved to Ireland in 2003 only to fall in love with the Emerald Isle, and decided to call it home. Saffa lives with her husband and sixteen-month-old daughter.

The Hardest Thing I Ever Did
Saffa Musleh

I never said I wanted to be a mother. I never heard the eternal tick tock that other women spoke of and didn't think I ever would. Call it selfishness, but I honestly never thought I would ever want to give my life away to another being. There were hundreds of things to do and places to visit, so why would I need a child in my life? It's not like you can take a break from having a child, so why do anything that takes that much commitment and effort when you have a chance not to?

It was interesting being the oddball and having the no-children-wanted conversation with my friends, but then I caught the love bug and got married. A beautiful wedding took place and married life didn't look too bad. It was a commitment and I had managed it well enough for the first few months, so when himself declared his yearning for a baby, I thought, Why not? This might be fun!

Ten months later, fun was an alien term to me, something I vaguely associated with my pre-married life. There was no fun in being pregnant. None. I was getting sick every day at the mere hint of food, any food. I was so enormous by my second trimester that a friend of mine called me an overstuffed penguin. My nights were spent tossing and turning with the Bump hindering my attempts at getting comfortable, and the days were spent in endless trips to the loo. Oh, how I hated being pregnant.

The birth was fun-less as well. I was blessed with two lovely midwives to talk me through the whole process, but that doesn't change the fact that it was an unpleasant experience, to say the least. I was late and so I had to be induced. The first couple of hours passed with me thinking, This isn't too bad, actually. If Pamela Anderson can do this with no pain relief, then I surely can. It was only after the intravenous drip was hung that I realised what pain meant. Here I was, afraid to go to the dentist for a root canal, not knowing what agonies reside in the maternity ward. Needless to say, I got the epidural and a few hours later a big baby boy called Raad came into this world.

Raad came with added benefits. I didn't just get the beautiful child. Along with him came the sleepless nights and the colic and the crying and the leaking breasts and the ever-present trace of sour milk down the back of your best jumper. I am not saying I didn't love my baby. I adored him. I just hated the rest of the package. I hated that I couldn't remember having a solid night of sleep. And what's with babies and the front door? How do they calculate their spits and bowel movements to co-ordinate with the minute you push the buggy outside? And why did no one tell me how loose and wiggly my tummy would be after birth? I mean, I read about the weight gain, but this was ridiculous.

I had read every single book the library had about child rearing, giving birth, eating right, blah blah blah. I was a nurse with six years' experience – I bathed babies, cleaned them, fed them. If anyone was to be ready for kids, I was, and yet I felt as ill prepared as a six-year-old showing up for an admittance test to Mensa. Motherhood and I were not getting along.

I heard that children thrived on routine, but mine didn't. Waking up whenever he thought appropriate, feeding on demand – there was nothing with me and Raad that had a schedule. But I checked all of that with his nurse and his doctor, I checked it online and I got the books from the library, of course. By all accounts, he was a healthy baby and I was a struggling first-time mother. Nothing to write home about, really. I thought I was doing a good job, even though I hated it. Motherhood and I never got along, but we tried to settle for a peaceful co-existence. And then everything changed.

Raad got sick and was hospitalised. A month of investigations later, we were sent home. We had no idea why he got sick and we didn't bother questioning it any more than we did during his month of stay in the hospital. Life was good. At least, that was what we determined back then. An obstacle was put in our way and we were going to get over it. They say denial is hugely underestimated.

My son was five months and thirteen days old when he died.

There is nothing in the world that prepares you for being a mother. And there is nothing in the world that even comes close to preparing you for being a bereaved mother. Here was everything I hoped for and wanted broken into a thousand shards and scattered all over the place. Here was my son, in his white clothes, taken away from me to rest in a hole in the ground. It didn't matter what the autopsy report said afterwards or what the mourners at the funeral told me. I didn't care that he was an angel in heaven. I didn't care about the disease that had been lurking in his lungs. I was frozen in my grief. I had two empty arms with no baby to hold.

You need not know about the grief and the pain. You need not imagine the sorrow and, most of all, the emptiness that wrecks your soul. To say that you feel the emptiness physically is an understatement. I felt it. I felt a hole within me and knew that nothing, just nothing in this world would ever fill it.

The world prepares you to be a mother in the most bizarre of ways. It shows you pictures of healthy babies and beautiful women who breastfeed and change nappies while watching *Oprah* and cooking a five-course meal. They never complain, are never tired and when they are, they can be sure that some miracle product you can buy for ten euros in Superquinn would solve that problem for good. But there are no pictures of grieving mothers in magazines and surely none ever pop on our television screens, except the ones in the ten o'clock news in some war-stricken country in the Middle East. By all means, I was alone in my grief and knew nothing about how I would ever trust life again.

Someone was kind enough to give me a hug in an airport terminal shortly after Raad's death. It was a lady waiting for her connecting flight. We had only exchanged a couple of words when I blurted out, 'My son died last Monday.' She didn't ask me much, and I didn't feel like talking all that much either. She hugged me instead and in our brief encounter she told me that refusing to ever have a baby again, which was my primary notion, was a betrayal to all the love I had for my little boy.

'You owe it to him to share that love with another child,' she said.

I didn't think much of it at the time. Too wounded and too raw, I put aside all thoughts of ever getting pregnant. I couldn't love someone that much again. I couldn't possibly ever fathom the idea of carrying a child in my womb and nurturing it only to have fate snatch it away from me as it did with Raad.

The days and the months went by in a daze. I was on autopilot, eating and drinking when I needed to, sleeping with the help of sleeping pills. Crying my eyes out the minute I was alone. I had wonderful help from two therapists, but I still couldn't find anything in my life worth getting up in the morning for. I got a job which got me out of the house for a few hours every day and tried to forget that there was actually more to life than the stupor I was in.

My gynaecologist saw me four months after Raad died. She advised me to go on the Pill and I obliged. The prescription for six months' worth of contraception was in my handbag when I noticed, in the way that most busy women do, that my visit to Boots may be for something other than pills. It took two tests to confirm it, but yes, I was pregnant.

The tears I cried while sitting on the toilet seat were not happy tears, nor were they sad ones. Just tears of yearning and anticipation. I was to hold a baby again, I thought. Am I ready to go through it all? And what if?

Hundreds of what ifs went through my head. They invaded my dreams, and amidst it all I knew that nothing was guaranteed. It actually could happen again. There was no logical explanation for my son having the disease that he had, so how would I ever know that this baby wouldn't meet the same fate? My husband and I had attended genetic counselling, which was supposed to have put our fears to rest, but it didn't. A part of my brain was asking me to be rational and consider the odds of lightning striking twice, as my GP described it, but I could not be rational. Not with my body carrying all the hormones it did. Not with my grief being that raw and new.

The hardest thing I think I had to face at the time was telling my husband. He was asleep that morning. I sat at the edge of the bed with the pregnancy test in my hands, trying to think of what to say. He must have felt me sitting there. As he opened his eyes, I held the test up, not knowing what to tell him. We held each other and said nothing.

The one thing we knew for sure was that no one was to know about the pregnancy until we were ready. It was almost six months before we told our closest friends and family. Telling people about the pregnancy, in our minds, equalled apprehension and responsibility. It meant that yes, we are ready for a baby. Yes, we have dealt with the loss of our son and yes, we are in total control of what is happening to us this time.

One more thing that nobody tells you when you have a child is that nothing is under your control. You can heat the bottle till it reaches the exact temperature, but you cannot make your baby drink it. Buying colic medicine from your drugstore is one thing, but having it relieve your baby's wind is a different issue. No amount of lullabies you sing to your baby is going to put him to sleep if he doesn't want to. You can do everything according to the book and follow each and every expert's opinion and still mess things up. I know I did everything right with Raad and so even when I did everything right this time, how was I to know that my child was not going to die? I never drank in all my life. Never smoked. Do not take medicines even for headaches and have no history of family diseases, and that didn't stop my baby from getting sick and dying. I had nothing under control and admitting that to myself was a real eye opener. Call it wishful thinking, but the only thing that comforted me during the long months of pregnancy was knowing that I had all these dreams of a healthy child, and that for once, my dreams were going to come true. The possibility of them not materialising into reality was not an option for me. That was the hope that helped me sleep at night. That, and the kicks I got from a very moody little thing that loved noisy music and hated me cuddling with her dad.

My due date was in March, and we often joked of how little Patricia may come a few days early in time for Paddy's Day. But Paddy's Day came and went with no signs of labour pains. Raad's anniversary was approaching. The fourth of April. I dreaded the possibility of having both the birth and the anniversary in the same month, and here was March twenty-eighth and no baby. Again I followed the experts' advice, and out came the curries and the long walks. I raided the nature stores for herbal concoctions that help induce labour and danced till my back almost broke in half. Still, no pains.

It was on March twenty-ninth that I had an appointment in the Coombe. Four days overdue; anxious and visibly disturbed by the possibility of having my baby in April, I asked the obstetrician whether the pain I experienced while sitting in the waiting area that morning was a sign of anything. He shook his head and said that I was to be induced in a week's time and that there was no possibility of me going into labour anytime soon.

That night, my son was ever present in my mind as the labour pains got more and more intense. I promised myself I would not complain about the pain or the fact that my midwife was anti-epidurals. I would endure whatever it took for me to have a healthy baby. And as the contractions grew stronger, the fear grew bigger and bigger. Was the baby going to cry when she comes out? Will she be pink? What will the APOGAR score be? Will she need hospitalisation? What if the on-call paediatrician did not show up as planned? What if she turns out to be sick like Raad?

It was fifty-five minutes after midnight, on the thirtieth of March, that my little Zada cried her lungs out as she lay on my chest. A healthy, pink, active baby girl. She was feeding ten minutes after being born. She was seen by a paediatrician almost every day for the first week of her life and each one of them was happy enough to say that my girl was as healthy as they come. She was all I hoped for, and a little bit more.

I didn't break down when the fourth of April came. I grieved for my son, with my daughter in my arms. We took her over to the burial site and had her say hello to her older brother. Things made sense then. The love I had for Raad was too big not to be shared with another child. I still hated the motherhood package, but I knew enough to count my blessings every time my little one cried or tossed and turned. She gave me hope and taught me that a mother can only do the best that she can do. And that that was more than enough.